PRIMAL HUNT

Applause for L.L. Raand's Midnight Hunters Series

The Midnight Hunt
RWA 2012 VCRW Laurel Wreath winner *Blood Hunt*
Night Hunt
The Lone Hunt

"Raand has built a complex world inhabited by werewolves, vampires, and other paranormal beings…Raand has given her readers a complex plot filled with wonderful characters as well as insight into the hierarchy of Sylvan's pack and vampire clans. There are many plot twists and turns, as well as erotic sex scenes in this riveting novel that keep the pages flying until its satisfying conclusion."—*Just About Write*

"Once again, I am amazed at the storytelling ability of L.L. Raand aka Radclyffe. In *Blood Hunt*, she mixes high levels of sheer eroticism that will leave you squirming in your seat with an impeccable multi-character storyline all streaming together to form one great read."—*Queer Magazine Online*

"Are you sick of the same old hetero vampire/werewolf story plastered in every bookstore and at every movie theater? Well, I've got the cure to your werewolf fever. *The Midnight Hunt* is first in, what I hope is, a long-running series of fantasy erotica for L.L. Raand (aka Radclyffe)."—*Queer Magazine Online*

Acclaim for Radclyffe's Fiction

"Medical drama, gossipy lesbian romance, and angsty backstory all get equal time in [*Unrivaled*,] Radclyffe's fifth PMC Hospital Romance…[F]ans of small community dynamics and workplace romance without ethical complications will find this hits the spot."—*Publishers Weekly*

"*Dangerous Waters* is a bumpy ride through a devastating time with powerful events and resolute characters. Radclyffe gives us the strong, dedicated women we love to read in a story that keeps us turning pages until the end."—*Lambda Literary Review*

"Radclyffe's *Dangerous Waters* has the feel of a tense television drama, as the narrative interchanges between hurricane trackers and first responders. Sawyer and Dara butt heads in the beginning as each moves for some level of control during the storm's approach, and the interference of a lovely television reporter adds an engaging love triangle threat to the sexual tension brewing between them."—*RT Book Reviews*

"*Love After Hours*, the fourth in Radclyffe's Rivers Community series, evokes the sense of a continuing drama as Gina and Carrie's slow-burning romance intertwines with details of other Rivers residents. They become part of a greater picture where friends and family support each other in personal and recreational endeavors. Vivid settings and characters draw in the reader…"
—*RT Book Reviews*

Secret Hearts "delivers exactly what it says on the tin: poignant story, sweet romance, great characters, chemistry and hot sex scenes. Radclyffe knows how to pen a good lesbian romance."
—*LezReviewBooks Blog*

Wild Shores "will hook you early. Radclyffe weaves a chance encounter into all-out steamy romance. These strong, dynamic women have great conversations, and fantastic chemistry."
—*The Romantic Reader Blog*

In **2016 RWA/OCC Book Buyers Best award winner for suspense and mystery with romantic elements** *Price of Honor* "Radclyffe is master of the action-thriller series...The old familiar characters are there, but enough new blood is introduced to give it a fresh feel and open new avenues for intrigue."—*Curve Magazine*

In *Prescription for Love* "Radclyffe populates her small town with colorful characters, among the most memorable being Flann's little sister, Margie, and Abby's 15-year-old trans son, Blake...This romantic drama has plenty of heart and soul." —*Publishers Weekly*

2013 RWA/New England Bean Pot award winner for contemporary romance *Crossroads* "will draw the reader in and make her heart ache, willing the two main characters to find love and a life together. It's a story that lingers long after coming to 'the end.'"—*Lambda Literary*

In **2012 RWA/FTHRW Lories and RWA HODRW Aspen Gold award winner** *Firestorm* "Radclyffe brings another hot lesbian romance for her readers."—*The Lesbrary*

Foreword Review Book of the Year finalist and IPPY silver medalist *Trauma Alert* "is hard to put down and it will sizzle in the reader's hands. The characters are hot, the sex scenes explicit and explosive, and the book is moved along by an interesting plot with well drawn secondary characters. The real star of this show is the attraction between the two characters, both of whom resist and then fall head over heels."—*Lambda Literary Reviews*

Lambda Literary Award Finalist *Best Lesbian Romance 2010* features "stories [that] are diverse in tone, style, and subject, making for more variety than in many, similar anthologies... well written, each containing a satisfying, surprising twist. Best Lesbian Romance series editor Radclyffe has assembled a respectable crop of 17 authors for this year's offering."—*Curve Magazine*

2010 Prism award winner and ForeWord Review Book of the Year Award finalist *Secrets in the Stone* is "so powerfully [written] that the worlds of these three women shimmer between reality and dreams...A strong, must read novel that will linger in the minds of readers long after the last page is turned."—*Just About Write*

In **Benjamin Franklin Award finalist** *Desire by Starlight* "Radclyffe writes romance with such heart and her down-to-earth characters not only come to life but leap off the page until you feel like you know them. What Jenna and Gard feel for each other is not only a spark but an inferno and, as a reader, you will be washed away in this tumultuous romance until you can do nothing but succumb to it."—*Queer Magazine Online*

Lambda Literary Award winner *Distant Shores, Silent Thunder* "weaves an intricate tapestry about passion and commitment between lovers. The story explores the fragile nature of trust and the sanctuary provided by loving relationships." —*Sapphic Reader*

Lambda Literary Award winner *Stolen Moments* "is a collection of steamy stories about women who just couldn't wait. It's sex when desire overrides reason, and it's incredibly hot!" —*On Our Backs*

Lambda Literary Award Finalist *Justice Served* delivers a "crisply written, fast-paced story with twists and turns and keeps us guessing until the final explosive ending."—*Independent Gay Writer*

Lambda Literary Award finalist *Turn Back Time* "is filled with wonderful love scenes, which are both tender and hot." —*MegaScene*

By Radclyffe

Romances
Innocent Hearts
Promising Hearts
Love's Melody Lost
Love's Tender Warriors
Tomorrow's Promise
Love's Masquerade
shadowland
Turn Back Time
When Dreams Tremble
The Lonely Hearts Club
Secrets in the Stone
Desire by Starlight
Homestead
The Color of Love
Secret Hearts
Only This Summer
Fire in the Sky (with Julie Cannon)

First Responders Novels

Trauma Alert	Wild Shores
Firestorm	Heart Stop
Taking Fire	Dangerous Waters

Honor Series

Above All, Honor	Word of Honor
Honor Bound	Oath of Honor
Love & Honor	(First Responders)
Honor Guards	Code of Honor
Honor Reclaimed	Price of Honor
Honor Under Siege	Cost of Honor

Justice Series

A Matter of Trust (prequel)	Justice in the Shadows
Shield of Justice	Justice Served
In Pursuit of Justice	Justice for All

PMC Hospitals Romances

Passion's Bright Fury (prequel)
Fated Love
Night Call
Crossroads

Passionate Rivals
Unrivaled
Perfect Rivalry

The Provincetown Tales

Safe Harbor
Beyond the Breakwater
Distant Shores, Silent Thunder
Storms of Change

Winds of Fortune
Returning Tides
Sheltering Dunes
Treacherous Seas

Rivers Community Romances

Against Doctor's Orders
Prescription for Love
Love on Call
Love After Hours

Love to the Rescue
Love on the Night Shift
Pathway to Love
Finders Keepers

Short Fiction

Collected Stories by Radclyffe
Erotic Interludes: *Change Of Pace*
Radical Encounters

Stacia Seaman and Radclyffe, eds.:
Erotic Interludes Vol. 2–5
Romantic Interludes Vol. 1–2
Breathless: *Tales of Celebration*
Women of the Dark Streets
Amor and More: Love Everafter
Myth & Magic: Queer Fairy Tales

Writing As L.L. Raand
Midnight Hunters

The Midnight Hunt
Blood Hunt
Night Hunt
The Lone Hunt
The Magic Hunt

Shadow Hunt
Rogue Hunt
Enchanted Hunt
Primal Hunt

Visit us at www.boldstrokesbooks.com

PRIMAL HUNT

by
L.L. Raand

2024

PRIMAL HUNT
© 2024 By L.L. Raand. All Rights Reserved.

ISBN 13: 978-1-63679-561-4

This Trade Paperback Original Is Published By
Bold Strokes Books, Inc.
P.O. Box 249
Valley Falls, NY 12185

First Edition: May 2024

THIS IS A WORK OF FICTION. NAMES, CHARACTERS, PLACES, AND INCIDENTS ARE THE PRODUCT OF THE AUTHOR'S IMAGINATION OR ARE USED FICTITIOUSLY. ANY RESEMBLANCE TO ACTUAL PERSONS, LIVING OR DEAD, BUSINESS ESTABLISHMENTS, EVENTS, OR LOCALES IS ENTIRELY COINCIDENTAL.

THIS BOOK, OR PARTS THEREOF, MAY NOT BE REPRODUCED IN ANY FORM WITHOUT PERMISSION.

Credits
Editors: Ruth Sternglantz and Stacia Seaman
Production Design: Stacia Seaman
Cover Design by Tammy Seidick

Acknowledgments

Thanks to all the readers who requested more of the Midnight Hunter universe (and for giving it a try when "paranormals" weren't their thing). These characters have allowed me to write romance, sex, and passion in a way that I couldn't when keeping to the constraints of the "real" world—plus I got to write about creatures and worlds that fascinate and delight me. Sharing these stories has been a great pleasure.

Thanks also to my editors, Stacia Seaman and Ruth Sternglantz, for managing the diverse cast of characters and intertwining relationships, and to Sandy Lowe for keeping me and the BSB house afloat while I wandered beyond the veil.

To Lee, for eternal patience

Chapter One

Timberwolf Compound, somewhere in the Adirondack Forest

Sylvan, silent and stealthy, slipped through the shadows, her wolf within watchful, on full alert, and ready to rise between one breath and the next. The heartbeats of hundreds of wolf Weres inside the Compound walls resonated in her depths—the warriors standing post on the fortifications and the inner buildings or asleep in the barracks, the maternals overseeing the young in the nursery, and the Pack members who had returned from their lives in the outside world to renew their connections with Pack. Even the distant *sentries* on perimeter duty miles away beyond the safety of the encampment shared a place in her consciousness and were never far from her protective reach.

All appeared quiet to any without the heightened sensitivity of an Alpha wolf intimately linked to their territory. She'd left the side of her mate well after the moon had reached its zenith, driven by the insistent pacing of her wolf within and the sense of impending danger. Wary of the false aura of peace that could shatter at any moment, Sylvan prowled the commons at the center of the Compound. The gathering points around the firepits and the training grounds were deserted in the deep hours between midnight and dawn, an unusual occurrence.

The moon had crested an hour before, and ordinarily with its call so strong, dozens of her Pack would be outside the fortified walls running in pelt or lingering on the commons in search of a tangle or a tussle, depending on their urge to couple or challenge. The perimeter patrols stationed throughout the thousands of acres of Pack land secured their territory so the Pack could run freely in safety along the many trails that threaded through the virgin forests. But not tonight. Tonight, by her order, no one passed outside the fortifications. Even her mate had left their den a mile from the Compound and slept in one of the rooms adjoining Sylvan's office in the headquarters building.

For the first time in Sylvan's memory, she was not certain her territory was secure. Not since a Gate from the world beyond the veil had opened a lance throw from her very walls and a royal Fae contingent had stepped out into the heart of Pack land. Not since border guards of the Snowcrest wolves, whose Pack adjoined hers on the northern border, had been attacked—killed or worse—at multiple locations by assassins who appeared and disappeared through breaks in the barrier between worlds. Not since Cecilia, the Queen of Faerie, had sought an alliance with the Weres and Vampires against an enemy none could name.

War was coming. Sylvan did not know when. She did not know from where. And she did not know in what form her enemies might manifest. But without doubt, war was coming. What she had to decide was whether she would wait or gather her forces and strike first.

Not a decision she could make alone. Not a decision she was even certain her allies would support should she call for forces to attack. But all her allies and their highest-ranking advisors, Were, Vampire, and Fae, had witnessed the agents of the enemy—reanimated abominations belched from a tear in the fabric between worlds, defilements of passive creatures transformed into ravenous beasts and ensorcelled Weres. These travesties of their former selves were forced to set upon their own kind even after death.

An army of such creatures would exact a toll she was not willing to pay in the blood of her Pack and her allies. When war was certain, allowing the enemy time to gain strength was a poor tactic. But first, she had to be certain beyond doubt that her Pack was secure. She had to ensure that, should she fall, the Pack would survive.

Clad in only a black T-shirt and black BDUs, barefoot and with the night as her shield, she dropped onto the far end of the porch fronting the two-story timber and stone warrior barracks and eased along the rough wood planks to the entrance where a familiar figure stood guard.

"Callan," Sylvan murmured.

The commander of her soldiers snapped to attention. "Alpha, how may I serve?"

"Stand easy." Sylvan brushed a hand down the center of his back, assuring him that no threat was imminent while establishing the touch contact all her Pack craved from her. She led not just by strength of will and muscle, but by the depth of the love she radiated to every member of her Pack. The tension in his muscles eased, but he kept his gaze directed outward, scanning the Compound, still vigilant.

"All quiet within?" she asked.

"Yes, Alpha. The cadets are tired and secretly welcome a long night in quarters," he said with a hint of laughter in his voice.

"Good, then they might be learning something. And the rest?"

"A few grumbles from the senior recruits who had been planning on a run and a tangle, but all accounted for."

"And the *sentries*? How are the warriors?"

"Ready to answer your call," he said briskly. "They are eager, Alpha."

Sylvan's wolf chuffed and curled into watchful waiting, satisfied for the moment. "And how is it that you stand guard and not one of your lieutenants?"

"If they come waging war," he said, "it will be at dawn. I want to be awake at that moment."

"Lord Torren tells me that the Gate that allowed the Fae entrance to our territory is gone."

"I trust Lord Torren to speak of what is of the Fae." Callan growled softly.

"As do I," Sylvan said firmly. "But you have concerns?"

"How do we know the Gate that allowed those creatures to enter our world is truly of the Fae? If they found a way to make one Gate into our territory, they could make another just as they have done in Snowcrest land. Or somehow force that one just outside our fortifications to open again."

"I understand your worry, but I have seen what came through the veil at Snowcrest, and those creatures were not of Cecilia's making. She sent her royal envoys through a Gate of her making into our territory to seek aid. I have made it clear another breach into our world will make us enemies."

"Yes, Alpha."

"I value your instincts at all times. I would not trust another to lead our warriors."

He ducked his head for an instant with a low rumble of pleasure at her praise.

Sylvan sensed his unease return a moment later. "Something else still troubles you."

"Some of the cadets are ready to be assigned to cadres."

"Even with battle imminent?"

"Yes, Alpha. A few have progressed quickly." He paused, uncharacteristically reticent.

"Callan," Sylvan murmured, "you need not fear to speak."

"It's Kendra and Kira, Alpha. I think they might be hard to hold back if we are threatened, but they are not fully trained."

Sylvan kept a leash on her wolf, who bristled at the implied criticism of her offspring. Every dominant wolf took pride in a strong young pup, and hers were among the strongest. "Are my young causing problems?"

"No, Alpha," he said briskly. "They are skilled and obedient."

"Obedient?" Sylvan laughed. "I remember being at their stage, and obedient is not a word I would use to describe myself. Arrogant and verging on undisciplined at times would be more accurate. I trust that you and your lieutenants can handle them."

"There is something else," he said.

Sylvan waited.

"They're not just acquiring new skills more quickly than I have ever seen, Alpha," he said. "They're advancing rapidly in every way. They shift effortlessly—faster than any of the other adolescents. They're already as strong and proficient as some of our recruits."

"Would you trust them to lead a cadre if one of your *sentries* fell? Because that day may come all too soon if you promote them."

"I don't think we could prevent them from it, Alpha. The others sense their strength and their place in the Pack already and look to them for leadership. They ought to be promoted and prepared for that day, should it come soon."

"I see." Sylvan sighed.

"Given our present state of readiness," Callan said, on firmer ground now when discussing the state of his troops, "I also recommend promoting Drea and Anya immediately."

Sylvan cocked her head. Young warriors, skilled but not seasoned in battle. "Drea has field experience, I agree. Why Anya?"

"She's our best tracker and among the strongest with telepathic abilities—she would be very valuable in combat."

"All right. See that both attend the council meeting. The Prima and I trust you to make the right decisions for all our warriors." She clasped his neck and stroked her thumb down the steely column of muscles to his shoulder. "As to our young, prepare them as you see fit. Better to test them now than in the heat of battle."

"I'll see to it," Callan said.

"Good," Sylvan said. "The war council convenes an hour after midnight. Assign them to post for now."

"As you will."

"Is the *imperator* in her quarters?"

Callan paused. "I don't know, Alpha."

A cautious answer from a loyal captain. Sylvan expected no less. "Good night then, Captain."

As he saluted, she leapt down from the porch and threaded her way across the commons to the barricades running along the top of the twelve-foot-high walls. The fortifications enclosed the Compound, the Pack's military encampment where her warriors trained, her young grew to maturity, and the healers cared for the wounded and injured. Surrounded by another thousand acres of densely patrolled forest deep in the heart of Pack land, the Compound was impregnable and highly defensible. In exchange for her pledge to protect this ground and all the members of her Pack, unto death, her Pack entrusted her with their loyalty and obedience. The Pack bonds forged by her power as Alpha united them, body and spirit.

She would not rest this night until she was certain all within were secure. She bounded up the scaffold to the walkway atop the wall with speed that verged on wolf-fast even while still in skin. Treya, the slender, tight-bodied blond *sentrie* on post, sensed her presence an instant later and snapped to rigid attention. She saluted with a fist to her chest. "Alpha! How may I assist you?"

"Stand easy, Treya," Sylvan said. "No disturbances outside the walls?"

"No, Alpha. Nothing visual in the area of the anomalous Gate."

"Good. The foot patrols are to hold position until I order otherwise. Open our gates only by my command."

Treya lowered her gaze as a faint shiver coursed through her.

Sylvan raised a brow. "Problem?"

"Ah, I believe the *imperator* is inspecting the area around the Gate at the moment, Alpha. Should I instruct the guards to open the minor port upon her return?"

Sylvan suppressed a growl. "How many in her party?"

Treya's gaze dropped to Sylvan's feet and her fear hormones spiked. "I do not know, Alpha."

"I understand." Sylvan cupped Treya's cheek, soothing her discomfort. The *sentrie* was not responsible for her superior's actions. Treya instantly settled with a faint sigh, assured that her Alpha was not angry with her.

"Carry on, *sentrie*."

"Yes, Alpha," Treya said with another salute.

Sylvan blurred along the barricade until she was far enough away from Treya not to pull Treya's wolf into a change as she let her wolf ascend. She dropped over the wall and landed in pelt on all fours in the forest outside the Compound. Prowling without disturbing the air or the night sounds, she circled well away from the site where the Queen of Faerie had somehow constructed a Gate to allow the royal Fae contingent to enter Sylvan's territory unbidden. After the recent assaults on the Snowcrest stronghold through a similar kind of Gate, she couldn't discount the possibility that the same kind of incursion could threaten her territory. Approaching the area of the Gate downwind, she arrowed in on Niki's scent. Niki's wolf would soon know she was coming, not because anything would give Sylvan away, but because Sylvan's bond with Niki was one of the strongest in the Pack. Not only was Niki her general and her Pack second, but she was Sylvan's oldest friend. Still, Niki had only a few seconds to prepare before Sylvan leapt over the last boundary of dense shrub and landed next to her.

The reddish-gray, green-eyed wolf bristled reflexively, an innate response to any close approach by another dominant wolf, Alpha or not. Sylvan clamped her jaws to Niki's neck with a growl and telegraphed her fury, wolf mind to wolf mind.

What part of my order to maintain high alert status was unclear, Imperator?

Your orders were clear, Alpha. Even in their silent exchange, Niki's edge of arrogance was easily perceptible to Sylvan's wolf.

Sylvan tightened her grip while Niki stubbornly stood her

ground, her chin level with Sylvan's. Had Niki raised her head, Sylvan would have brought her to the ground and straddled her. She hadn't dominated her friend and general in many years, not since they were both adolescents striving to advance their positions in the Pack. Niki had never challenged her for the Alpha position, but when they were young and Sylvan's father had been alive, they had fought frequently for places in his royal guard.

Why? Sylvan asked. *Why are you out here alone, in direct disobedience of my orders?*

I am charged with protecting the Pack, just as you are. Niki's muscles bunched and quivered as she struggled not to fight back, the effort clear in every tremor rippling through her shoulders.

You have not answered my question. Sylvan growled, low and threateningly. *Why are you out here?*

We don't know the Gate is gone, Niki replied.

And the sentries *are aware and charged to monitor the area. By my order.*

Niki huffed as well as she could with the pressure from Sylvan's jaws on her throat. *Precious time would be lost waiting for visual confirmation.*

And what would be lost if one of those creatures or a dozen of them came through a Gate while you were out here alone? Sylvan tightened her grip, and with the power of her will alone forced Niki's head lower than hers. *You are my general and my friend, but you cannot disobey my orders.*

Niki gasped, her forelegs buckling as Sylvan straddled her. *My mate sleeps inside this Compound*, Niki signaled silently, *and my young. My duty to them comes before all.*

Tell me why I should not relieve you of your command, Sylvan said.

Niki stilled, and a faint whine tore from her throat, telegraphing her distress and her submission to Sylvan's will. Sylvan released her.

The red wolf shook herself, as if shedding water from her pelt. Her gaze flickered quickly across Sylvan's eyes, never settling long enough to bring challenge. *I would die for you or any other wolf in our Pack.*

I know, Sylvan said. *But beyond your allegiance, I need your obedience. The* sentries *on the barricades know you are out here, in direct disobedience of my orders. By rights, I could exile you.*

Sylvan shed pelt, and the force of her transformation pulled Niki into skin with her. In the moonlight, Niki's eyes held the residual gold of her wolf. "I can feel it, Alpha. Something is coming. Something… wrong."

"Then you know what you should have done. You should have come to me. I need all my warriors united, Niki. Whatever we're going to fight will be something none of them have ever seen before. If you cannot stand with me, as I see fit, you cannot serve the Pack either."

Niki dropped to one knee and lowered her head. "I'm sorry. This is the first time since I've had a family that I've been afraid."

Sylvan's chest tightened. She settled a hand atop her friend's head. "Don't you think I'm frightened every day?"

"If you are, you carry it in secret."

"Not entirely," Sylvan murmured. "My mate knows. And were I anyone else, so would my Alpha."

Niki lifted her chin until her cheek lay in the curve of Sylvan's palm, her gaze still fixed on the ground in front of her. "I should have come to you. I thought if I did…"

"What?" Sylvan murmured.

"You would think me weak."

Sylvan rumbled low in her chest and gripped Niki's shoulders, pulling her upright.

"Look at me," Sylvan said, the Alpha command in her voice something no wolf, no matter how dominant, could deny. Niki's gaze slowly rose, touched Sylvan's, and she shuddered. "You are one of the strongest, bravest wolves I've ever known. Love does not make you weak. Love makes you stronger than before. Tell me, *Imperator*, can I trust you with the lives of my Prima, my young, my Pack?"

Niki whispered, "Yes, on my life. I swear."

"Then speak with the commander of the watch—double the patrols if you think it's necessary. No one—including you—patrols alone here or on the perimeter. In pairs, close contact, check-ins every hour. Experienced soldiers only. Am I clear?"

"Yes, Alpha," Niki murmured. "It shall be done."

"See to it." As quickly as she had shed pelt, Sylvan transformed again and raced off into the night. She had done all she could do, and now she needed her mate. Niki wasn't the only Were who feared for those she loved.

Chapter Two

Snowcrest territory, on the northern border of Timberwolf Pack land

Trent's wolf alerted to the inner pull of her mate shifting into pelt, and she came awake instantly. Even as she roused, her heartbeat exactly attuned to her mate's and a fine dusting of pelt already flowing down her torso, Trent knew Zora had already disappeared into the night. Trent sensed her direction through the mate bond that had formed the moment they were bonded, the intimate, singular link that joined her with Zora and, through Zora, the Pack Alpha, to every other Were in their Pack. From the instant they'd bonded, Zora's duty became hers, as did her loyalty and devotion to the Pack. She had been born Timberwolf and would always remain so in her core, but her heart and loyalty were Snowcrest now.

As Trent lay sweat-soaked and trembling with the need to be by Zora's side, Zora raced on through the dense forest surrounding Cresthome, covering the rugged terrain with the agility and speed that only an Alpha Were could display. She had left their quarters on the upper level of the barracks through the open window above the bed, and when she'd let her wolf ascend, she hadn't invited Trent to join her on her run. As much as Trent's wolf snarled and paced—unhappy to be left behind, worried that some harm might come to her mate, demanding to shift with her claws deep into Trent's psyche—Trent resisted.

She could easily have followed her mate, but to do so would've suggested she did not trust her mate's strength, skill, or ability. Now, especially now, after they were so newly mated and she was an out-Pack Were who still didn't have the full trust of Zora's Pack, she could not undermine Zora's authority. Nor would she ever. Zora was her Alpha as well as her mate. She would not follow unless warned of danger through the mate bond. She might as well announce that Zora was not fit to lead were she to chase after her when the Alpha chose to run alone.

Trent rose, pulled on a pair of BDUs, and, in the heat of the late summer night, didn't bother with a shirt. She strode out onto the deck adjoining their quarters and greeted the other Were she'd scented outside. "Loris."

"Prima." Zora's *imperator*, a dark-haired, dark-eyed male a decade or so older than Trent, muscular and broad-chested, wore black BDUs like her, but unlike her, also wore a tight black T-shirt and combat boots. His gaze remained slightly below hers, his only sign of concession to her dominance. Trent could have forced his submission with the added power her link to Zora instilled in her, and had she sensed any true resistance to her authority she would have. But he had been at Zora's side when she emerged victorious from the challenges she'd had to face to secure her position as Pack Alpha and had remained a staunch defender when the rare Snowcrest Were grumbled that Zora was too young or too inexperienced to lead. He had been opposed to their mating and would have been glad to stand in Trent's place by Zora's side, but Zora had not wanted Loris as a mate.

She had chosen Trent, an out-Pack dominant not all that different than some of the Snowcrest dominants in power and skill. Except Trent had been the only one not deterred by Zora's need, nor afraid to reveal her own. They had chosen each other, and that was enough to place Trent at the pinnacle of Pack hierarchy, a position she respected and intended to keep.

Loris, however, was no threat to her, and Zora relied on his strategic experience and command of their soldiers. Zora had never mentioned Loris's desire to mate with her, but Trent could sense it. Had he given the slightest indication of challenge, she would have faced him without hesitation. But he had not, and out of respect for Zora, Trent accepted his position in the Pack as her second. They might never be friends, but they were united in their loyalty to Zora.

"*Trent* is fine when we're alone," Trent said. "Are the *centuri* aware the Alpha is running?"

"Yes, they're following at a distance."

"Good." She walked to the rail and stood beside him, searching the night in the direction Zora had run. To her left, rows of barracks formed one border of the rectangular central parade grounds, and the hum of activity carried on the still air. "The motorcade is ready?"

"Yes, Ash has chosen the best of our soldiers"—he caught himself—"*warriors*…to accompany the Alpha to the Timberwolf Compound."

Trent hid her smile at Loris's faint concession to the changes in the forces he commanded as Zora's general. Snowcrest was a mercantile Pack, not a warrior Pack like the Timberwolves. They had soldiers, as did every Pack, to secure their borders and provide escort for their merchants and traders through dangerous territory. Their guards and security forces were not trained for war, although every wolf Were had the natural instinct to fight for its mate, its Pack, and its territory— dominants or not. After the abduction and murder of several of Zora's border guards, Trent had been sent to Snowcrest territory to oversee the training of Zora's fighters, to train them as warriors. Loris had resented the presence of Trent and the other out-Pack Weres in his territory, especially when his Alpha showed sexual interest in one of them. Trent didn't blame the Snowcrest Weres for resenting the presence of a force of warrior class Weres in their midst, but the training had been essential. "And you're satisfied with Ash's choices to accompany the Alpha?"

"I am." He paused and his tension radiated in the air between them. "If I might speak?"

Trent let out a long breath. "Loris, Zora has always valued your counsel, and as she does, so do I. Your advice is always welcome."

"The Alpha has only recently secured the loyalty oath of all the Pack," he said carefully, "and should she leave our territory while some still hold resentment over her…choices—"

"Meaning me," Trent said dryly.

Loris nodded. "As you say, Prima. I do not think it wise for her to be absent while the Pack is still uneasy, especially not to lead our forces into foreign territory. I am her general, and I should take that risk."

"Are you aware of any of our Weres planning to challenge, or encouraging others to do so?"

"No," Loris said, "and if I were, I would handle it myself."

"We don't know what the war council will decide, or even if Zora will choose to send Snowcrest forces into battle—should that even come," Trent said calmly. "But as the Alpha decides, so shall she lead. And *all* of us shall follow, whether into another realm or securing Cresthome."

"Yes, Prima," he said flatly.

Trent didn't necessarily disagree with him, but she let her wolf rise with a faint warning rumble. She would always prefer that her mate not be in danger. But she had mated the Alpha of a wolf Were Pack. The Alpha held her position through power and will. To disobey or question her command was tantamount to challenge. Zora, like every other Alpha, would fight to the death to preserve her position. And Trent would challenge Loris or any other Were before she let that happen.

Loris ducked his head. "Our Pack is loyal, on this I swear."

"Good," Trent said briskly. Her mate bond thrummed with energy, and a charge of excitement rippled through her. "The Alpha returns. Alert Ash that we will depart shortly."

"As you will." Loris pivoted and disappeared before Zora emerged from the forest.

Once back in their quarters, Trent stripped off her pants and sat on the side of the bed, shaking with the need to couple and to reestablish her connection with her mate. Zora's sable-pelted wolf bounded through the window, and in a blur, Zora stood before her, naked and glorious. Her skin shimmered with the excitement of the run and the powerful erotostimulants she exuded as she called Trent to her.

Trent gasped at the rush of sex hormones flooding her blood. "You summoned me?"

Zora's amber eyes glowed with a feral glint, her wolf still prowling close. "I did. I want you."

"I am always ready," Trent said, her throat thick with need.

Zora gripped her by the shoulders, spun her down onto the bed, and straddled her hips.

"You are as beautiful in skin"—Zora's canines skimmed over the pulse in Trent's neck, a dominance show that made Trent's engorged clitoris thrum—"as you are in pelt. I pictured you like this on my run." She rocked over Trent's taut abdomen, coating the faint dusting of pelt below Trent's navel with sex pheromones. "Only you drive me mad to release on you. Only you." Zora braced her arms on either side of Trent's shoulders and bit her throat lightly, not enough to trigger her engorged glands to erupt. Just hard enough to edge her to the brink. "I need to take you soon."

Trent arched her neck, a move her dominant wolf would make for no other. "I am yours to take. But hurry. I am close to exploding."

With strength that belied her slender appearance, Zora drove her thigh between Trent's. The hard muscle of her leg crushed Trent's tense, distended clitoris, and the glands beneath it turned to stone. Trent growled deep in her chest. Her hips lifted, allowing Zora to settle between her thighs and notch her engorged clitoris tightly beneath Trent's. Trent shuddered, a whine rising unbidden. Only for Zora would her wolf surrender.

Zora smiled, a dangerous smile as her wolf's eyes bored into Trent's. A fine dusting of pelt spread across her torso. Zora's wolf rode close to the skin, ready to complete their coupling. Zora kissed her, a hint of canines scraping her lip, and the bite sent a jolt into Trent's sex.

"Be careful. I'll release all over you," Trent groaned.

"Oh, you will, when I say."

Too close to wait, Trent rocked upward, and Zora met her at the peak, their joining effortless and swift. Trent's stomach clenched as Zora's still blunt-tipped claws dug into her shoulders. The mate bite on her throat throbbed.

"I need you." Zora shuddered, poised at the pinnacle for Trent to welcome her.

Trent's heart soared at the words Zora would never speak to another. "And I you, everywhere, always."

Trent gripped Zora's hips at the first warning spasms of release. She let her claws emerge and scored Zora's hips.

Zora's head snapped back, a growl of pleasure deep in her throat. "You're so full, so ready."

"Only for you." Trent's jaws ached as her wolf rose to the call of Zora's need. She thrashed, forcing Zora deeper until the pressure on her glands was too much to hold.

Zora laughed, her eyes wolf-gold, her skin shimmering with the sheen of their sex pheromones and the power of her call. Everywhere in the camp, Weres felt the wild power.

"I'm about to spill," Trent gasped. "I need your bite. Please."

"Always."

Zora struck at the mate bite on Trent's throat, and Trent stiffened. The glands buried deep beneath her clitoris erupted, and her essence burst forth. As she flooded Zora's sex, she claimed the spot on Zora's breast that belonged to her. Her bite triggered Zora's release, joining them as only a mated pair could join. Zora rode her as the storm raged, her eyes wolf wild. When at last Zora emptied, Trent caught her as she collapsed against her.

"Thank you," Zora murmured, drained and sated.

Trent laughed. "Not for that, my love."

Zora eased up onto an elbow and toyed with Trent's nipple. Trent hissed as her clitoris pulsed.

"No, not for that," Zora said. "For not following me when I could feel that you wanted to."

"Ah, that."

Zora kissed her. "Mm. You are a wise mate."

Trent framed Zora's face and watched as Zora's wolf receded, satisfied for now. "You are my Alpha. You are my mate. And my love. I would die for you, and I will follow where you lead."

"I never expected you." Zora kissed her. "I never knew I could want this way. Love this way."

Trent raised a brow. Her wolf preened. "Good."

Zora slid her hand between them and clasped her sex. "I want you again."

Trent rumbled and made no move to stop her. "We'll be late."

Zora leaned down and nipped at her mouth. "Not very."

❖

A glen in Faerie, close to the fading knowe

"Lord Cethinrod," Francesca crooned as she stepped from the mist shrouding the Gate connecting her hiding place to greater Faerie to greet the Night Lord of the Southern Realms. "How very good to see you again."

She hid her fury over the degrading circumstances that forced them to meet in a clearing in the ancient forest like two common mercenaries rather than the ruling powers they rightfully were. At least in this world she could walk beneath the cerulean sun without danger of facing true death. Had she remained in her seat of power in the human world, she would have granted him an audience while she sat on her throne, surrounded by a phalanx of her Vampire guards with her blood slaves prostrate on the floor at her feet. But there were more thrones in the universe than the one she'd had to abandon. Here, in Faerie, she was the petitioner, even though she would never allow the true extent of her weakness to show, least of all to one with whom she hoped to form an alliance.

"Your Grace," Cethinrod murmured in a tone that might have been the wind rustling through the slender branches of the delicate latticework above their head. He used the Olde title for a reigning monarch, one Francesca had not heard for centuries. The dark-haired male bowed, his obsidian gaze beneath slashes of black-winged brows a liquid inferno as it slid over her. His silver tunic, adorned with a black bird of prey on the breast, flowed like mercury over his slender form. His skin, like that of all the royal Fae, glittered in a constantly shifting array of opalescent colors, as if a rainbow was trapped beneath the pale surface.

Francesca found him quite beautiful, and a surge of hunger bled into her eyes as her incisors lengthened. The essence of her thrall enveloped him in a hypnotic cloud of sexual stimulants that would have brought any human and many Weres to their knees at her feet, imploring her to strike and, with her bite, release the hormones into their bloodstream that would drive them to sexual ecstasy.

Cethinrod merely smiled as he took the hand Francesca offered and kissed her fingers. Only the most powerful of the Fae had the strength to resist a Master Vampire as practiced in the art of seduction as Francesca. "I am well-pleased, Your Grace, to find you looking even more beautiful than the last time we spoke."

"And you, My Lord, are nearly as gracious as you are handsome." Francesca accepted the compliment as her due, despite knowing she was fast approaching the point where the human servants and blood donors she'd managed to escape with could no longer sustain her at full strength. Or at her most alluring.

"Tell me," she continued, linking her arm with his as they turned together to walk to the edge of a shimmering golden pool beneath whose surface fish with long magenta fins darted amidst delicate green fronds. As she watched, a long needlelike tentacle exploded from the largest of the fronds, impaled a fish, and pulled it into the center of the vegetation. She found the act satisfyingly efficient. While she enjoyed toying with her prey, when the moment came to turn pleasure into something quite different, she preferred to strike when least expected. The shock made the blood so much richer. "Tell me, to what do I owe the good fortune of your visit?"

She had received a carefully worded invitation to meet with Cethinrod, brought to her on the wing of a large black bird that might have been an enchanted crow…or any of Cethinrod's court in their true form. Despite the delicate wording on the paper that dissolved into raindrops as she read it, she very clearly recognized the message as a summons. In the world where she had reigned with absolute power, she would have ignored such a message and found a way to remind the petitioner that only those she deemed worthy received an audience. But she had no power here, not yet, so she endured the charade. And the insult. The only consolation to her pride was the reminder that Cethinrod sought *her* out because he needed her just as she needed him.

The Fae raised an indolent shoulder, his gaze on the pond, as if his words meant little to him. "I bring news of Cecilia's court."

Francesca hissed. Cecilia, the traitorous bitch, would be one of the first she would slay when she led her army to victory here before moving on to conquer the frail human world. "What has your Queen done that might interest me?"

The muscles in the arm she still clasped tightened as Cethinrod reacted to the insult *your Queen*, a reminder that he was still a vassal to the throne, no matter how he liked to pretend that the Southern Realm was a land unto its own.

"She has had interesting visitors of late." Cethinrod's tone gave no hint of the resentment Francesca knew he carried. With her superior forces and ancient power, Cecilia held an iron grip on his land, one he ruled only by her largesse.

"Oh?" Francesca kept her tone as unconcerned as his. "And who has she been entertaining?"

"Sylvan Mir and Master of the Hunt, Lord Torren de Brinna."

Ice slithered through Francesca's veins. Two powerful enemies. "Are your sources reliable?"

"Quite. My sister Rowena, who unbeknownst to Cecilia was raised away from the Southern court due to an unfortunate lapse in parental judgment that resulted in a less than desired lineage, is a lady of the chamber in Cecilia's court."

"How very fortunate. And has your sister reported the purpose of this meeting?"

Francesca carefully kept the fire of her rage banked. Sylvan Mir along with Vampire Liege Jody Gates were among her greatest adversaries. Sylvan ruled over the largest and strongest wolf Were Pack in the Northern Hemisphere and, when in league with Francesca's Vampire enemies, posed a nearly insurmountable foe. That Sylvan should deem to travel beyond her territory into Faerie was an ominous sign. Torren de Brinna had long been exiled from Cecilia's court and might be one of the few Fae ancient and powerful enough to challenge for the throne. For Cecilia to grant de Brinna safe passage in Faerie, the circumstances must be unusual indeed.

"Alas, no," Cethinrod said with a sigh, "Rowena was not privy to the conversation, but she did report that some great surge of power made the very land tremble during their visit."

"Meaning?"

"I fear some union between Cecilia and her visitors may have been forged, which suggests new alliances may be at hand."

Ah, at last they had come to the purpose of this visit. "I imagine you do not wish to see any bolstering of Cecilia's strength now."

Francesca kept her pleasure at this news to herself. If Cethinrod felt pressed by Cecilia's growing power, he would be even more in need of what she could provide. And what *she* needed now was blood. "Fortunately, my…forces…have proven quite successful against Weres and, of course, humans, should Cecilia seek to add them to her defenses."

"I'm sure your confidence in victory is warranted," Cethinrod said. "However, I believe we should strike before midsummer night, when Cecilia will also be at her strongest."

"Any attack must be a coordinated one," Francesca pointed out. "We must strike Cecilia's court, the Vampire stronghold, and the Were Pack lands at the same time. The solstice is only weeks away."

Cethinrod met her gaze in a rare show of directness. "Can your army be ready by then?"

"I will need more material for my Mage to transform. Many more than my hunters can provide in such a short timeframe." She let the thrall swirl about her. "And I will need blood donors. *Were* blood donors, alive and unspoiled."

"And if I told you I can enlist Fae willing to secure what you need?"

"At what cost?" Francesca murmured, her tone belying her sudden interest.

"What we all seek—power over our dominion once victory is at hand." Cethinrod's form shimmered for a heartbeat, and beneath his glamour, a towering avian predator with a vicious curved beak, massive talon-tipped feet, and eyes of molten lava rent the air with knife-edged wings.

Francesca smiled as Cethinrod's form reappeared. He wanted her assurance that she would support his claim to the throne of all Faerie once Cecilia was defeated. And why shouldn't she make that promise now? After all, the future might bring many changes, and promises were easily lost. "Bring me Weres to nourish my minions and captives for my Sorcerer to transform, and I will give you an army before which the Queen of Thorns will quake."

"It shall be done," Cethinrod murmured.

❖

As soon as Cethinrod disappeared in a shower of color, Francesca hurried to the cave in the depths of the knowe. A Vampire soldier—one of the few she had kept awake with as infrequent feedings as possible—bowed at her approach. Crista, among the oldest of the soldiers who had escaped the purge of Francesca's seethe, had been turned at barely twenty. Slim and dark-haired with luminous dark eyes, her beauty was barely diminished by the hunger that haunted her gaze. Francesca allowed her to feed only enough to prevent her from succumbing to the ennui that had immobilized most of her remaining followers when their blood slaves expired.

"Mistress," Crista said, "have you need of me?"

Crista served as a bedmate prior to feeding, and the need in her tone revealed the urgency of her hunger. But then, a little hunger only made them more eager to please. Francesca kissed her. "Later, my darling. I will send for you, and we will feed together."

Crista trembled, her eyes glowing embers. "Yes, Mistress. I am your servant."

Francesca slipped deeper into the depths of the knowe and materialized beside the Sorcerer who had chosen to follow her into exile for the promise of power and pleasure. "Tell me, Maester Finngar, how soon will we be ready?"

The Sorcerer, or Mage, as the practitioners of the dark arts preferred to be called—as if that somehow gave them an aura of respectability—bowed as if he really meant to pay homage, replying in his unctuous tone, "Mistress, I did not expect you."

"Of that I am quite aware." Francesca smoothed one hand down her scarlet gown, one of the very few she had been able to escape with during that traitorous night at Nocturne, drawing his eyes to her barely covered bosom. Inwardly satisfied as she saw his obvious reaction, she said sweetly, "I've been waiting for your report and thought I would come see your progress for myself."

She glanced around the holding cells, moderately satisfied to see that the numbers of creatures had swelled. Many of the large grottos previously used for storage of goods that supported the inhabitants of the long-abandoned Faerie Mound were now filled with creatures the Sorcerer had transformed into killing machines. Distorted forms of wolf and cat Weres snapped and clawed at each other, their eyes wild and senseless. Once set upon the enemy under Finngar's spells, they would kill until killed. "I had hoped to see more."

"I could move faster," he said apologetically, in a tone Francesca recognized as completely false, "if I had more material."

"By *material*," she said, "you mean more creatures to transform. My retinue makes nightly forays beyond the veil at great risk to themselves to bring you fresh specimens."

"Yes"—and this time his gaunt features took on genuine pleasure—"I have discovered that the life force of Were creatures is far more amenable than that of any lower beings we might find in Faerie."

"And that matters why?" The fire of her anger flared whenever she thought of her ancient enemies. Weres and Vampires had once been uneasy allies when they'd banded together to escape the human purges a millennium before. While the humans were still a danger, they were weaker than the Praeterns, and the Vampires no longer needed to treat the Weres as equals. As blood donors, they were far superior to humans, however. Once defeated and subjugated, the Were blood would add to the strength of her Vampire minions. And if she controlled the source of the blood, her power would increase a thousandfold. All she had to do was convince the Fae to support her in her quest to defeat the Weres and their traitorous Vampire allies. For that, she needed to provide Cethinrod with the ensorcelled killers.

"Even after death, their essence remains strong for a longer period of time, allowing me to perform the rituals to reanimate them with even greater power. Of course," he said, bowing again with all sincerity, "Were subjects are difficult to come by."

She didn't point out to him that their numbers would always be smaller, smaller even than their Fae allies, and they would be at a disadvantage if he could not produce these magically enhanced soldiers in sufficient quantities to convince her enemies *and* her allies she was too strong to challenge. The fact that her soldiers were dead was of no matter—after all, Vampires were often thought of by the ignorant to be dead. Imagine their surprise when they learned otherwise. Her army of ensorcelled undead would soon be feared on both sides of the veil.

She was running out of time, however, with Cethinrod pushing to strike in a matter of weeks, while her position grew weaker rather than stronger. Her hunters had reported that locating the entrance to the knowe after a raid beyond the veil had become more difficult, which could only mean the knowe was finally, truly dying—or that it planned to eject them, leaving them exposed and defenseless in greater Faerie. Cethinrod's promise to provide her with Weres would solve many problems, as long as her Sorcerer could work his pitiful magic. "I will see that you have more specimens very soon. And I expect that you will have my army ready by midsummer."

Finngar tried to hide his shock. "I…but of course, Mistress."

She stepped closer, letting the mist of thrall envelop him. "You won't disappoint me, will you?"

"Never, Mistress," he croaked. His eyes traveled with a hunger he could never disguise to her mouth, where she allowed the gleam of her incisors to show. When she deemed his need had heightened sufficiently to be painful, judging by his erratic breathing and the state of the ridiculous robe he insisted on wearing when employing his tenuous skills, she smiled and drew him closer. His blood addiction gave her all the control she would ever need, but with the decreased numbers of her retinue, she too must take advantage of every source of sustenance. When she took his vein without ceremony and released the stimulants into his blood that would trigger his sexual release, he convulsed.

She drank with no satisfaction. As she released him, he whimpered, eyes dazed, and sagged against the bench covered with his potions and crystals. When Cethinrod brought her Were donors to produce the army she needed, she would no longer need to abase herself with this pathetic specimen.

She turned away with distaste, calling as she swept away, "When next I meet with our Fae allies, I'll expect to bring them the news that we are ready to go to war."

Chapter Three

The instant Sylvan landed in the Compound, she shed pelt. Even in transition, her wolf alerted to a sensation that should not exist in the heart of her territory—the low, steady thrum of power from another Alpha. Had she not just completed her surveillance of the entire inner commons, her first thought would have been that Zora Constantine had arrived early for the war council. No other wolf Were Alpha was close enough to have arrived in the short period of time she had been beyond the fortifications—even if her *sentries* had somehow been compromised in some way to allow a foreign Alpha entry. That thought was just as quickly discounted. This was not Zora's elegant, knife-edged whip of power that she sensed, but something more exuberant, forceful but as yet untamed. This Were had no idea how much danger they were in, and that alone told her all she needed to know.

Sylvan's wolf growled a warning and, unhappy at the suggestion of another Alpha anywhere near, pushed for ascendency. Sylvan's jaw grew heavier, her canines longer, and a fine dusting of shimmering silver pelt slid down her arms and torso. She cocked her head, nostrils flaring, and scented again. Rumbling with discontent, her wolf paced within, sending sharp tendrils of urgency deep into her psyche, demanding to meet whatever challenge threatened. Sylvan held her wolf at bay, tempering the flood of aggression pheromones boiling in her blood, before she pulled every dominant Were within the Compound into a shift. With her fingertips tingling from her claws pressing beneath their surface, every sense on guard, she eased along the perimeter of the commons in the shadows of the fortification, testing the air as the scent she sought wavered and floated, almost as if the Were she tracked had no control over their power, or no knowledge that they broadcast it. The signature—a brisk, bright pulse of unbridled force—resembled an avalanche gathering momentum as it cascaded down a mountainside. The wave of power rose abruptly, strong enough to bring Sylvan's pelt rolling beneath the surface and her canines to elongate, before it simply disappeared.

She paused at the nearest guard station just long enough to pull on yet another shirt and pair of BDUs before following the quickly dissipating foreign signature to headquarters. She bounded onto the broad wood-plank surface where the guards, one on either side of the arched double doors, saluted sharply and said as one, "Alpha. At your command."

"Stand easy, soldiers." Sylvan surveyed her offspring, both in dark green camo, each with a hand on the hilt of the black baton sheathed at her belt. Kira, blond hair nearly as light as Sylvan's, eyes as winter-ice blue, and dark-haired, dark-eyed Kendra. Twins who bore an unmistakable likeness to each parent. Both dominants, both fiercely loyal to the other, they were rarely apart.

Callan had lost no time assigning them to guard duty and, wisely, had not separated them on their first stint at standing post. They should begin as they would undoubtedly go forward, training and fighting together. Both would need to appreciate the strengths of the other and learn to accept the fine dance of power they would need to live with. Sylvan studied them in silence, pleased when both stood within the hurricane force of her regard without flinching. A lingering hint of fine white-gold pelt shimmered in the moonlight on Kira's exposed skin. Her chin jutted just a fraction lower than Kendra's as they faced her, the slight difference in their stances telling her all she needed to know. Kendra was instinctively ready to react to any threat with force, while Kira would take just a moment longer to assess before striking, displaying exactly the kind of measured force a strong second provided.

"Problems?" Sylvan asked, her gaze tracking from Kira to Kendra. Something had alerted Kira's wolf. Her signature scent of wild thyme and blackberries lingered in the still air.

"No, Alpha," Kendra answered, speaking for both, as she naturally took the lead. "All quiet."

Kira's silence signaled her assent. Theirs was a unit born of blood and instinct. Their wolves would need to learn to navigate the tumultuous forces of their nearly identical powers. One, as was always the way of the Were, would need to grant supremacy to the other. Kira had instinctively yielded to Kendra's will since birth, even while challenging her relentlessly in skin or pelt, just as any good *imperator* would. Sylvan recognized the dynamic. Niki, though not her sibling but as close as one, had been the same with her when they were adolescents. Kira and Kendra, well into adolescence now, would undoubtedly tussle many more times before they reached adulthood and assumed their place in a Pack.

Sylvan's chest tightened, remembering her own struggles as she came into her power. Controlling an Alpha wolf—one whose every instinct was to dominate, to demand the mantle of responsibility and the risk that came with it—especially in a Pack where another Alpha still ruled, was a difficult and painful struggle. She'd had no desire to take her father's place in the Pack, but there had been times when her wolf, her primal *self*, had brought her within a heartbeat of challenge.

Kendra would have to face that struggle alone. In this, Kira could not help her. Nor could Sylvan. They were of her blood and Drake's. But they were dominant wolf Weres before all else, and in that, their wolves held more sway than any other power.

Sylvan allowed her power to rise, satisfied when both young dipped their heads. "I'll be with the Prima until I convene the council. None are to enter until I give the order."

"Yes, Alpha," they replied and saluted in unison.

❖

Sylvan pushed through the huge, fortified outer doors barring the entrance to headquarters as if they were merely curtains, bounded through the great room with its towering stone fireplace and scatterings of leather sofas and chairs, and leapt up the stairs to the room where her mate waited. Drake's uneasiness radiated throughout the long, wide hallway. Sylvan let herself in to the sparsely furnished, unadorned sleeping quarters, the strength of their bond growing stronger the closer she came to her mate. The connection soothed and excited her.

Drake sat on the edge of the bed, a shimmer of gold splintering the obsidian of her eyes. "What is it?"

"You feel it," Sylvan said, closing the door behind her. She didn't bother with a lock. None would dare enter, and when the Alpha pair tangled, all would feel their call. She pulled off her shirt and tossed it aside, coming to stand before Drake.

"Yes," Drake said, "something new, of Pack, but...*not* of Pack." Drake rose, scored her fingertips down Sylvan's abdomen, and kissed her. Her canines skimmed Sylvan's lip as a finger flicked open her pants. "I would have come in search of you, but I felt your wolf watching. Just...watching. But not entirely happy. What happened?"

Sylvan ran a hand through her hair and dropped down onto the bed, pulling Drake into her arms. She drew deeply of her mate's scent, absorbing the unique mixture of pheromones and neurochemicals uniquely Drake and, now that they were bonded, uniquely them. She closed her eyes and, for just a moment, let herself forget the cloud of war, the threat to her allies, and possibly the ultimate challenge to the sovereignty of her Pack that bore down on her.

Drake caressed her nape and brushed down the center of Sylvan's naked back, the slight touch enough to tighten Sylvan's sex and bring a sheen of pheromones to her skin.

"How is it you leave in one set of clothes and return in another?" Drake asked mildly, her hands relentlessly caressing Sylvan, claiming her as she aroused her. "You've run in pelt, more than once tonight. What called your wolf?"

"Niki was outside the fortifications, against my orders." Sylvan arched her back with a rumble of pleasure. Drake knew how to tame her with a touch, setting her on the hunt for something far more satisfying than a quick tangle. "I tracked her to the Faerie Gate."

"Ah," Drake said. "I'm sorry."

"Why?" Sylvan rolled onto her back and Drake settled atop her, their bodies molding effortlessly. Sylvan was the Pack Alpha, and quite probably the most dominant wolf Were in the Northern Hemisphere, but she willingly gave her body—and her throat—to her mate. She loved the feel of Drake above her, between her thighs, as close inside her as she could be, just as she knew her mate craved the same. Drake quickened, her heat and essence signaling her need, and Sylvan fought not to join with her instantly. She'd been full and ready since her wolf had awakened her an hour earlier with a sense of urgency she hadn't been able to locate.

"Why? Hm. I'm sorry that Niki disobeyed you," Drake said, "and for whatever troubled her enough to bring her to do so. I'm sorry that she earned your censure and your disappointment. And I'm sorry that you needed to discipline her. Is she all right? Are *you*?"

"I didn't exile her." Sylvan spread her fingers through Drake's hair and drew her down for a kiss. She absorbed Drake's essence from the sex-sheen that coated her skin, in the taste of her kisses, and in the ready slick of her sex. Drake's strength filled her, bringing solace and desire and madness all at once. Sylvan shuddered, already half-mad with need. "Does that make me weak?"

Drake tugged at Sylvan's lip and drew a fine piercing point of blood. "You could never be weak. But you *can* be honorable and wise."

"But I need," Sylvan rasped, the pressure in her loins, the tense ache in the glands beneath her sex, reminding her just how weak she was, "for you."

"And I for you." Drake fit her body more closely to Sylvan's, the muscles in her thighs bunching as she thrust. When she arched her neck and the moonlight slashed across the mate bite at the juncture of her throat, Sylvan took her with a swift lunge, burying her canines deep enough to trigger Drake's release. Drake roared as gold eclipsed her eyes, her wolf joining her at the moment her sex exploded, her image flickering between wolf and Were.

The fire of Drake's essence exploded between Sylvan's thighs, and her sex filled to the brink. All she needed was Drake to claim her, to complete their bond, to finish her. "Now, Drake, now."

Sylvan's power lashed the air with fingers of flame as Drake struck the mate bite on Sylvan's chest, pushing her to the edge and beyond. Their essences merged, their pleasure peaked and rolled, and their call flooded through the Pack. All who felt it drew satisfaction from knowing their Alphas were one, and there for them.

Long moments later, finally drained, Sylvan settled back with Drake cradled against her.

"What is it we sensed?" Drake slowly stroked Sylvan's chest. "I can still feel your wolf on edge, readying for a fight. We all can."

"There will be no fight this night," Sylvan said quietly. "But there is another Alpha in the Compound. My wolf is understandably unhappy."

"An out-Pack Alpha, here?" Drake's wolf came to attention with a sharp growl. "I would have sensed that too. Who would have the audacity to violate our territory? And why are we not tracking them down!"

Sylvan stroked her hair. "No, not out-Pack."

"I don't understand," Drake said. "We have many dominant Weres, but I don't recognize this one. Has one of them challenged?"

"No, not yet. Hopefully not ever." Sylvan kissed Drake's temple and sighed. "It's Kendra."

Drake stiffened. "How can that be? She's—both of them are—still too young."

Sylvan shook her head. "They're maturing much faster than we expected. Callan says every time they shift, which has happened during training—and we've seen it ourselves since they were pups—they advance much faster than usual. We've always known she would be the more dominant." Sylvan relayed her conversation with Callan. "I've told him to put them on post where they can begin formal training. They're on guard duty downstairs right now."

"I know I shouldn't be surprised," Drake said. All young Weres matured rapidly, their biology much more attuned to the wolf part of their nature than to that of any ancient human ancestor. Once they began to shift, they followed the same accelerated trajectory when not in pelt. "They left the nursery for the barracks far sooner than other pups of the same chronologic age. I've always thought Kendra's and Kira's physical and emotional development followed a faster timeline as a result of some combination of your Alpha-dominant genetics. But she's still an adolescent. Surely your wolf recognizes that."

"Kendra may have inherited her Alpha nature from me," Sylvan said, "but your DNA is likely the cause of their steep growth curve. After all, your transformed DNA is what has allowed you to survive the transition from human to Were." She laughed softly. "Of course our young *would* demonstrate some new behavior."

"We don't have any others like them to compare to," Drake said softly. "My only consolation is as quickly as they're maturing into adulthood, their lifespans won't be shortened. All Weres reach maturity quickly."

"They're not human," Sylvan said. "None of us are or ever have been. Ancestrally, perhaps, but that was eons ago."

"What will you do about Kendra? What does it mean?"

"A wolf Were Pack needs dominant wolves. They form our warrior legions—they protect us all. Some of our most dominant Weres—Niki, Max, even Callan—could rise to Alpha status, but they are content to serve my wolf."

"And if she isn't?"

"She'll want her own Pack, or mine."

Drake rested her forehead against Sylvan's. "I love her, both of them, more than any others in the Pack because they're mine, but so are you. You are my mate, and my Alpha. I would rather see her go before a challenge."

"We're not there yet. We may never be." Sylvan pulled her closer and kissed her again. She could offer no other comfort and would keep her worries to herself. She could not chart Kendra's course—that was for Kendra and her wolf to decide.

Chapter Four

The Vampire seethe, Dominion of the Night Hunters

Rafe surveyed the Vampire guards she had chosen to accompany her and their Liege to the Timberwolf Compound for the war council. She and the guard had accompanied Liege Gates there many times in the past, but she prepared for each encounter as she would for any mission in enemy territory. She had lived centuries and had learned never to trust any ally, regardless of how long their association or how common their goals. She'd seen family members betray each other, queens betray kings, countries betray neighbors, and lovers each other most of all. She trusted no one other than her Liege.

  She had been hesitant when Viceregal Zachary Gates had reassigned her from his guard with orders to protect his heir. At the time, Jody Gates had been young in the terms of the Vampire and not yet Risen—a living Vampire who was vulnerable to true death unless bonded to a host whose blood would provide them eternal life at the moment of their first death. But Jody had no bond mate and seemed not to want one despite being in danger daily. She had insisted on mingling with humans, working as a detective even when the human forces did not respect her or honor her station. Rafe had accepted her orders to serve Jody Gates and dedicated herself to keeping her alive, just as she had with all the liege lords who had come before. But in all that time, she had never felt anything other than duty for them. Vampire society was built on power and force—loyalty was not demanded or required. When the chain of command was broken, those who disobeyed were executed. When a liege was defeated, all their Vampires, minions, and blood servants were routinely destroyed to prevent a later uprising. Rafe's only charge had been to secure the continuance of the liege she served.

All that had changed when Liege Jody Gates proved to be unlike any liege lord Rafe had ever known. Time and again, Liege Gates proved willing to sacrifice herself for those who followed her. She had risked true death to save a member of her guard when she'd put herself in the path of a bullet meant for him. Rafe would return that bond in kind and die for her if need be. Until that moment came, her sole purpose in being was to protect Jody, and now her consort, Becca Land. When Liege Gates named her *senechal*, Rafe accepted the place as Jody's second only if she could continue to lead the guard.

Now she had to ensure her soldiers were prepared to defend her.

"Once we enter Timberwolf territory, we will be outnumbered by dominant Weres, but we are stronger, faster, and more deadly." Rafe surveyed the six guards she had hand-chosen for their prowess in battle, their unshakable pledge to protect their Liege, and their absolute willingness to face true death in the performance of their duties. Several hissed, displaying their disdain for creatures most Vampires considered inferior to them. "The stronger Weres can detect our thrall, but not many can resist it. Identify your targets and test their susceptibility to your obfuscation carefully. We do not want to be accused of instigating hostilities."

Her smile sent the message she intended them to hear—opponents who were off-balance, lulled by attraction, and distracted by sexual excitement were easier to subdue. War had no rules.

"Of the Fae who may be present, Lord Torren de Brinna is the most dangerous. Do not underestimate her. Even outside Faerie, her power is considerable and her magic ancient." She nodded to a blonde with ice-blue eyes and a svelte body encased in the formfitting black leather that Sabine preferred when fighting. "Sabine, de Brinna is your target."

Rafe went on to indicate which guard would focus on the members of the council she deemed most dangerous, including the two Alpha Weres, their mates, and the Timberwolf *imperator*. She had spent time—or what passed as time in Faerie—with Sylvan Mir and her *imperator*, Niki Kroff. She trusted them more than any other predator, even liked them, but her job was to serve Liege Gates. The Alpha and her general would fall to her to incapacitate if the need arose.

"We leave within the hour," she said as she finished the assignments.

"Why must we travel to them?" asked Alfred, a relatively young Vampire of only two hundred years, turned in his early twenties, blond, blue-eyed, and classically handsome. In his black silk shirt and knife-edged black pants tucked into knee-high black battle boots, he looked more fit for a fashion runway than the battlefield. Rafe knew him to be swift to detect danger, lethal with a blade, and one of the few guards who enjoyed the kill. He adhered to Liege Gates's strict injunction against bleeding a host to the point of death, but he fulfilled his desire to bleed an enemy when the opportunity arose in battle. As long as he refrained from draining their human servants and blood hosts, Rafe saw no reason to censure him for an atavistic instinct that had allowed their species to survive millennia of being hunted by humans and Praeterns alike.

His question betrayed his youth.

"Liege Gates prefers that we reveal as little as possible about our headquarters and our living arrangements to potential enemies," Rafe said, "and that includes Vampires from other seethes. To acquaint outsiders with the layout of our stronghold and the locations of the entrance and exits is to offer the opportunity for attack at some future point."

She shouldn't need to tell any of them how critical it was that their seethe remain impregnable, not when even the strongest among them would be close to coma during daylight hours. The living Vampires among the guards could function for brief periods of time when exposed to ultraviolet light, but the Risen—herself, Sabine, and Marrott—could not tolerate sunlight for more than a minute, if that. The ferrous compounds supplied by hosts and essential to carry the oxygen in their blood lacked the stabilizers present before first death, and any further disintegration would lead to almost instantaneous second, and final, death. Even should their bonded blood mate be on hand, the likelihood of resuscitation was almost nil. Liege Gates, whose power exceeded that of any Risen Rafe had ever known, had only moments to survive in sunlight.

"Watch the shadows. That's where the Weres will position their strongest fighters. Never underestimate the Alpha and her Prima. If I judge Liege Gates in danger, I will give the order to evacuate, and your sole responsibility—until not one of you remains alive—is to get Liege Gates and her consort into the protected vehicles and out of the Compound. Should they fall while any of you remains, living or Risen, I will end you."

The six guards snapped to attention and saluted, fist to left shoulder. "On our honor, *Senechal*."

"It's time to feed. I need you all at your strongest."

"Will we bring hosts with us?" asked Julian, a muscular dark-haired, dark-eyed male whose typically pallorous Vampire complexion still contained a hint of the sun-kissed islands where he had been born, and where he had been turned by a Vampire missionary.

"Some of our human servants will wait in the vehicles should any of us be injured and require blood. Go now, feed and prepare. You are dismissed."

Rafe waited until her guards filed out to lock and seal the central hexagonal chamber where meetings were held. From each of the six sides, hallways led to resting and feeding chambers, all of which were patrolled during daylight hours by human guards. One doorway, larger than the rest with access by a code known only to Rafe, led via a passageway fortified with impregnable walls to Liege Gates's private quarters. Rafe passed through an adjacent door into the passage to her own quarters, leaving the door behind her unlocked so her Liege could find her at any time. The corridor, lit by wall sconces at intervals, ended at the entrance to her resting chamber. That door remained open whenever she was not inside, and from twenty feet away she sensed the rapid heartbeats and sexual excitement of the two female blood servants who awaited her in a large four-poster bed that sat against one wall, centered on an ornate Persian rug of deep blues and reds. Amelie and Pru, human servants who had hosted for Rafe's previous liege for close to a century. Their aging had been so slowed by the intermittent exchanges of Vampire blood that they still appeared as the full-breasted, vivacious, sensual twenty-year-olds they had been when they'd first offered their blood in exchange for pleasure.

Both naked, they pulled apart slowly as Rafe entered, turning to her with sloe-eyed, dreamy expressions. Amelie, the redhead, her creamy skin sprinkled with freckles, her lips swollen from the kisses she'd been sharing with Pru, smiled and sat up, the sheet falling to her thighs. Her breasts were as milky white as some Vampires' but held the luminous flush of life that was distinctly different. Her rosy nipples were tight and her breathing rapid. "Lord *Senechal*. We await you."

"I can see you've been anticipating me."

Both females laughed, continuing to caress each other as Rafe unbuttoned her shirt, rolled up her cuffs, and left it hanging open. As she crossed to the bed, she unsnapped her trousers and slid the zipper down. Pru, brunette and voluptuous, lolled on her pillow while slowly stroking Amelie's breast and watching Rafe's every movement with avid interest. Rafe scented Pru's arousal growing with each step she took toward the pair. She slowly unleashed her thrall, letting the seductive hormones float around them in an ever-thickening invisible cloud of potent pheromones and mind-altering chemicals. By the time she was ready to feed, all they would know was the overwhelming need for sexual release, a craving deeper than that for any drug. Rafe wanted them deep in the throes of sexual need before she fed. She took no pleasure from the discomfort they would feel otherwise—pain did not stimulate her, nor did the pleasure that accompanied her feeding. What drove her now was not desire, not in the sexual sense. The pain that arched along her spine and coalesced like a furnace of broken glass in her center was bloodlust.

What she craved was the exhilaration of life—of power—rushing through her body as she consumed what only their blood could give her. The sexual satisfaction that followed was automatic and irrelevant and barely made an impact on her consciousness. The distant pulse of physical arousal that accompanied her need to feed would not lead to sexual potency without the power of the fully oxygenated, ferrous-rich blood she would consume. That she was not physically potent at this moment mattered not at all to these two humans.

Her bite and the pheromones she would release into their blood systems, inciting orgasms beyond any they could achieve in any other fashion, was what *they* craved. They were blood servants, voluntary hosts, and they hungered for what only she could give them, just as she hungered for what they ached to provide her. Vision clouding with the red haze of bloodlust, she settled on the bed between them and drew each to her. She cradled a breast in each hand as they undulated against her, their skin damp and hot with unbridled need. They stroked her torso in a choreographed dance, pushing her open trousers lower and dipping between her thighs.

Rafe's throat contracted as her incisors punched down. The pain in her loins stabbed into her psyche, ice picks of flame. She had only seconds of control left before she tore into them like the animal some believed the Vampires to be.

"Amelie, Pru. Are you ready?" She always asked, even though the question was irrelevant. Encased in her thrall, they were lost to the dreams that rose unbidden from their subconscious minds, allowing them to float in a world of their own conceived pleasures. Their only desire now was for completion.

But she always asked.

"Yes, please," Amelie moaned, one hand pushing Rafe's trousers down so she could press her center against Rafe's bare thigh. "Oh please, please hurry. I'm burning. I'm burning inside. Please."

Her nails dug into Rafe's midsection, leaving bloodless crescent wounds already turning purple.

Rafe kissed her, allowing the erotostimulants released as her incisors lengthened to flood Amelie's system, heightening her need and her arousal.

"Soon," she whispered, toying with Pru's nipple, switching her attentions between the two of them, teasing and toying with them until her own lust blinded her to anything but her need. A hand crept between her thighs, grasping her slowly pulsing clitoris, and she felt only the pain. Need, the mindless need of a trapped animal willing to do anything to survive, pounded through her, a thousand blades searing her consciousness, slashing her free from any bonds of reason. She buried her incisors in Amelie's throat, opening her jugular. She groaned, her hips thrusting, as the first rush of life poured into her. She swallowed, each rhythmic pulse igniting her flesh until her heart beat full again, her sex engorged, and her clitoris hardened in quick jerks.

The hand between her thighs—Pru's? Amelie's?—stroked her clitoris, and Rafe vaguely registered the sensation, but her pleasure was not from that. The flush of life that rocketed through her ignited an orgasm not of pleasure, but of power. She drank and orgasmed in a synchrony of power and passion, while Amelie writhed and screamed with the never-ending release. When Rafe had drunk to the point where any more would threaten the survival of her host, she turned to Pru. She wasn't finished. As her power grew, so did her need for blood. More, she needed more. She slid on top of Pru, and when Pru arched in her false embrace, keening with sexual need, Rafe drove her thigh between Pru's and took her throat. Blood poured into her, and this time, nearly at full potency, she orgasmed instantly.

Pru, head thrown back, eyes wide and unseeing, chanted, "I'm coming, I'm coming, oh, I'm coming."

The roaring in Rafe's head, the fingers of flame racing along her spine, drove Rafe to take more. Just a little more—just enough to stop the pain. Rafe held on to a fragment of her will. The pain would never truly abate. The lust would never be assuaged. And she would not kill her host.

Rafe pulled away, a groan wrenched from her chest.

"Oh please, don't stop, please don't stop," Pru pleaded, one orgasm cresting and immediately building into another. "It feels so good, I need to come so much. Please, please don't stop."

Heedless of the pleading Rafe knew would never stop, Rafe sealed the wound and rolled away. She breathed now, although her body didn't need to. Her skin was coated with the release of the females. Her sex was full and still ready. She slid a hand down her chest, paused where she could feel the steady beat of her heart, then traced lower between her thighs. Grasping her engorged clitoris, she stroked until the spasms subsided and the pressure resolved.

Staring at the ceiling, she listened to the two women whimper softly, the last waves of orgasm coursing through them even in their insensible state. When at last they quieted, she stood, pulled off her clothes and tossed them aside, and showered quickly. Fully vital now, with the lust tempered to a slow-burning flame in the pit of her stomach, she dressed in another set of formfitting black shirt, pants, and calf-high boots, strapped on her double-holstered weapon harness, checked her weapons, and settled them against her sides. Then she slid on a black blazer, one of many in exactly the same cut and color, designed to give her easy access to her weapons. Before she went out to assemble the guards, she punched the intercom for another of the human servants. "Bring food to my chamber for when they awake."

"Yes, My Lord *Senechal*," the disembodied voice replied.

❖

Becca gripped Jody's shoulders, a cry escaping as another orgasm flooded her senses, leaving her mindless, aware of nothing but the pleasure that struck deep into the heart of her.

"Don't stop," she whispered, threading her fingers through Jody's black hair with one hand, holding Jody's face to her throat with the other. "I love the way you feel."

Jody trembled, the heat from her newly invigorated body pouring from her, warming Becca with wonder and relief. Jody's body was so often cool to the touch, never cold, but a constant reminder that Jody's existence was fragile despite her tremendous strength. Her pale skin lost heat as the night wore on and her need for the blood that sustained her grew. Becca's blood. Becca lusted for the pleasure of Jody's bite, but nothing could be more arousing than sustaining her beloved with her own blood.

"Don't stop, my love," she murmured. She trusted Jody implicitly, knowing Jody would never harm her. Knowing too that in the throes of ecstasy, just like any host, she would beg Jody for more. She had even more reason than a blood servant to want more. Through her bond with Jody, in that moment when her blood—and hers alone—gave Jody life, Jody's power roared through her, uniting them in a way that no joining with a blood servant could ever replicate.

"I can't take any more from you right now, as much as it pleases me." Jody gently slipped her incisors from Becca's throat, sealed the wound, and kissed her. "There will be another time."

Becca laughed, hearing the tremor in Jody's voice, knowing Jody craved what she craved—the intimate blood rites of a bonded pair. Just those simple words—*another time*—made her heart soar. For so long, Jody had resisted making a life with her—resisted *her*. But no more.

"I'm stronger than you think," Becca said, nipping at Jody's lip. When she drew a bead of blood, she licked it. Jody tasted of midnight mist, copper, and earth. Power beyond imagining. A fraction of that power transferred to Becca each time they bonded. Jody would open a vein for her and give Becca all she wanted if she asked, but she didn't need Jody to do that. The blood they shared when they joined was enough for her to feel the changes already. She was in no hurry to discover exactly how far away from being human she would go. She didn't fear what was to come, but her humanness was part of what allowed Jody to express the emotions that Vampires weren't thought to have. And not just humans and other Praeterns believed the Vampires incapable of love—the majority of Vampires believed it too. Teaching Jody differently was a challenge Becca enjoyed every day.

"I want you to do something for me," Becca said.

"Anything, my heart." Jody rolled onto her back and drew Becca into her arms. Becca rested her head against Jody's heart, and she sensed Jody's smile.

"You're listening to it, aren't you?" Jody murmured, stroking Becca's shoulder, sending shivers down her spine.

"I like to hear your heart. You know, even when you're resting, I can hear it."

"You're convinced it beats even then? That I'm not dead?"

"Believe me, my darling, you are not and never have been dead. When you are at rest, you are always there. I feel you in my soul." Becca kissed Jody's breast and caressed her bare torso. Jody's skin flushed a faint pink, and her pulse bounded, as if she'd been running. The muscles in Jody's deceptively slender abdomen quivered beneath her fingertips, and Becca's sex tightened. "Mm, and now that you are full and very much awake, I want you again."

Jody closed her eyes and drew Becca even closer. "You're determined to keep me from becoming what I truly am."

"You mean a heartless, emotionless, soulless Risen Vampire?"

"Yes," Jody said.

"I have no doubt that there are some like that. I've met them." Becca raised up on an elbow and looked into Jody's obsidian eyes, slashed through now with shards of red that never disappeared. Her eyes were those of every Risen Vampire, eternal beings capable of being destroyed, but only with tremendous difficulty. She traced the knife-edge of Jody's jaw and kissed her. "But that is not you. And you should know, whoever you become, I will love you."

Fire danced in Jody's eyes—mesmerizing, consuming, unimaginably erotic. "If I ever become someone who cannot return that love, you must leave me."

Becca frowned. "What are you worried about?"

"Rafe's reports of what she witnessed while in Faerie, and all she suspected was being hidden." Jody sighed. "The war stirring in Faerie threatens us. Should we be forced to defend our Dominion here in this realm, the battles, the battle lust, and the blood that I will shed may change me."

"We don't know that Francesca is even alive—or in what state she currently exists—in Faerie. And we don't know she's coming here."

Jody said, "The creatures Rafe observed are killing machines—their only purpose, once unleashed, is annihilation. If Francesca amasses an army like that, here? All of humankind will unite to destroy us and every other Praetern species if that ever happens."

"Then why would Francesca risk that?" Becca shook her head. "She would be hunted just like all of us."

"Because she's a narcissist, and she thinks that nothing will ever defeat her. That all of us may perish, but she'll survive and establish a new Vampire world order." Jody grimaced. "She's been lucky, and so far she's been right."

"Then we must see that whatever evil she is brewing never crosses into this realm," Becca said, "and that Faerie remains our ally."

"We may be drawn into a war not our own in order to prevent a greater danger." Jody grimaced. "My Vampires may die to save those who revile us."

"If Sylvan asks for forces to return to Faerie," Becca said, "I must ask for your promise."

"What would you request of me?" Jody said with a hint of caution in her voice.

"I don't want you to go."

"I am the leader of my Dominion," Jody said with the edge of finality she took on when her mind was set. "It is my obligation to lead—"

"Darling," Becca said lightly, "I call bullshit."

Jody frowned as if she'd never heard the word before. "I believe you're insulting me."

"I realize that's something you're not used to." Becca dropped a kiss on Jody's throat, enjoying the faint hiss of pleasure Jody couldn't hide. Oh, her lover was not done feeding yet, whether she wanted to be or not. "You are indeed the leader of your Dominion, and your Dominion is still in turmoil after the coup at Nocturne. That, coupled with your father's part in attempting to destabilize the Weres, makes this an unwise time for you to be away from your Vampires. And"—she hesitated, the tightness in her chest belying her calm—"you have no heir."

"I would name an heir before I put myself in serious danger."

"That is possible, of course, but not the most assured way to create stability throughout your Dominion. An heir of the blood would be far more unifying, aren't I right?"

"Yes, but—"

Becca drew a breath. "I would like to give you an heir."

Jody stiffened. "I...you wish to bear a child?"

"I carry your blood inside me," Becca said. "Any child born to me would be of *our* blood. A blood heir. I want to do this."

"You know, with what you carry in your blood from my DNA, what kind of child we would have."

"Of course I know." Becca met Jody's gaze—saw turmoil and hope in the dark well of her soul. "Do you think I could love you and not be able to love a child like you?"

"I'm not being insulted," Jody whispered, a wave of bloodlust striking her with demanding urgency. "I'm being seduced."

Becca's heart soared as her body quickened. She knew her lover. She knew when Jody was pleased and not sure how to show it. And she knew what they both needed now.

"You're being loved." Becca slid on top of Jody, pressing her sex to Jody's thigh. "Feel how much I need you."

She pushed back her hair and bared her throat, aware of what the sight of her pulse rippling beneath the skin would do to her lover. "Take what is yours."

In seconds she would be beyond knowing anything but the craving for Jody's bite and the rush of Jody's erotic essence inside her. "And give me what is mine."

"Always, my love," Jody murmured and struck.

Chapter Five

When Rafe appeared in the central chamber, her cadre of guards were arrayed as she expected them to be, each outfitted in a black shirt, tailored pants, and high black boots. Like her, each wore a weapon harness with their personal choice of handgun, and like her, they each carried an array of concealed weapons, depending on their fighting style. She carried a knife sheathed on each forearm. Sabine favored shuriken and kept the razor-sharp throwing stars in a special compartment on her belt, while Marrott's in-close weapon of choice was a silver spike, which when punched into the eye or skull of a Were would prove fatal if the victim could not shift immediately. And sometimes, even then. Rafe carried one other weapon in the event her enemy proved to be Fae—two slender iron short swords in a back sheath. A strike with cold iron might not kill them, but their magic would fall, giving her time to deliver a lethal blow.

A quick glance also confirmed the guards had all fed. Their complexions bore the flush of new blood, and the fathomless black pupils fixed on hers roiled with the red glow of hunger. Hungry not for sustenance now, but for battle. These were predators, born to live by the hunt or die. Centuries in hiding had not changed their genetic predisposition, even if living among humans in civilized society had taught them to be careful. They had all simply become more stealthy hunters.

Satisfied that her guards were ready, Rafe nodded to Hugo, the shortest of the six, muscular and brown-skinned, with thick black hair and a disarmingly pretty smile. "Hugo, see that the blood servants are escorted to the vehicles and then direct the motorcade to proceed to the main exit."

"Yes, *Senechal*," he snapped, saluting briskly before disappearing down the nearest passageway.

"The rest of you," Rafe said without breaking stride as she crossed to the passageway leading into the mansion—the sprawling marble edifice that had once served as the state governor's mansion and now served as Liege Gates's home and headquarters—"with me."

She led the way through the warren of tunnels and alcoves that beehived the underground complex. Unknown and invisible to anyone studying the outer footprint of their headquarters, the many rooms provided sleeping quarters for the human servants and resting chambers for the Vampire minions who fulfilled multiple functions in the seethe or who simply sought shelter from the dangers of the outside world. Only the most trusted senior guards knew the entire map of the intersecting hallways, stairways, and concealed passageways that led to the first floor of the mansion, which to the world outside appeared to be Jody Gates's home. Anyone watching or recording the movements of visitors entering and Vampires leaving would assume the vulnerable areas for a strategic strike would be aboveground. Today, the ubiquitous photographers and the spies posing as such would see what Rafe wanted them to see—the motorcade carrying Liege Gates and her entourage leaving from the garage adjoining the main building, the dwelling where the Liege was presumed to live.

In reality, none of the areas in that structure were inhabited, nor were they occupied at all during the potentially lethal daylight hours. No one used the mansion except during meetings with human representatives on official business with the Viceregal. The Vampires of *Chasseur de Nuit*, the Night Hunters, lived as they had for millennia, deep in the shadows and the safety of the night.

At the last intersection before the elevators leading to the upper levels and the garages, Sabine wordlessly signaled for the guards to turn right. As the cadre disappeared, Rafe turned left down the final hallway and slipped through a door coded to her retinal scan. She entered a foyer carpeted in thick Persian-weave rugs and furnished with several high-backed leather sofas, a Louis XV sideboard set with silver wine goblets and decanter, and a marble fireplace now dormant. The sitting room adjoined Liege Gates's apartments and had once been occupied by blood servants waiting for Jody to rouse at sunfall and feed. No one had been brought to this area under an amnesic thrall since Liege Gates and her consort had formed a blood bond. Liege Gates did not sate her thirst or her lust with servants or slaves, as many in power did.

Rafe took up a station adjacent to the inner apartment door and waited. Minutes, hours, time itself were meaningless to her. She had lived centuries, watched families and loved ones disappear into the mists of time, and entire civilizations crumble to dust and be forgotten. She occupied her mind with reviewing the thoroughness of her preparations for a meeting she had reluctantly agreed they should attend. Despite the increased danger to Jody whenever she ventured beyond the protective confines of the seethe—which was far too often for Rafe's liking—Francesca's plans would embroil the Vampires in a war with humans. After witnessing the ensorcelled creatures loosed in Faerie and set upon the Snowcrest Weres, Rafe had no doubt the former Mistress of the City intended an eventual assault in this world. The Vampires in absolute numbers were the smallest of the Praetern population, although in terms of power and strength they were equaled by none. Still, the humans had vast resources, militarily, monetarily, and in sheer numbers, and would exact a heavy toll if arrayed in force against the Praeterns. No—Francesca must be ended, true ended, and that would require as much power as could be marshaled. Rafe could not counsel Liege Gates to avoid the coming fight, but she could do everything in her power to ensure she did not perish in it.

❖

Timberwolf barracks, two hours until the summit meeting

Anya rumbled softly as the weight of a body sliding onto the bunk beside her brought her from a light doze to instant readiness. Moonlight filtered through the high horizontal windows that ran beneath the eaves of the long, narrow barracks. As one of the *sentries*, she slept in the common room with twenty other Were soldiers. Weres, like most shifter Praeterns, viewed sex in the same way as they viewed hunting or eating— as essential to life, natural and instinctive. While the pheromones that signaled sexual readiness were registered by every Were for leagues around, only the unmated and a match within the dominance hierarchy would respond. And any Were, dominant or submissive, could decline the invitation. When not on duty, if Weres wanted a tangle, they found some private space, not to hide their activity, as frequent coupling for Weres, mated or not, was intrinsic to Pack cohesiveness, but to give the others the opportunity to sleep.

This night, though, they'd *all* been ordered to remain in the barracks, which didn't translate into refraining from a quiet—or as quiet as Weres ever got—tangle. Those who weren't coupling just ignored the pervasive flow of pheromones and curled down with their wolves to rest. Anya had spent herself in a pleasant tangle with one of the older soldiers earlier that had left her relaxed but with a restless urge inside that had become more and more frequent in recent weeks. Her releases more often than not left her hungering for something… more, and she'd learned to just ignore the sensation. Now, though, she had company, and judging from the wave of pheromones and the slick glide of sex-sheened skin over her bare back, her visitor was close to the pinnacle of readiness. Smiling to herself, Anya turned on her side and looped an arm around Genta's waist. "You should take off the rest of your clothes."

Genta caressed Anya's breast and put her mouth against Anya's ear. "Should I apologize for waking you?"

"Why would I want to sleep when you're so close to erupting all over me?" When Genta shivered and whined low in her throat, a helpless, desperate sound of need, Anya chuckled and brushed her fingers along the curves of Genta's hip. "Off."

As Genta hurriedly pushed her briefs down, Anya continued to stroke along her thigh to the delta between Genta's legs. The hot essence of Genta's desire welcomed her, and her sex tensed in response.

"You're always welcome," Anya murmured, "but I thought you'd found Michael earlier."

Genta, recently promoted to *sentrie* but only barely out of adolescence, entwined her legs with Anya's, pressing her heated sex to Anya's hand. "He's sleeping."

"Hm. Tired, is he?" Anya rolled onto her back and pulled Genta above her, clasping her hips and urging Genta to straddle her upright thigh. Genta braced herself above Anya on extended arms as Anya cupped her sex and teased the hard length of her clitoris. "He's young yet."

"I can't sleep. I need…yes, that. I need…that." Genta's tawny eyes glowed in the moonlight as she arched her neck, her tousled blond hair fanning around her neck and shoulders. Her breasts, full and firm and upright, glistened with sex-sheen.

Oh yes, she was very close already.

Anya tightened inside, her sex beginning to pulse. She was only a few years older than Genta and her sex drive every bit as rampant as that of the barely out of adolescence Were, but she'd learned to hold her need at bay a little bit longer. And Genta was not the first to visit her bunk that night.

"Squeeze me," Genta said.

Anya gripped her and stroked. Genta growled and thrust harder. Anya let her claws erupt and scored the flesh beneath her hands. Jolted by the pinpoints of pain, Genta jerked and drenched Anya's hand and stomach in her essence. The cascade of pheromones, hot and potent, brought Anya to the brink of orgasm with a shuddering groan. Her erupted canines throbbed, and the urge to bite brought her wolf snarling to the surface.

Now. Now. She needed to bite. She needed…needed. Claim her. Claim her. Claim her and release.

Anya pulled back, shocked. Not Genta. Her wolf had never fought to claim another Were before, and this felt wild, uncontrolled, and impossible. Anya clamped her jaws tight and wrenched her head away when Genta collapsed against her. Anya's sex pounded, her glands swollen to bursting. She gripped Genta's shoulders, refusing the call of the tender juncture of Genta's neck and shoulder where a bite would invite a joining, and pressed her sex to Genta's hip until she spent enough to ease her need.

Genta shuddered in her arms. "You make me release so hard."

Anya forced a laugh through her strained throat, her stomach clenched and her sex still throbbing. "You came to me already on the edge."

Genta laughed softly. "I knew you would finish me finally."

"Are you? Finished?" Anya murmured, ignoring the fullness in her sex that reminded her she was far from done.

"Mm. Yes."

"Good. You should get some rest before Callan announces the cadres form up outside."

"Can I just stay here?" Genta asked on a long lazy sigh. "I might be ready again soon."

"Some other night," Anya murmured, not trusting her wolf. Whatever it was that had unleashed that urge, she didn't want to risk it again. Genta was not for her. She knew that with absolute certainty.

With a sigh, Genta groped for the shirt she'd pulled off when she crawled into Anya's bunk. "I suppose you're right."

"If we didn't have to muster in an hour, I would want you again," Anya said to soften the rejection.

Genta rumbled in pleasure and leaned down to kiss her. Her canines tugged at Anya's lip, and Anya's clitoris instantly hardened. Too sensitive. Too ready. Too close to being out of control. Anya gently pushed her away. "Go now. Get some rest."

Genta moved away into the still barracks, and Anya turned on her side, curling into herself, willing away the tension deep within that demanded she…that she what? What was it her wolf demanded?

A hand gripped her shoulder, and she jerked around with a snarl, canines jutting and pelt racing down her torso.

Callan backed away, both hands in front of him. "Sorry."

Anya sat up quickly and ran her hands through her hair. Bare-breasted, her pants open, still shivering with sex-sheen and rushes of hormones, she drew a long breath. "My apologies, Captain. I was… surprised."

"Meet me outside." Callan's expression suggested he knew exactly what had her on edge.

"Of course." She stood, pulled on a shirt, and followed him outside. She mentally reviewed everything she'd done on her last duty tour and couldn't recall any particular problems.

Callan closed the barracks doors and halted.

"Sir?" she said.

"I know this isn't the best way to do this, but we don't have time for formalities. You're now the lieutenant in charge of the third cadre."

She straightened to attention and saluted. "Yes, sir. Thank you."

"The Alpha requests your presence at the war council."

Anya blinked. Newly promoted lieutenants did not join the Alpha's inner circle, especially not at a war council. "Yes, Captain."

"And Anya," Callan said, grinning, "you might want to grab a shower beforehand and cool off. Your call is strong enough, I felt it outside all the way out here."

"Ah, I was about to do that." Anya carefully kept her eyes above the level of his midsection. Callan was mated, which did not mean he and every other Were in the vicinity wouldn't respond to her call, at least involuntarily.

"Good. Join me here, and we'll go over together."

She saluted briskly, vaulted over the side of the porch, and made her way to the outside showers. The icy water did little to temper the heat that fired within her, scorching her in a way she'd never experienced before. She wasn't ready to decipher what message her wolf was sending. She could only hope to ignore it and keep her wolf under control.

❖

Chasseur de Nuit *seethe*

Rafe straightened to attention as the door separating the waiting chamber from Liege Gates's quarters opened, and Becca Land, followed closely by Liege Gates, stepped through. The Liege's consort wore a fitted maroon shirt open to between her breasts and tailored black pants with black heels. Rafe's Liege was dressed entirely in black, absent of color save for the red in her eyes.

"Hello, Rafe," Becca said.

Rafe bowed, her gaze still focused on the pair. "Good evening, Consort. My Liege."

"Rafe," Jody said softly. "Are we ready?"

"Yes, my Liege, all is in readiness." Rafe saluted, ignoring the faint grimace that her Liege often got when she did. Liege Gates had told her the salute was unnecessary when they were alone, as was the use of her title, but that was one of the rare occasions where Rafe disagreed. Formality was a sign of respect as well as a way of maintaining order among predators who lived in close quarters and often were forced to share scarce sources of sustenance. Another consequence of living openly among humans, who were once seen primarily as prey, was the inevitable penalty for the death of a host, whether the host had willingly offered their vein or not. Among members of the seethe, the oldest and strongest fed first, followed by the newlings who had no control but a voracious hunger, and only then did the others feed. A healthy seethe was one in which the hosts were cared for and the members allowed to feed fairly.

Rafe fell in just in front of Liege Gates's right shoulder where she could quickly cover her at the first sign of hostilities. Becca walked to Jody's left, and Jody kept a hand in the center of Becca's back, poised to redirect her in the event of danger.

As they strode to the elevators, Rafe added, "You and Consort Land will ride in the third car."

"Very well."

The official protocol provided to the media and other officials stated that the Liege traveled in the heavily fortified lead car, which was never actually the case. Rafe determined which car the Liege and the Consort would ride in immediately before the motorcade assembled. No one else in the guard or any outside sources was informed of that in advance. Zahn Logan, the head of security, a human servant of ancient lineage and unquestionable loyalty, was the only other among them Rafe had informed.

When they reached the garage level, the eight vehicles in the motorcade, all identical black limousines, idled in a line in front of the half-open garage doors. Overhanging impregnable steel doors blocked line of sight as passengers embarked.

The lead vehicle bearing the flag of Liege Gates's Dominion on the left front fender slowly rolled out, followed by the second car. Before the second car had cleared the garage, the doors on the third vehicle swung open, and Liege Gates and Becca Land stepped into the back with vampire speed, and Rafe slipped into the front passenger seat. The slight delay as the driver slowed just enough to allow everyone to enter would be imperceptible from two hundred yards away, the inner perimeter currently patrolled by Vampire security. Human lookouts had been posted throughout the day at several outer perimeters along the exit route from the city, one which was varied every time the Liege traveled. At several hours before dawn, the streets were empty or nearly so, and monitoring traffic both via ground and air surveillance was not difficult. Nevertheless, Rafe opened her channel to the lookouts.

"Check," she said.

"Checkpost alpha, clear. Checkpost beta, clear. Checkpost charlie, clear..." The responses continued with no evidence of unusual activity.

Still, Rafe did not relax. Assassination attempts on the Were Alpha and Liege Gates had already been made and nearly proved fatal. The Humans First movement, a radical group, had been vocal as to their position that Praeterns were not people, and therefore violence against them, including homicide, was not a crime. And humans were not their only enemies. Vampires, like all apex predators, held their position through power and force. Every time Liege Gates left the safety of their seethe, she was in danger, and unfortunately, unlike many Vampires who held power, she insisted on performing her duties personally, which often required her to travel. Her Liege made Rafe's duties more difficult, but her existence held no other meaning after all these centuries alone.

As they passed through the quiet Albany streets, Rafe scanned the surrounds despite the all-clear reports. A well-placed hand-held rocket burst from someone who stepped from a hiding place where they might have been hiding for weeks, just waiting for this opportunity, could demolish the vehicle. The occupants would likely survive unless the rocket was incendiary. Fire would surely kill the Consort, and possibly even the Risen Vampires. Rafe caught glimpses of the occasional police vehicle trailing them on side streets. As their motorcade did not adhere to any speed limits on the way out of the city, she was obliged to advise the local law enforcement agents in advance of their itinerary. She had argued this egregious breach in security with Liege Gates on multiple occasions, but Liege Gates had been firm. The law was the law, and they would adhere to it.

Rafe grimaced. Not *her* laws—and why should the Vampires be bound by human laws when many humans denied them the very right to exist? If Vampires didn't control so much of the world's wealth, acquired over centuries of investment and economic advancement, she doubted most nations would even try to intervene in genocidal wars. Rafe and every other Vampire knew the police were not their friends, but they did have some allies within the ranks and higher. When they crossed the boundaries of the city, they diverted to a route which they had not informed the officials of.

"Aerial check," she said into a second channel.

"All quiet," came the reply.

At the speeds they were traveling, they would be under cover of forest on Pack land in less than an hour. Until then, they would be shadowed by their own security helicopter. The helicopter would have to turn back at the border of the Were territory or risk assault from Were forces on the ground at least, or open warfare at most.

A few moments later, she detected the sound of vehicles—several—less than a mile behind them and radioed the helicopter. "Aerial check. Vehicles to the rear. Identity?"

"Roger that. Three Rovers. We've had them on radar for seventy-two minutes. Snowcrest Weres."

"Very well, thank you."

After turning off the interstate onto a secondary road and navigating along progressively narrower roads, switchbacks, and turns, the driver of the lead vehicle slowed.

"*Senechal*," Sabine reported over the channel reserved for the guards and Rafe, "we have reached a gated guard post. There are two armed Weres in view." A pause. "At least another pair in the forest within line of sight to our vehicles."

Rafe opened a channel to the other drivers. "Hold your positions. On my command to evacuate, vehicles one and two will provide a screen for the Liege's car to turn and retreat. Any vehicle still operable will follow to cover the rearguard action under Zahn's command. Acknowledge."

The affirmatives sounded, and Rafe stepped from the vehicle and strode toward the concrete bunker and adjacent guardhouse. A tall, sharp-eyed blond Were in khaki camo BDUs approached, a rifle resting casually by their side. Rafe wasn't the least bit fooled by the casual pose. Given the rapidly decreasing distance between them, she could disarm and disable the Were in the time it took the guard to fire. In all likelihood, she would be wounded, potentially lethally, but her Vampire guards would have time to evacuate Liege Gates and her Consort.

"Rafe," the blond Were said, "how many?"

"Drea," Rafe said. "Four per vehicle."

The Were continued to walk forward, and Rafe turned to join them, placing her body between the *sentrie* and the vehicles.

"No problems on the trip?" the *sentrie* asked when she reached the last vehicle in the row of vehicles and turned to walk back. She would have scented the human servants within, but the Vampires would have shrouded their presence, making it difficult for even a Were to scent them.

"Quiet."

The Were nodded. "Good. Just the way we like it. You're clear to proceed."

Rafe rejoined the Liege's vehicle and gave the order for the motorcade to advance. The deeper they progressed into Timberwolf territory, the greater the danger that they could be trapped and ambushed. Despite their Vampire speed and immunity to lethal injury, they *could* be killed. Her senses sharpened as the taste of battle lust filled her mouth. Her incisors lengthened and hunger turned her vision crimson.

"Rafe," Jody murmured softly, "we are among friends."

"I have no friends." She spoke not from regret, but with the surety of a millennium of witnessing betrayals.

Jody sighed. "You have me."

Rafe turned to meet Jody's gaze. "You are my Liege."

"Then trust me on this. There may be danger here, but the Weres are not the source. Try not to incite them to challenge you." Jody smiled, shards of crimson alight in her eyes. "I do not wish to explain to an angry Alpha why my *senechal* drained one of her wolves."

Rafe grinned. "More than one." She eased back in the seat and tempered the thirst that always burned in her depths. "As you wish, my Liege."

"Thank you." Jody slid an arm around Becca's shoulders and settled back on the wide leather seat.

The motorcade moved on through several more checkpoints before pulling up to the main fortifications. As expected, the captain of the Timberwolf warriors emerged from an opening in the stockade barricade and walked with a loping stride toward the vehicles. He was unarmed, which meant nothing. Callan was fast and wouldn't need a weapon to shift and attack. He smiled when Rafe stepped out and glided to meet him.

"Welcome," he said. "You're the first to arrive."

"Snowcrest is close behind us," Rafe said. "They turned off the interstate five minutes after we did."

"We have them," Callan said with a smile. He signaled the *sentries* on the barricades, and the tall main gates slowly swung open. "We have arranged parking by the east wing for your vehicles. A *sentrie* will show your drivers and other members to a private waiting area."

"Very well." Rafe gave the order for the motorcade to proceed inside, and the vehicles entered the Compound, followed the circular path around the perimeter, and halted in front of the main headquarters building. Once again, Rafe stepped out of the vehicle first, but this time each pair of guards exited the remaining vehicles. She quickly scanned the area, saw only two young Were soldiers standing post, and opened the rear door. "You may exit."

The Liege and Consort stepped out, and the Vampire guards instantly formed a semicircle around Rafe, Liege Gates, and Becca Land, moving forward in well-choreographed synchrony in a protective shield as they crossed to the entrance.

Rafe took in the two young Weres on post, who briskly saluted. The Alpha's young, by their scent. Interesting.

Kira, the blonde of the pair, said, "Liege Gates, Consort Land, Lord *Senechal*, welcome to the Timberwolf Compound."

Jody slowed to briefly meet Kira's gaze. Not long enough to challenge, but directly enough to establish her status as the reigning Vampire in the region. "Thank you, Kira."

The young Were's eyes brightened for an instant, but her expression remained formal. The dark-haired twin leaned over, opened the doors, and everyone proceeded inside.

Sylvan Mir came forward, hand extended, and said, "Jody, how are you?"

Jody gripped Sylvan's hand for an instant and then let go. "Very well. I see your young have progressed in their duties."

"That and more." The wolf Alpha grinned, leaned forward, and kissed Becca Land on the cheek. "Becca."

"Hi, Sylvan," Becca said.

"This way." Sylvan gestured toward the rear of the two-story great room where a fire burned in an open hearth twice the height of the tallest among them. A scattering of leather sofas, chairs, and heavy wooden tables occupied the space before the fireplace. Were soldiers lined the side walls. The Timberwolf *imperator* and the *centuri*, Sylvan's personal guard, fanned out to the sides of the hearth. Niki Kroff met Rafe's eyes across the expanse, and while Rafe knew Niki was mated, she recognized the pulse of hunger Niki would never be able to subdue.

Rafe saw no reason why the Were, or any of them, should be concerned by their nature. She nodded briefly and carefully controlled her thrall. When she fed, it would not be from an unwilling host, no matter how strong their desire—or her hunger.

Chapter Six

The war council convenes, Timberwolf Compound

Zora slid closer and curled her fingers around the inside of Trent's thigh as the Rover prowled through the gates of Sylvan Mir's fortress stronghold. She had no better or more appropriate word for the encampment. The Timberwolves were a warrior Pack, their protective and aggressive instincts running back to the dawn of time. While she had every confidence in her Weres to defend Cresthome in her absence and her soldiers to fight wherever they might be needed, here in the heart of Timberwolf Pack land, she and her *centuri* were vastly outnumbered by far more experienced warriors. Her wolf was wary and on guard. Her Alpha instincts made this an uneasy meeting, not just for her, but for her mate. Trent was returning to Timberwolf territory for the first time since their mating, when she had assumed the mantle of power as the Snowcrest Prima. Her allegiance to Snowcrest was unquestionable, but her ties to the Timberwolves ran through her DNA as well as her soul. Were she challenged or a Snowcrest Were endangered, Trent would retaliate. Zora would expect no less, even though such aggression in a foreign Were's territory was tantamount to an act of war and none of them would likely survive. Such was the way of the predator.

Your wolf is bristling, Trent voiced along their internal avenue of communication, taking care that Ash and Jace, who rode with them, could not overhear. The Alpha needed to project an air of certainty and fearlessness, or every one of their Weres would be uneasy, edgy, and ready to shift at the first hint of aggression from any Timberwolf. They might be allies, but they were all still wolf Weres, and a room full of edgy dominants was a firefight waiting to ignite.

She's fine—just wary, as she should be, Zora replied, exerting her mental dominance to reassure her wolf that all was well. *Your wolf seems calm enough, not that I'm surprised. You're rarely worried about anything—not even the threat of an Alpha wolf who might take issue with your impertinence.*

I was never impertinent. Only unwilling to be chased away. Trent covered Zora's hand where it lay on her thigh, squeezing gently, and said aloud, "Besides, I have no quarrel with these Weres, and they should have none with me. I'm with you, where I belong. Any Were can see that." Trent nuzzled Zora's neck and kissed the angle of her jaw. "I trust the Timberwolves, but should they behave foolishly, they will discover I am ever and always your champion. I don't expect a fight today, but if one comes, I'm ready."

Zora's wolf chuffed. She had chosen Trent long before Zora was willing to accept the undeniable rightness of their bond and the mating frenzy that had nearly driven her mad when Trent had first appeared at Snowcrest—arrogant, dominant, irresistibly sexual, and set on having Zora despite the obstacles. Zora's sex tightened with urgency as Trent's mating scent engulfed her. She nipped Trent's lip, causing her to grumble at the provocation. "You're always ready for most things, my love."

"I'm always ready for you…right now as much as ever. I can feel your wolf teasing me, which might not be wise considering where we are."

The motorcade slowed as they approached the great lodge, and when their driver halted, the vehicles carrying Zora's guard pulled into line behind them.

"Mm," Zora whispered, her mouth close to Trent's ear. "My wolf doesn't care where we are or what meetings we have to attend. She wants what she wants, and that has always been you. Now that I have you, waiting is…annoying."

Trent rumbled, a low, seductive sound. "As soon as we're done here, I promise to do something about that."

Zora played her fingers higher on Trent's thigh, caressing lightly between her thighs until Trent growled, a deeper, more aggressive sound.

"Now you're just playing with me," Trent complained, but her voice held only pleasure. She *and* her wolf loved to play, and being teased by her lover was the ultimate game.

Laughing, Zora moved away as the shadows of the *centuri* moving into position flickered over the windows of their vehicle. "I suppose now that we're here, we should see what Sylvan asks of us." She kissed Trent one last time. "I have no desire for war, but know that I will not hesitate to commit our soldiers if it means stopping whoever has sent those monsters to prey on our Pack."

"I and every Snowcrest Were know this and support you," Trent said as the door beside her opened.

Ash, the muscular, dark-haired captain of Zora's guard, stood just outside, shielding them from view of the Timberwolf Weres Zora sensed nearby. "A moment, Alpha."

Ash's mate, Jace, another Timberwolf Were who had yet to choose where her loyalties would fall—with her mate's Snowcrest Pack or the Timberwolves—stood by her side, her blue eyes shimmering gold. Unlike Trent's, Jace's wolf remained conflicted and agitated, and Zora wouldn't be surprised if some of the Timberwolves sensed her uncertainty and challenged her. Zora mentally shrugged. Challenges among a wolf Were Pack were essential to maintaining the cohesiveness of the hierarchy. Jace would stand to the challenge or she would relinquish her position with the Timberwolves. Her mate bond would not break, of that, Zora was certain.

"Thank you, Ash," Zora said, at a nod from Ash that all was clear, and stepped out. The *centuri* who had exited the remaining vehicles formed a cordon for Zora and Trent to pass through to the entrance. She brushed the back of her hand over Trent's as they walked side by side between the line of *centuri* up the stairs, where two young *sentries* guarded the doors. Both saluted, right fist to left shoulder, at their approach.

"Alpha Constantine, Prima," both said, their eyes straight ahead. "Welcome to the Timberwolf Compound."

"Thank you, *sentries*," Zora said as they passed through the arched doorway.

Niki Kroff waited for them just inside, her gaze flicking to Trent's and holding for just a moment longer than was proper, or wise, with a Prima Were. Before Trent's wolf responded to the challenge, Niki dropped her eyes a fraction and faced Zora, appropriately avoiding direct eye contact.

"Alpha," adding after a pause, "Prima. If you'll follow me."

"Thank you, *Imperator*," Trent said coolly, projecting enough power to catch Niki by surprise. Trent was no longer a lieutenant, but a mated Prima, and with that bond all the power of the Snowcrest Weres became available to her.

Niki caught her breath, slowly nodded, and replied formally as she should have done upon their entrance, "We welcome the Snowcrest Alpha and Prima to the Timberwolf Compound."

Zora smiled to herself as she and Trent walked through the great room. She didn't worry about her mate. Trent knew who she was, had always known her strengths and her worth regardless of rank or title, which she'd proved when she'd relentlessly pursued the Alpha of a neighboring Pack. Zora glanced at Trent, who grinned as if reading her thoughts. With their mate bond growing stronger every day, she probably was. They were so recently mated that the drive for them to join was constant. Trent sensed the flow of her pheromones, and her eyes glowed gold.

Zora shook her head and dragged her mind back to the business at hand. There would be time later to have what she wanted and needed from her mate. First, above all else, Pack.

❖

Torren de Brinna stepped from the vehicle her Lady kept for the occasions when they needed to travel by conventional means. The non-Fae mistrusted those who could move between realms through tears in the fabric of matter, which the humans had termed Gates. The ancient Fae, born of other pure-blooded Fae, could create those portals at will, but reminding one's allies of that power within their own territory was never wise. Riding in a vehicle with even a small percentage of iron in its frame was akin to a form of poisoning, one she could endure but preferred to avoid. As soon as she was free of the confining iron box, her magic flooded back, and the dimension beyond the human world flickered through the veil. She took a long breath and, when the constrictions in her chest eased, leaned into the rear compartment with an extended hand. "Ready, my Lady?"

"Are you all right?" Misha asked quietly as she slid across the plush leather seat and took Torren's hand. Her mahogany eyes telegraphed her worry as she smoothed down the diaphanous folds of her pale blue silk shirt. Her black tights and gleaming, thigh-high black boots matched Torren's black trousers and high collared royal-blue and gold shirt, the colors of Torren's house. "The journey took longer than I expected. I'm sorry."

"You need have no concern. I much prefer traveling via the Gates, but I thought the Weres would object to another opening in their territory just now." Torren leaned closer. "I do find the human vehicles irritating, however."

Torren laughed, that melodic sound that thrummed with power and never failed to stir Misha's need. Her wolf came awake with a sudden rumble, and desire coursed through her. Torren, of course, knew exactly what she'd done to her, and for an instant, her countenance shimmered and a great eagle peered down at her. She never feared Torren's other forms but enjoyed eluding her hunt as much as she did being caught. Her wolf preened with satisfaction, knowing her mate hungered for her.

"Stop," Misha whispered with little conviction. Her pleasure at the return of Torren's magic after the deadening effect of the iron rivaled her desire. Neither of which she could celebrate while surrounded by Timberwolf Weres. "I do not choose to share even a taste of your power with another."

"Until later, then," Torren said, offering her arm. "I'll temper my efforts for now."

Misha slid her fingers through the angle of Torren's elbow as they walked. "You might want to keep your beasts under cover as well before you frighten the wolves."

Torren laughed again, and the air around them vibrated with color. "As you say, my Lady."

❖

Alpha Raina Carras watched the royal Fae and her wolf mate enter the great lodge as their vehicle pulled around the circle to the lodge. She slid an arm around her mate's shoulders, not bothering to sheathe her claws. "The Fae consort—you know her, don't you?"

Lara hissed at the prickle of pain as Raina's claws slid through her blood-red silk shirt. Her mate, like all cat Weres, was territorial and possessive. And Raina's possessiveness often led to the fierce coupling that fed Lara's bloodlust as well as her sex frenzy. Lara had learned exactly how to play her mate's cat games, and answered offhandedly, "Mm. Yes. We were trainees together."

"Trainees," Raina murmured. "What exactly were you learning?"

Lara turned and kissed her, her incisors scoring a line along the inside of Raina's lip. She licked the faint line of blood and let a whisper of thrall mist Raina's face. "Hunting. Tracking. Combat."

"Coupling," Raina snapped, her green eyes spiraled with gold as her cat growled low in her throat. Her canines jutted, as large as any wolf Were's, and tawny pelt dusted her throat.

The long, elegant feline throat where Lara thirsted to feast. Bloodlust roared through her, and she pushed away.

"Raina," Lara gasped, "any more, and I'll need to feed. I hunger for you."

"You can wait," Raina soothed, playing her still bared claws along Lara's thigh. "But now you'll only see me when we're surrounded by Vampires and Weres."

"I only ever see you," Lara said. Their mate bond was unbreakable, but not what Raina's cat had expected. Lara's Vampire/wolf Were chimeric DNA, unknown to any Were or Vampire, had created a unique bond between her and the cat Alpha. She needed blood, just as any Vampire, to survive, and she was driven by potent sex pheromones to couple, just as every other Were. Lara knew her mate accepted her Vampire needs. More than accepted them. Raina loved to taunt her with the promise of reigniting their blood bond, especially when she was newly awakened and thirsting for sustenance. Raina's cat was powerful and strong and could feed her as often as she needed, but still, Raina was not a Vampire and could not flood her with the potent sexual stimulants that only a Vampire's bite could deliver. "I am *of* them, but I *belong* to you. I hunger for you. I spend my essence only for you."

"When we leave here," Raina said as their vehicle rolled to a stop, "I will be yours and you will drink until I empty you of every drop."

Lara shuddered, lust simmering in her depths, and unleashed her thrall. When she sensed Raina struggling to contain her need, she smiled and pushed the door open. "Then *you* will see only me until then."

Lara slid out, laughing silently as Raina snarled. Her cat mate enjoyed games even when she wasn't in control. The muscular Were waiting beside the vehicle nodded a greeting. The glint in his eyes said he knew exactly what had just gone on between them.

"Callan," Lara said, "good to see you."

"Prima." He tipped his head to Raina, in deference to her rank. "Alpha Carras. I trust you had a good trip and no hostilities in your ranges?"

"Everything is quiet on our borders," Raina said. "Our scouts have not reported any aggressions."

"Excellent."

"That is not to say," she said, "that our territory will not be the next invaded. If I didn't know that, I would not be here."

"Of course. And we are grateful that you and your cats have joined us."

Raina nodded and slipped an arm around her mate. Lara would need to be in the shielded vehicles or another protected area before sunrise. "And the accommodations for our vehicles?"

"By the west portico. Shielded for your departure should the meeting not adjourn before dawn."

"My captain will inspect it if one of your *sentries* takes him around."

"Of course." Callan waved over a small redhead in khaki pants and a black T-shirt that accentuated her sensuous curves. The wolf Were's gaze lingered a moment on Lara as Callan instructed her to escort the motorcade.

"And that one?" Raina said. "You *trained* with her too?"

Lara laughed. "Anya? No, she was a cadet the last time I saw her."

"I do not like this arrangement." Raina's cat prowled uneasily, irritated to be out of her territory so close to sunrise and surrounded by predators of all kinds. Shields would do little good if the Compound came under attack when the Vampires were incapacitated, as most would be after sunrise, Lara included. Cats and wolves were uneasy allies at best. Her mate was no longer fully Were, no longer fully wolf, and yet not completely Vampire. There were those in every camp who would prefer she be exiled. Lara knew it and had tried to resist their mate bond. Raina snarled inwardly. As if she or her cat would have been denied. But she would not rest easy until they were back in the high country, in their den with their Pride.

"I'll be fine," Lara murmured as they followed Callan inside. "Alpha Mir will not allow any hostilities at this meeting."

"*I* will see to your safety," Raina answered with a show of canines.

"I know." Lara leaned closer. "As I will see to yours."

❖

Once directed to the meeting hall, Rafe assessed the potential field of battle. The wolf Alpha had set up a long trestle table to seat all the leaders and their mates. Sylvan Mir sat at one end of the table with her Prima to her left side. The *imperator* stood behind Sylvan's left shoulder. At the opposite end of the table, Liege Gates sat with Becca on her right side. Rafe glided into place behind her Liege's left shoulder. One side of the table held Raina Carras, the cat Alpha, with her Prima, the wolf Vampire Lara, and Lord Torren with her Lady, Misha. Opposite them, the second Wolf Alpha, Zora Constantine, and the Prima, Trent. Alpha Constantine's captain, Ash, stood to her left facing the cat general, Ian Frederick, in position just behind Raina Carras. The cadres of soldiers formed a semicircle of wolf Weres, cat Weres, and Vampires behind their leaders. Rafe scented others in the shadows throughout the cavernous great hall.

Only the royal Fae had no second or accompanying warlord. Rafe couldn't remember ever seeing a Fae royal with a general or warlord. Even in Cecilia the Queen of Faerie's court, there were no such powers. Advisors perhaps, but none trusted with the secrets of the throne. Cecilia had sent her consort away before revealing to Sylvan and the others exactly why she sought their aid. The Fae were solitary, secretive, and treacherous. When they bonded, they bonded for millennia. Beyond that, they rarely formed alliances beyond the political, and in a society with few offspring and fewer deaths, those alliances shifted as fluidly as the Fae themselves, depending upon the circumstances. That the wolf Alpha appeared comfortable with Torren de Brinna—the Master of the Hunt and an ancient Lord of Faerie—within her territory spoke to Sylvan's power as much as her confidence.

The power gathered in such a close space along with the Fae's magic and the thrall emanating from every Vampire brought the gathering of predators to the brink of aggression. Rafe's blood burned with battle rage, and the taste of bloodlust scoured her throat. At least half the Weres showed subtle—and in some cases, not so subtle—signs of their emerging beasts. Only the royal Fae looked relaxed, her Lady's hand resting delicately on her forearm, despite shimmering with visible power. Rafe wasn't fooled. She'd seen what the Master of the Hunt became in battle and the speed with which the Hound changed form to the Eagle, and once in a bare flicker of an eye, to an opalescent Dragon. The Master of the Hunt needed no second. She doubted if even with her strength and speed she could defeat de Brinna, but she would face true death trying. Torren glanced over, caught her gaze, and smiled. After centuries and countless lovers and blood servants, Rafe was immune to physical beauty, but the light emanating from de Brinna's countenance warmed her like the sun she hadn't seen in a millennium. She hissed softly and, to her great consternation, heard a whisper where there should have been no voice but her Liege's.

You need not look to me for an enemy, my Vampire friend. Best to look among your own. I have no desire for your master's throne.

In years past, Rafe would have attacked anyone seeking to enter her mind and roll her will. But de Brinna was already gone, leaving only a cool breeze behind. She scanned the array of soldiers and guards, satisfied that her Vampires had chosen their targets as ordered and would respond with lethal speed in the case of hostilities. As her gaze passed over the Weres, her speculative perusal stopped short on one of the Timberwolf Weres who gazed directly back at her. A redheaded female, unusual among the wolves but not unheard of, whose piercing green gaze somehow spanned the distance between them and bored into Rafe's. Most other species avoided direct eye contact with Vampires, wisely wary of the possibility of being enthralled.

This wolf seemed to have no such concern and continued to assess her with bold abandon. Ordinarily, Rafe would've dismissed the scrutiny, but the sheer audacity of a wolf who appeared to be only a few years out of adolescence surprised her, and that was a sensation so foreign to her that she paused in her surveillance. Paused and studied the female.

Young, as she'd first surmised, full-breasted, with a tapered waist and a flare to her hips obvious even in the uniform all the Were sentries wore—khaki BDUs and formfitting black T-shirts. Muscles were obvious as they were in every Were, but her body seemed made for seduction. The thought brought Rafe up short. If the Were had been another Vampire, she'd think she'd been enthralled. Her concentration and her focus had been diverted from her duty, and that never happened. Mentally grimacing, she broke eye contact and returned her attention to Sylvan Mir. Even as she looked away, she imagined the female's gaze still on her.

"All of you know why we're here," Sylvan said. "What many of you may not know, and I see no reason not to share the news, is that Cecilia, the Faerie Queen, has directly asked for our aid. That is an extremely unusual request and one that on the surface is hard to understand."

Of course, Rafe knew the reason and, as Sylvan went on to explain to the others, saw the surprise on the faces of those who had not known that the Faerie Queen was pregnant. No doubt, many of those in the room thought the advent impossible. But the Fae *did* reproduce, although extremely rarely, and the news of a royal birth would travel through Faerie like a cannon shot. Rivals would be immediately on guard, knowing that any child of the Queen would solidify Cecilia's power on the throne. Anyone maneuvering to replace her needed to move quickly before the child was born. Once an heir was born, all of Faerie would rally around the Queen and the royal child, whose very presence proved Cecilia's power and rightful place on the throne. Cecilia, knowingly or not, had made herself both a target and a God.

"Perhaps," Sylvan said, "Lord Torren can explain some of the politics and why Cecilia reached out to us."

Torren smiled, and as with all Fae, the beauty of her visage rippled through the air like music and rippled over the skin like a seductive touch. Vampires tended to be more resistant to the magic of Fae than any other species, but Rafe felt the stirring of lust, not for sex, but for blood. She watched her guard and saw the glint of red pass through the eyes of several before they brought their lust under control. She'd been careful not to choose anyone less than several hundred years old for exactly this reason. Were blood was potent, and that was enough to hunger even Vampires who had recently fed. But the presence of any Fae, let alone a royal Fae of ancient power, affected them all. Her glance was drawn unexpectedly to the young redheaded Were she'd noticed moments before. Like then, the female was focused on her, a tinge of gold in her eyes, a glint of canines exposed against her full lips. Her breasts pushed against the tight black shirt, the outline of her nipples firm and tight. Rafe's hunger surged, unbidden and wild, a storm of need flashing through her with searing force. Her incisors punched down, and her vision hazed to red. Had she been younger, less controlled, she would have been at the female's throat in an instant. As it was, she had to forcibly drag her gaze away. A quick check of her guards assured her that they were all under control. Whatever pheromones this female exuded appeared to affect only her.

"Cethinrod," Torren continued, "has often claimed that the Southern Realm had equal claim to the throne as Cecilia, and now his claim will be weaker."

"How are these internal Fae problems relevant to us?" Raina Carras said. "The Fae have never been quick to support us, not even when the humans hunted us across Europe and Canada and throughout the rest of North America. The humans are a common enemy, and yet the Fae stood by while we died. This *trouble* has undoubtedly been brewing in Faerie for eons." She shrugged, an insolent roll of her shoulders distinctly catlike in its dismissiveness. "I fail to see why we should care about yet another power struggle in Faerie."

Lord Torren appeared unconcerned by the criticism. "Cecilia has held the throne for centuries, and she's made no overt move to extend her power beyond the veil."

"Overt, as you say," Liege Gates put in, "but she has certainly maneuvered behind the scenes to weaken the political positions of both the Vampires and Weres in our realm. Were there an opportunity to extend her reach into this world, I am sure she would."

Torren nodded. "Of course. That's what queens do."

Zora Constantine chuffed, a disgusted sound that relayed her displeasure. "We seem to be forgetting that these politics and Cecilia's problems are not the most critical items to be discussed. We've been attacked in our own territory repeatedly, and some of you at this table have seen the enemy. Those creatures came from Faerie, and if they're not Cecilia's, then there is another enemy who needs to be neutralized."

Several of the Weres grouped behind Zora Constantine grumbled in assent.

Sylvan replied, "You're right. Protecting our borders and destroying the enemy who has attacked us is essential, but I believe in this instance our enemy and Cecilia's enemy may be one and the same."

"I've fought what came through the veil," Torren said. "Those are not Fae creatures. They were ensorcelled, which speaks of a Mage powerful enough to control the dead."

"A necromancer," Zora spat. "And why couldn't that Mage be in league with Cecilia?"

Drake, Sylvan's Prima, said, "If that were the case, Cecilia would not solicit our aid. If those were her agents, she would deny it, of course, but she certainly would not ask for our presence to intervene."

Zora slid a hand over Trent's. "My mate has been beyond the veil and has seen the creatures. She's felt the dark power and nearly died from the poison in her blood." She turned to look at Jody Gates. "Everything points to a Mage in collusion with a Vampire."

Rafe stiffened at the thinly veiled accusation, and several Vampires hissed.

"All evidence points that way, I agree," Jody said calmly. "And I think we all suspect the same thing. Francesca escaped across the veil and is being harbored in Faerie. The extent of her power is uncertain. Her strength will depend upon how many Vampires and blood servants she was able to bring with her."

"How long can she maintain control of her minions if she cannot feed them?" Trent asked.

Rafe stiffened. Vampires guarded the secrets of their survival closely, for of all the predators, they were most vulnerable during their forced quiescence. To be questioned about something as essential as the ties between a Master Vampire and their minions was tantamount to challenge. The Vampire guards arrayed behind Jody extended their thrall, a subtle infusion of power and potent pheromones evolved over eons to lure and pacify prey. A prelude to instantaneous translocation and attack. At the merest signal from Rafe, the meeting would erupt in bloodshed. Their only advantage was to attack first.

"Jody," Sylvan murmured.

Rafe cut her gaze to the wolf Alpha. Sylvan's posture hadn't changed, but her jaw had grown heavy and her eyes shone brilliant gold. Beside her, the Prima also appeared on the verge of change. So the Alpha and her mate could sense the Vampire thrall.

Jody swiveled to face Trent, raising one hand in a casual gesture that nevertheless signaled her guard to hold their position. She smiled, the magenta flames totally eclipsing the obsidian depths of her eyes. "Never doubt that Francesca will find a way to hold on to her power, even if that means feeding from her allies."

"Can't be a very happy alliance, then," Trent said, seemingly undisturbed by the lethal cold in Jody's tone.

Becca placed a hand on Jody's wrist. Jody looked down, covered Becca's hand with hers, and let out a breath. The gesture was unnecessary, as she didn't need to breathe, but a sign for the others at the table to relax. "As you say. And perhaps to our advantage."

Rafe mind-spoke to her guards that the danger had passed, and the heavy cloud of battle lust and blood fever abated.

"What about the Mage?" the cat Alpha asked impatiently. "Do we know who this is?"

"No," Sylvan said. "Someone powerful enough to reanimate and control Weres."

"And someone foolish enough to join forces with Francesca," Drake added.

Sylvan took a deep breath and let her gaze move around the table. "The longer we wait, the more time we give Francesca and whatever Fae she has on her side to grow in power and build an army. I believe they will come through the veil in force if we don't stop them."

Rafe knew what her Liege would decide. Francesca was an ancient enemy, and her first move would be against the Vampire elite. She would never be weak, and allowing her to gain more strength would only make it more difficult to stop her later.

The debate was short. Predators all, their nature was to drive other predators from their territory before they could gain a foothold, even when those predators were of their own Pack. While each would prefer to fight alone, an alliance presented the best chance for swift victory.

Zora Constantine spoke up. "We will need some time to prepare our soldiers. When do you propose we move?"

Sylvan said, "If the attacks resume or escalate in your territory or"—she glanced at Raina Carras—"anywhere else on this side of the veil, we can't wait. But even if things remain quiet, a matter of weeks."

Liege Gates spoke first. "My Vampires will honor our alliance."

Raina Carras said, "And my cats."

Zora Constantine echoed the pledge. "The Snowcrest Weres stand ready."

Lord Torren de Brinna, the Master of the Hunt, laughed softly. "What a battle this will be."

Chapter Seven

Anya stood at attention with the other cadre lieutenants at the head of the phalanx of *sentries* arrayed behind her in the shadows thrown by the huge chandeliers that hung from enormous beams high overhead in the rafters of the great room. A fire flickered in the open hearth on one side of the chamber. Automated steel shutters darkened the floor-to-ceiling windows on the opposite wall. Crossbeams as thick as her thigh rested in iron clamps across the center of each shutter, an added measure to ensure that the Vampires were safe from the sudden exposure to sunlight should the Compound be attacked. When she'd walked by Callan's side onto the parade ground a few moments before and been directed to the fifteen *sentries* who now formed the cadre under her command, the enormity of the change in her status became starkly evident as each warrior saluted her. These Weres were hers to lead, to protect, and to die for.

The Alpha rose and glanced around the table, meeting the eyes of each member of the war council. "The Timberwolf Pack pledges to meet the enemy on any ground and fight until our territories, our Packs, our Dominions, and our seethes are secure." She nodded, smiling faintly to Torren de Brinna, whose stake in the upcoming conflicts was known only to her. "And for the lives of our friends."

The Were Alphas, the Vampire Liege, and the royal Fae saluted the Alpha, and the pact was made.

Raina Carras said, "Moonfall is soon upon us, and I wish to return to my territory before daybreak. If there's nothing else, Alpha Mir?"

Sylvan glanced at Lara, who had once been hers but was no longer. "The presence of the Alpha and Prima of the Catamount Clan has been appreciated."

She turned, her gaze falling on Anya, and Anya felt the power of her attention like a hand gripping her shoulder. Her heart raced.

"Lieutenant," the Alpha said quietly.

As if drawn by an invisible force, Anya stepped forward. She would have found a way to answer that silent order with her last breath. She saluted briskly. "At your command, Alpha."

"Alpha Carras, Lieutenant Kozlov is our communication specialist. With your permission, she and your Prima can communicate through Pack bonds over significant distances. Should any danger occur in your territory, you may signal her, and we will respond."

Raina stiffened and glanced at Lara, a move so subtle that most might not have appreciated it, but Anya did. The look Raina gave her was that of a mate who had suddenly been told her Prima shared an intimate link with someone other than her. The faint curl in her lip and the ruffling of the golden pelt along her bare forearms revealed her displeasure. Raina's gaze raked over Anya's face, and if that glance had been claws, she would have bled. "I see."

Anya carefully did not meet the cat Alpha's gaze. Her heightened ability for mind-to-mind communication had become apparent in early adolescence, a genetic trait that had been passed down through her maternal bloodline. Until now, she'd never been called upon to use it in any official way. She had not expected the command nor even considered the ramifications of what her Alpha had just ordered. She rarely mind-linked with other members of the Pack, primarily because to do so would be an intrusion and, more importantly, would open her up to potential scrutiny. She had no desire to be known in such a way. When she needed intimacy, she favored sex. She didn't want or need to share anything else.

Lara spoke up, her hand lightly curled around Raina's nape, a sign of possession and assurance. "The Timberwolf Alpha is correct—our Pack bonds, once formed, never disappear unless by her will. My allegiance to the wolf Pack, however," she said, facing her prior Alpha, "has ended. My body, my heart, and my allegiance belong to the Catamounts and my Alpha."

"Of course," Sylvan said. "And I and all my wolves honor that."

Raina growled softly in her throat, her stare still riveted on Anya. "Very well. Your assistance, Lieutenant Kozlov, is accepted."

"As you wish, Alpha Carras." Despite what Raina Carras inferred about her bond with Lara, she had never tangled with her. Lara had been a *centuri* when she was just a recruit. She would've liked to have tangled with her, but then, she liked a tangle with most Weres, particularly one as dominant as Lara. That time had passed—no Were would attempt to couple with a mated Were. Anya preferred young, vigorous partners who looked for nothing but a quick, uncomplicated tangle that ended with a hard release for all involved.

As Anya stepped back to the edge of the shadows, her wolf alerted and a wave of pheromones rushed through her. Her sex tightened and pelt rippled beneath her skin. The call was foreign—and for an instant she imagined it was Lara, but the silky shiver of arousal coursing through her depths was not Were. Her jaw ached with the rise of her wolf. She *knew*, without understanding how, where to look. The Vampire *senechal* who stood just behind Liege Gates stared back at her, her eyes a furnace of glowing flames. The force of her gaze was like a thousand caresses streaking over her body, filling her with need so painful she wished only to spend instantly. Anya struggled for control, her wolf wild to break free, to bite and... No. This was not the one. This was not the time. Sex-sheen soaked her skin. Her glands pulsed, hard and full. She would need to couple, and soon.

Anya stifled a whimper and marshaled all her strength to pull her gaze away. She was a Timberwolf lieutenant, a warrior, and she would not succumb to a Vampire's thrall. *She* would choose on whom she would spend her *victus*. She focused on the war council and prayed the formalities would soon end. Daybreak was not far off. The Vampires would surely leave before that.

Torren lifted Misha's hand, placed it gently on her forearm, and rose with Misha flowing upward bedside her with a grace more Fae-like than Were. "We will take our leave as well, Alpha Mir. I have...friends... on both sides of the veil who may provide valuable intelligence, but it does require some time."

Sylvan nodded. "As you see fit, Lord de Brinna." Sylvan glanced at Misha, another of her Weres no longer completely hers. "Misha. Safe journey."

Misha nodded. "Thank you, Alpha."

The pair turned and, with a glimmer of light that Anya might have imagined, were gone. The cat Weres and their Pride left as well, leaving only the Snowcrest Weres and the Vampires.

Liege Gates said, "A word, Alpha?"

Sylvan nodded. "I'll need a minute with Alpha Constantine. Do you have time to wait? The adjoining antechambers are well shielded."

"Daybreak is yet several hours away. We accept your hospitality." Jody took Becca's hand and motioned to the *senechal*, and seconds later, they too were gone.

Zora stiffened, as if not completely happy with her new Vampire allies, but said nothing until the room had emptied of all but the wolf Weres. "You have business that affects my Pack to discuss?"

Sylvan nodded. "Both our Packs. It's time we made a decision regarding the status of our senior warriors. With what we face, there can be no confusion as to allegiance."

Trent stiffened, her chin coming up until her gaze met Sylvan's. "There is no question about my allegiance, Alpha Mir. It is to the Snowcrest Weres and my mate, completely."

"If you do not mean to challenge me in my own territory, you will be careful," Sylvan murmured.

Trent shuddered. "To suggest I would not be one hundred percent committed to my Alpha and my mate is a challenge."

Zora gripped Trent's forearm but kept her eyes directly on Sylvan's. "My mate speaks only the truth, but if there is a challenge here it will be mine."

"None was intended," Sylvan said with a faint sigh. "You've chosen well in your mate."

"I know that without being told."

"As of this moment, as witnessed by my Prima and my *centuri*," Sylvan said, a roll of power so forceful Anya felt the pull of a change come over her, "I relinquish all claim to Trent Maran."

"So witnessed," the Prima said quietly.

Trent jolted at the severance of the tie that had existed since the moment she first drew breath. She came to attention, the planes of her face stark as the bonds to the Snowcrest Pack filled her with new power.

"I'll see to Liege Gates and her guard," the Prima said and slipped away.

"And finally," Sylvan said, her voice still heavy with command, "we must settle the issue of my *centuri* and your captain."

Zora turned to Ash, the captain of her guard, and Jace, the

Timberwolf *centuri* Ash had claimed as her mate. "Alpha Mir is correct. The time has come."

Behind Sylvan, Jace's twin brother Jonathan took a step forward. "Jace," he said, a faint pleading in his voice, "you are one of *us*."

Jace, blond and blue-eyed like Jonathan, a seasoned warrior and a member of Sylvan's elite guard, took Ash's hand. "I will not give up my mate."

Ash turned to Zora. "I have ever been your Wolf, Alpha. My heart has always been Snowcrest." She took a deep breath. "But now my heart is Jace's. She is my mate. She has never asked me, but by your leave, and with Alpha Mir's permission, I would—"

"Wait," Sylvan ordered. "If you agree, Alpha Constantine, until this threat that we face is defeated, I will accept Ash in my Pack if it is agreed that Ash follows my command and mine alone."

Zora said, "Ash, tell me, if you had to choose between the life of your Alpha or that of your mate, who would you choose?"

Ash's chin came up. "I would choose my mate, Alpha."

"As you should. If Alpha Mir agrees, go with your mate, Ash. Your heart and your allegiance are already Timberwolf."

"I do," Sylvan said.

Zora held Ash's gaze. "You are among my strongest and my bravest, and you have chosen well." She turned to her Prima. "Summon the motorcade around. It is time to go home."

❖

The Alpha waited until the Snowcrest wolves exited the meeting hall before turning to face Jace. "You will resume a command position as a captain. Callan will decide which squadron you will command."

Anya glanced at Jace as a low murmur spread among the senior warriors still in attendance. The Alpha's gaze swept over the ranks, and the warning in her eyes brought instant silence. Jace, who along with her twin had only recently been elevated to *centuri*, the elite guard and the highest honor for a Were warrior, gave no sign that the demotion was as painful as Anya could only imagine it to be. Jace came to rigid attention and saluted. "Yes, Alpha."

"Your mate will serve as a lieutenant, but without command responsibility."

"Ash is the captain of the Snowcrest forces, second to their *imperator*," Jace said.

"Not anymore," Sylvan said, her wolf half-amused and half-annoyed by Jace's objection. Jace was protecting her mate, as she should. But she was also out of line. "Ash made a choice, as did you. You both knew the consequences of an out-Pack mating. If and when Ash earns a command, the *captain* of our forces will see to the promotion."

Sylvan's tone made it clear the discussion was over, but Jace bristled. Anya's wolf raised her head, anticipating a challenge.

Ash spoke before Jace could force the Alpha to discipline her. "I am happy to serve in any capacity, Alpha Mir. All I ask is that I be allowed to defend my mate and your Pack."

Sylvan took a step closer and gripped Ash's shoulder. "Your Pack now."

Ash shuddered under the force of the Alpha's gaze, a soft whine reverberating in her chest. "As you command."

"Good. You're both dismissed." She turned to Callan and the remaining *centuri*. "Come with me. Lieutenant Kozlov, as well."

Anya hid her surprise. She had expected to be dismissed along with the other lieutenants and *sentries*. She fell in beside Dasha Baran, one of the newest *centuri* who had recently taken Jace's place.

"Congratulations on your promotion, Lieutenant," Dasha murmured, her arm brushing Anya's. "I'll look forward to seeing you more often."

Dasha's pheromones tingled on the back of Anya's throat and stirred heat in her loins, a not-so-subtle invitation to join her for a tangle once they were dismissed. In another time and place, Anya would've been very interested in Dasha's attention. Dasha's superior rank was no issue—Anya was no longer an adolescent but a warrior in her own right, and rank was not a barrier to Weres coupling. Only the mate bond could do that. The timing now was wrong—she had other responsibilities, including the need to review the duty assignments with her squad leaders as soon as she was able. More than that, her wolf showed no interest in coupling and curled up as if to go to sleep. Anya had no explanation for that, as usually such a pointed attraction from another Were inevitably led to sex. She could add this odd behavior to the many other instances when her wolf acted in ways she couldn't understand.

"Thank you, *Centuri*, I am proud to serve." Her failure to directly address Dasha's call signaled she was not available.

"Another time." Dasha laughed softly at the very careful rejection and moved slightly away as they loped down the long corridor to the antechamber where the Vampires waited with the Prima.

Sylvan, at the head of the wedge of Were warriors, pushed through the huge double doors, strode directly to the Prima, gripped her nape, and kissed her. The Prima growled softly in welcome. The *centuri*, at a sign from the *imperator*, flanked the exit, and Anya followed Callan to the far side of the Alpha pair. The Vampire Liege and her *senechal* stood on either side of the fireplace, and the consort occupied one of the two facing, long leather sofas ringed by the half dozen Vampire guards. The Vampires watched the Were forces enter with unreadable expressions. Anya's wolf prowled warily as Anya judged the distance to the nearest Vampire. She could change in midair if she needed to. She might even be able to take the Vampire's throat before it could take hers.

If need be.

A flash of heat coursed over her throat, as if she'd already been bitten, and she instantly knew the source. The *senechal* regarded her with a raised brow, an amused look as if she'd known exactly what Anya had been thinking. Anya curled her lip and turned away, despite her wolf's resistance. Being anywhere near the Vampire was like the pull of the moon on the night of the hunt, exhilarating, irresistible, exciting. Her body thrilled in anticipation, and she had no idea why, leaving her as confused as she was aroused.

"Jody," the Alpha said, pulling the attention of every Were in the room to her, "a problem?"

"More an…inconvenience." Jody scanned the Weres who had accompanied Sylvan. She knew all of them and had fought side by side with most of them. Several of the lieutenants were new, but not strangers to her. Under most circumstances, she would not discuss Vampire issues in an open forum like this, but she would be disclosing no secrets of consequence, and the matter needed to be settled before she could commit her Vampires to battle. "If I am to send a Vampire force into Faerie, they must have a means of sustenance."

"What of their human servants?" Sylvan asked. "Humans can pass through the veil."

"Physically our blood servants could accompany them, but they would also be susceptible to Fae magic, easily seduced by even the weakest Fae. Unless secluded and constantly guarded, which would be difficult with a battle force on the move, they would become a security risk or victims themselves."

The Prima said, "Your vampires have already been to Faerie. Did *they* suffer ill effects?"

Jody glanced at Rafe. "Lord *Senechal*?"

"My Liege," Rafe said in a low voice, sounding reluctant to reveal anything to non-Vampires.

"If you please, Rafe," Jody said, her tone definitely not a request.

"Yes, my Liege." Rafe addressed the Prima. "Our time in Faerie was brief, and I am more tolerant of long periods without sustenance than many…younger…than I. The Fae are resistant to our bite, and their blood does not carry enough of the necessary elements we require to serve as hosts."

"How long could you stay?" Drake asked.

"And still remain in full force?" Rafe lifted a shoulder. "I, perhaps days, even a week. Many of our guard, a shorter time, and the decline in strength and power would be unpredictable."

Sylvan waved a hand. "Obviously, we would not expect you to go without sustenance. If you cannot bring humans, then the solution is obvious. You will need Were hosts."

"Yes," Jody said.

Now Anya understood why the conversation was being held in private, and why the Vampires were reluctant to disclose the problem. No predator wanted another to know of its weaknesses. The admission that a Vampire's powers diminished unpredictably without feeding was akin to a Were in pelt exposing their soft underbelly.

"How many?" Sylvan asked.

"It depends upon the strength of the Were and needs of the Vampire," Jody said. "If one of us is injured, more than one host might be needed to supply enough blood to reverse the damage quickly. Otherwise, a strong healthy Were should not suffer any noticeable consequences from ordinary hosting."

"As a safety measure margin?" the Prima asked. "Any injury in battle must be tended to quickly to restore the warrior to full strength as quickly as possible."

Jody nodded. "Possibly more than one host would be needed if the injury is substantial."

"I can't order my Weres to host," Sylvan said.

"That is understood," Jody said flatly, the dark wells of her eyes emotionless and blank.

Anya's wolf whined softly at the cold, foreboding depths of the Vampire's power. Unable to resist, she looked to the *senechal*. Rafe was watching her. She always seemed to be watching her.

Callan said, "By your leave, Alpha, I will solicit donors from among our ranks and be sure that we have adequate numbers available."

The *imperator* stepped forward. "This is a bad idea. Most of our Weres have never encountered Vampires, and those who have, rarely if ever hosted." Gold snapped in her eyes. "The effect on them will be unknown and will put them at risk in the field."

Jody studied the general dispassionately. "I agree. Anyone who volunteers must have had experience hosting before the need arises in Faerie. We cannot afford to have an injured warrior without a host."

"And if we can't supply…hosts?" Niki said.

"Then I will not send my Vampires into battle at a disadvantage. You will need time to decide, but I would not take too long, especially if assault is imminent. We want any potential hosts to know what to expect."

"*I* know what to expect," Niki growled, taking another step closer, her pelt shimmering along her bare torso beneath her leather vest, "and I say no Were should be put at risk to feed—"

Sylvan snarled. "Enough. You insult our ally and my guest. You will stand down."

Niki shuddered. "As you command."

She spun on her heel and pushed her way out of the room.

Jody signaled to Rafe and the guards. "Summon the drivers. We are done here."

Just as quickly, the Vampires were at the exit, although Anya hadn't seen them move.

"I will volunteer," Anya said.

Jody turned back, and the Vampires behind her settled into a protective semicircle. "Have you experience?"

Anya's chin came up. "I'm a Were."

She heard a soft laugh and knew it came from the *senechal*. This time she managed not to look at her.

Jody smiled. "Undoubtedly you have some *experience*. Have you fed a Vampire?"

"No, Liege Gates. But I very much doubt it would be all that different than a vigorous tangle with a Were."

"Perhaps you have something to learn, then." The smoky voice of the *senechal* washed over her, and Anya finally cut her gaze to her.

"Really? And you would be the one to show me?"

Again, the indolent shrug, as if Rafe couldn't care one way or the other that Anya was offering to feed her. "Should my Liege desire."

Anya knew she should keep her silence, but the arrogance and the dismissal irritated her too much. "I shouldn't think you would need permission for that."

Heat washed over her again, unexpected and almost unbearably arousing. Sex-sheen burst on her skin, and her wolf climbed into her throat with a growl.

"That's enough," Jody snapped.

Rafe nearly disobeyed. The Were was beautiful and alluring and annoying, and she wanted to taste her. She eased her thrall, despite her blood surging with lust.

Anya said, "If we are to request volunteers, then at least one of us should be able to report what to expect."

"Then you should return with us tonight," Rafe said, knowing this would put an end to her unnatural thirst for the far-too-troubling Were.

Chin raised, her wolf prowling in her eyes, Anya took a step closer to the second most powerful Vampire in the Dominion. "If my Alpha commands."

Chapter Eight

Six *centuri* stepped forward as one, and six voices spoke in unison. "We will volunteer, Alpha. It is only right that our warriors should support the Vampire guard."

Max, the Timberwolf Pack's third and leader of the *centuri*, added, "And we will not be in danger of weakening should we need to offer blood."

The Alpha glanced from her *centuri* to the Vampire Liege. "Will that satisfy?"

"While your wolves' confidence is appreciated and not unexpected," Jody said flatly, "there is no guarantee that they will in fact be suitable hosts." She scanned the line of Were warriors. "Who among you has hosted?"

None replied.

Jody faced the Alpha. "No volunteers can be assumed to be acceptable until trialed. I suggest we match your Weres with my Vampires and settle the question as soon as possible."

"I can speak for mine," Sylvan said tersely, "and I know that each is capable without question. However, we have agreed that a trial is… safest. Max will not be trialed, as he will not be part of our forces. We will replace him with a volunteer from our senior ranks."

The dark-haired, muscular Were jerked at Sylvan's words. The tightening of Max's jaw and the gleam of gold below the surface of his black eyes were the only signs of his displeasure. Anya admired his control and realized she was far, far less experienced in every way than the group she had suddenly become a part of. Her wolf was young, brave, exuberant, and often driven by instinct, as proven by her extreme and inexplicable reaction to the Vampire *senechal*'s thrall. She would have to have iron control to survive the coming challenges.

Sylvan said, "When and how do you suggest we proceed?"

"Half my guard will remain here with the *centuri* you assign to them, and half of your *centuri* plus your lieutenant will return with us tonight. Our critical strengths will be diminished by only half for a brief time." She paused. "The Weres will need to host for our Vampires at moonfall and sunfall. That should assure they'll have no…ill effects from the frequent feedings."

Jonathan scoffed. "As if something so minor could diminish our power."

Jody studied him, a faint smile skating across her pale, ascetic features that only made her eyes appear colder. "I've seen you fight, so I know you are brave. Strength and bravery are not the same."

Jonathan grumbled but made no comment. Every Were in the room quietly huffed. As if a Vampire could sap their power so easily. Anya wasn't so sure—she'd felt the force of the *senechal*'s thrall and the irresistible need to surrender to the promised pleasure. Her sex still throbbed with the urgency to release. If a Vampire's demand for blood was as strong as the hunger that filled her even now, her wolf might be beyond controlling.

Sylvan sighed. "My Weres are capable of meeting any challenge. Let's see to this so we can prepare our forces and put an end to the evil that has been stalking us for too long."

Drake added. "Until sunfall, we shall be honored to host your Vampires."

Jody nodded. "And we welcome your *centuri* to the seethe of the Night Hunters."

The Alpha turned to the line of *centuri*. "Dasha, Jonathan, Mila. You will accompany Liege Gates and the Vampire guard tonight."

Each saluted briskly and joined Anya in the circle of Vampires.

Jody said, "Sabine, Hugo, Lily—you will remain."

Three Vampires, each slender, pale, and with far-too-perfect features belying they'd ever been human, stepped forward. With a salute, they said in unison, "As you wish, my Liege."

None gave any indication they were bothered by remaining behind despite dawn being just a few hours away, when they would be dependent upon the Weres to protect them and provide the blood they needed to survive. Anya had never been in such a vulnerable position. She'd always been surrounded by Pack—even in the midst of skirmishes. Her insides twisted as she realized she was about to be as vulnerable as these Vampires—she would be cut off from Pack, at least physically. And when she was alone with Rafe? Would she truly be able to withstand her demands? Would she be able to meet her needs in the most essential way? She set her jaw, her wolf prowling on the edge of change. She would *not* fail, no matter what the demands.

Jody glanced at Sylvan. "My Vampires will need security during the day."

"Of course. They will not be the first Vampires we have sequestered here. The *centuri* who host for them will stand guard."

The Vampire called Lily—a bronze-skinned, black-haired female who moved like a prima ballerina—spoke up. "There's time for us to feed before moonfall. Once at strength, we will be able to remain awake for a few hours after sunrise."

Sylvan said, "Quarters will be provided immediately."

Drake said, "I'll take you there now. Victor, Tasia with me. Callan—bring the last volunteer to the barracks as quickly as possible."

"I'll see to it, Prima," Callan said and hurried away.

The three Vampires who were to remain looked to Liege Gates for orders, and she nodded her assent. They followed the Prima and the two *centuri* out through another door at the rear of the room.

Jody nodded to Rafe. "Instruct the drivers we wish to depart and to make speed on our return."

"Of course, my Liege."

Rafe led the way out of the building, Anya and the three *centuri* following the Vampire guards. The Alpha walked out beside Liege Gates. Rafe stood by the third car with the Consort and gestured to Anya. "You will ride here."

Jonathan, Dasha, and Mila entered other vehicles in the line, each accompanied by one of the Vampires.

Liege Gates approached and held out her hand to the Consort. "Ready, my love?"

"More than ready to be home," Becca said and slid into the limo.

"If you please," Rafe said in an unexpectedly formal tone and cupped Anya's elbow.

Anya settled across from Liege Gates and her Consort. Rafe

entered, pulled the door closed, and said into her radio, "Car one, you may proceed."

"Understood," a female voice replied.

Rafe said, "Air control, check. We will be at the interstate in twenty minutes."

"Air control. Copy that. We'll be waiting. Nothing unusual in ground activity."

Anya leaned back in the seat as the limos pulled out through the main gates. As the night closed in around them, the interior of the limo seemed to shrink, as if they were adrift. Her wolf surged, sensing danger. Instinctively, she sought the Pack bonds, and when the power of the Pack filled her, her wolf quieted.

"We travel under blackout conditions," Rafe murmured, "and the vehicles are soundproofed."

"Of course," Anya said. "You don't have any trouble seeing in the dark, do you?"

Rafe smiled, the same slightly amused smile Anya was coming to expect. "No, we don't. But then, a wolf wouldn't either."

"We always have the moon," she said and realized that was what had so disturbed her wolf. The limos had some kind of shields that blocked light, even moonlight.

"Don't worry, it's still there. And our journey will not be long."

"Of course." Anya steadied her breathing and soothed her wolf. She didn't intend this Vampire to know she was uneasy. Or uncertain. She had never been this close to Rafe before and hadn't known what to expect when she climbed into the back of the heavily armored limousine, but it hadn't been to accompany the Liege and her consort along with the *senechal* on the trip back to the Vampires' seethe. She'd assumed she'd be sequestered with the Vampire warriors, if not actually under guard. Now she sat a few feet away from the most powerful Vampire in the Northeast and her Consort, while another Vampire nearly as powerful sat close enough for their legs to touch. As the motorcade picked up speed despite the utter blackness of the night around them, Becca Land leaned forward and held out her hand.

"We've never formally met. I'm Becca Land, Liege Gates's spouse."

"Of course, Consort," Anya said, taking her hand. "It's an honor."

Some Weres had human partners, and Anya had tangled with

humans once when she was much younger. She was acquainted with the frailty of their bodies and was surprised to find that the Consort's strength was far greater than she anticipated. And beyond that, a tingle of undeniable power spread through her. Foreign, but not uncomfortable. Her wolf perked up in interest, and the *senechal* laughed. Anya leaned back quickly, releasing the Consort's hand.

"Your youth betrays you, Lieutenant," Rafe said darkly. "If you respond like that when we reach the seethe, you'll find I'm not the only one at your throat."

Anya's wolf bristled and rumbled softly in her chest. "And you make assumptions, Lord *Senechal*. I choose who I want, even when it comes to you."

Rafe shifted on the seat to face her, and shards of red slanted through the opaque black of her eyes. Anya tensed, half expecting an attack, but instead was hit with another wave of heat and a stirring in her deepest reaches that instantly readied her. She'd only felt power like that from the Alpha's call, when every Were was instantly ready to hunt, to battle, to tangle, or to mate. She should not be affected this way, but her jaw tensed and her canines ached to erupt.

Rafe leaned closer. "You have much to learn and little time. You must be very careful, little wolf."

Liege Gates said softly into the thick pheromone-heavy air, "Lieutenant Kozlov has proved her bravery already, especially since it appears she'll be spending the night with you."

Becca laughed softly. "Perhaps Lieutenant Kozlov would prefer one of the others of our guard, Jody. This is, after all, voluntary."

Rafe hissed, a dangerous sound that brought pelt rolling down the center of Anya's body. Her claws punched through the tips of her fingers.

"That will not be the case," Rafe said. "She will accompany me to my quarters." She glanced at Jody. "My Liege, we must judge the hosts very carefully. We cannot risk our elite guard with inexperienced or unsteady hosts."

Anya snarled. "Unsteady? Are you suggesting that any Were warrior would crumple under the stress of battle or—"

"I'm not talking about battle," Rafe said, her voice soft but as razor-sharp as a claw. "I'm talking about the terror of having my mouth at your throat, my teeth in your vein, drinking you, draining you."

"If it was so terrifying, I doubt there would be so many willing to host." Anya glanced at the Vampire Liege, who seemed content to let them argue their way to some kind of truce. "I understand that killing the host is forbidden. And if that's so"—she looked back at Rafe—"and your servants continue to serve, there must be *something* enjoyable about it."

Rafe laughed, surprised by the beautiful young Were's attitude. But then, the wolves always thought highly of themselves, far more than they generally deserved. In all likelihood, this one too would tremble and pull back when she realized exactly what it was like to be the prey of a stronger predator.

"We shall see if you find it so," Rafe said and leaned back to stare straight ahead. Her body burned with need. A hunger she hadn't known in centuries ravaged her, tearing at her reason. Bloodlust made her tremble with urgency. She would have to find one of the servants and take them first to sate some of her wild hunger before she came to this one. She did not trust herself alone with her when her need was so great. For the first time in centuries, she did not trust herself to stop before her thirst drained her of all reason.

❖

Rafe's thrall permeated the close confines of the limousine, full and unrestrained, wild even. In the Timberwolf Compound, Jody had watched her closest advisor and confidant struggle to contain her bloodlust while surrounded by the potent call of the dominant Weres but, most especially, the young Were female seated inches away from Rafe now. All her Vampires had been affected, despite having recently fed, but she wouldn't have expected Rafe to be so volatile. She hadn't needed the warning that Sylvan had given her as they stood waiting for her Vampire guards to escort the Weres into the waiting vehicles. She'd already been on guard.

"Your senechal has taken a considerable interest in Anya," Sylvan said. "Even I could feel the force of her thrall."

"That's because you are an Alpha Were. Most of the others would not have registered it."

"That may be, but Anya will not be prepared if Rafe cannot control her hunger."

Jody met Sylvan's gaze. "That is not your concern now, Alpha Mir."

"It's always my concern when it's one of mine. Can you guarantee her safety?"

"Can you guarantee that my Vampires will be protected at moonfall for twelve hours when the sun is high? Can you guarantee that one of your wolves will not change in the midst of the feeding, pushed to the edge by the pain and the fury at being dominated? Even my Risen Vampires are not completely invulnerable."

Sylvan growled. "It seems we must both trust each other." She watched Anya climb into the car with Rafe. "She's young, but she is not without power. She is destined to be a centuri."

"We are all destined for something," Jody said. "It may not be what we expect."

Sylvan laughed softly. "Are all Risen Vampires so morose?"

Jody laughed. "That's quite possibly true."

Sylvan gripped Jody's shoulder. "We can't always choose our fate, but that doesn't mean we are not who we are meant to be. Your Consort's waiting."

Becca stood by the limo with Rafe and Anya. "Yes, she is."

"Becca will change your future."

"She already has," Jody murmured and escorted Becca into the back of the limousine.

She brought Becca's hand to her lips now as Rafe's thrall receded. As long as Rafe could control her need, Anya would be safe with her. Jody would not want to come between Rafe and her chosen host, not when the challenge might end in a banishment, at best, and true death at worst.

❖

Sylvan found Drake in the isolation wing of the infirmary, an area specifically designed to sequester rogue Weres or to protect Vampire guests. The windows had the same protective shields to block sunlight while also doubling as enclosures for Weres who could not be trusted not to change and rampage. The six rooms could each accommodate several occupants comfortably for an extended period of time. With the shields up, however, Weres could not shift and leave the room by the windows. The rooms could become traps for Were and Vampire alike. Presently, two doors were closed, the Were and Vampire pairs already inside.

Sabine stood by an open door, her arms folded, an implacable expression on her face. Sylvan didn't know her, but she recognized the outline of the sheath crossing her torso beneath her black silk shirt. The Vampire didn't bother to hide the shuriken she carried. Sylvan had seen them earlier and presumed all the Vampires carried multiple weapons. She could have pointed out the breach in etiquette to enter a meeting between allies ready for battle, but she understood their uneasiness when outnumbered three to one.

"The Vampires have just left," Sylvan told her mate.

"Callan has gone to find a volunteer," Drake said.

"There are no problems with the others?"

Drake shook her head. "No."

Sylvan sighed. "I'm not sure any of the *centuri* would have considered tangling with Vampires if it hadn't been for this."

"From what I understand," Drake said neutrally, "the encounters are not altogether unpleasant."

Sylvan raised a brow, her canines lengthening as her wolf bristled. Her previous interludes with Vampires were no secret, but her mate should never think anything could compare to what they shared. "I can tell you a Vampire offers nothing like tangling with another Were, especially your mate."

Drake chuckled. "Do you think I don't know that, Alpha?"

Sylvan leaned close and let her teeth graze her mate's neck. "Just checking."

Drake rumbled, her wolf preening. "You should show me instead."

"I—" Sylvan halted as Callan strode down the hall with Drea at his side. Blond, well-muscled, a dominant with an unusually calm temperament that made her an excellent security officer, prone to consideration as well as action. She was a good choice, on the surface. Who was to say how her wolf would respond when a more powerful predator inflicted that first stroke of pain before the pleasure wiped out any desire to fight back? Sylvan had never relinquished control even when under the influence of the erotic power of a Vampire's bite, but she was not an ordinary Were.

"Drea," Sylvan said to the lieutenant. "You understand if you host for one of the Vampires, you will be coming with us into Faerie."

Drea's eyes sparkled. "Yes, Alpha. Perfectly. I'm honored to be included."

"Very well then. Come with me."

Sylvan escorted Drea to where Sabine waited. "Sabine, Lieutenant Drea Carr has volunteered."

Sabine held out a hand to Drea, and as she did, Sylvan felt the warm glide of thrall skate over her skin. While it stirred her blood, the neurochemicals impossible to block, her sex did not ready. Only her mate could arouse her. Drea, however, shuddered, and a fine dusting of tan pelt feathered her chest in the opening of her camo shirt. Sylvan extended her power as her lieutenant struggled to control her Wolf, her canines exposed and her jaw growing heavy. With a growl, Drea leashed her wolf.

Sabine laughed. "Hello, you will be fun."

Drea took Sabine's hand. "Call me Drea."

Sabine looked past Drea to Sylvan. "Don't worry, I won't hurt her." She drew Drea through the doorway, and as the door closed, Sylvan heard her murmur, "Much."

Turning, Sylvan shook her head and rejoined her mate where Drake waited with Callan. "Callan, post guards at the end of the hall. If there's any difficulty, you have my permission to open the doors."

"How will we know?"

Sylvan blew out a breath. "We'll all feel a wolf in distress. Short of that, let them all be."

He saluted. "Yes, Alpha."

As they walked out together, Drake said, "I don't think we've ever had quite this situation before."

"None of us have ever been in this situation before. I hope this wasn't a mistake."

Drake looped an arm around Sylvan's waist. "It was the only decision we could make, or forgo the Vampires as allies. *That* would've been a mistake. Cecilia needs to know that regardless of how powerful she becomes, the Weres and the Vampires would stand against a Fae incursion into the human realm. We might be her allies now, but she mustn't think us fools."

Sylvan laughed. "You're the politician I could never be."

Drake nipped at her jaw. "I am the mate that you chose. You rule our warriors and guide our Pack, but I know what I am to you."

Sylvan stopped, turned, and gripped Drake's nape. She kissed her, her canines already extruded, catching Drake's lip with an edge and drawing a small point of blood. Drake whined softly as her wolf responded, her claws punching out and raking Sylvan's back through her shirt.

"I would have you now," Sylvan said. "Here, in this moment."

"Would you," Drake murmured. "I think what you need even more than that is a run."

She pushed Sylvan away and, with lightning speed, shifted. The black wolf shot Sylvan a cheeky glance and streaked through the nearest open window. Laughing, Sylvan changed in midleap and followed her through into the Compound. As she landed, she caught a glimpse of Drake leaping up onto the barricades followed by two other wolves nearly the same size. Kira and Kendra, called to pelt by the Prima.

So that's the way it would be.

Sylvan gave chase, the lightness in her heart ignited by the love of her mate and her young. She would take chase now in the last moments of joy she might have before her only thought would be battle.

Chapter Nine

Sabine had fed upon rousing at sunfall the evening before, and again after the *senechal* had briefed them for the trip to the Compound. Her hunger was far from sated, and the idea of seducing the Were added an edge to her lust. When decades turned into centuries and centuries into uncountable years, the thrill of the chase dimmed. And now that they lived under the edict that they might hunt but not have the pleasure of completely taking their prey, feeding had become necessary, but far from satisfying. She wouldn't be able to subdue this one completely either, not if she wanted to leave at nightfall with her head. She had won countless battles, but the Timberwolf Alpha would be a formidable challenge and one she doubted she would win should she have to face her in combat. She'd seen the Alpha's half-form, a massive warrior with the shape of a Were but the form of a wolf with the cunning and speed and power of both. The first time she'd witnessed the transformation, one she'd yet to see demonstrated by any other Were, she'd known real fear for the first time in memory.

Despite the risks, taking this Were excited her in a way she hadn't expected. Drea offered her blood out of duty rather than the addiction to the pleasure Sabine could provide, like the blood servants in the seethe or the humans at Nocturne's feeding grounds. Sabine surveyed the Were's body and features, something else she rarely bothered with any longer. Hosts had become faceless, nameless vesicles whose pleasure was not of her making, but only an aftereffect.

Drea stood just inside the door in the dark—the shields on the windows blocked all light, but she was clearly visible in tones of silver and black, her eyes glowing amber, like embers in a banked fire, her body taut and poised to spring. Sabine smiled. The wolf was on guard, it seemed. That was interesting—and exciting.

"Are you afraid?" Sabine asked as she strolled to the surprisingly large and comfortable-looking bed pushed against one wall. She unbuttoned her shirt and shrugged it off. She wore nothing beneath it, save for the leather holster that crisscrossed her torso between her breasts and held her throwing stars. She heard the quick intake of breath from her soon-to-be prey, and the sound brought her incisors down on a surge of bloodlust. The hunger rose, swift as a knife to the heart.

"No," Drea replied. The half-naked Vampire was exquisite, taller than Drea by half a head, slender but sculpted, her muscles undoubtedly far more powerful than her lithe physique suggested. She'd moved across the room without Drea realizing it, and that was a warning signal. This was an apex predator. But then, so was she. In her wolf memory, she ran across the tundra and through the mountains with her Pack, knowing that if they were caught and surrounded by the Vampires, they would be destroyed. In those ancient times, two apex predator could not share the same territory, and as the humans spread relentlessly deeper into the unpopulated wilderness, the predators became prey. She was alone in a cell with a superb predator now, and she probably should be afraid. Her wolf was wary, but her skin slicked with sex-sheen and her clitoris tightened. Not fear, arousal.

"What then?" Sabine asked, casually unstrapping her weapon harness and draping it over the rail at the foot of the bed.

"Curious."

"About what?" Sabine unbuckled her belt and pushed off first her boots, then her pants.

"How is it," Drea said, "to be dependent on feeding?"

Sabine laughed. "We are driven by our instincts, aren't we? How is it to know that something as simple as a silver blade could end even the strongest of you?"

"We train to be strong…and smart," Drea said. "I don't fear battle."

"This will not be like any battle you have ever known." Sabine stretched out on the bed. "You don't have to take your clothes off," Sabine said, "but you might find that you want to. If we were in the midst of battle, there wouldn't be time for anything except my mouth at your throat or any other part of your body I might want to take. But we don't have to rush now."

Drea unlaced her combat boots, pushed off her trousers, and unbuttoned her shirt but left it on. Clad only in skintight briefs and the camo shirt, she strode the length of the room and lay down beside the Vampire. Sabine was testing her, and she did not plan to fail, not only because she'd sworn to her Alpha she was up to the task, but because the Vampire excited her. She was dangerous, beautiful, and deadly. Her wolf liked a challenge.

Sabine traced a finger along Drea's jaw and down the pulse in her throat. "I can taste your need in the air."

"We won't have time in battle, you said," Drea murmured, aware of the drowsy arousal spreading through her. This was not the pressured need that filled her glands when the pheromones of another Were flooded her senses. This was something different, something making her need exquisite, but her mind compliant. She wanted to release, endlessly, and struggled to think.

"No." Sabine slid one hand beneath Drea's shirt and stroked her breasts. "I will take what I need, then, unless you stop me. If you can."

Her thumb glanced over Drea's nipple, and Drea rumbled, a sound she hadn't expected to make when tangling with this foreign creature. Her clitoris lengthened in readiness, and her sex pounded with the essence about to release. She was no stranger to tangling, but she hadn't been prepared for the force of her need. This was how Vampires lured their prey—with the erotostimulants they emitted to ease the pain and terror their prey experienced.

"Don't use your thrall," Drea said, resting her hand on Sabine's hip. "Take me the way you would have to do it when we had no time, the way you would need to if your life depended on it."

"My life," Sabine whispered and bent her head to press her mouth to Drea's breast. "Your heart beats so fast. So strong."

The erotic haze lifted, but Drea's urgent need did not. Sabine caressed her, one hand between her thighs now, knowingly, expertly massaging her. Drea arched, her canines fully extended, her claws extruded, her wolf already wild to couple.

"Tell me," Sabine said, her mouth now at Drea's neck, steadily stroking her, the pressure in exactly the right place to make her release, "are you ready?"

"Yes," Drea groaned, "do it."

Sabine's incisors plunged downward, and she pierced Drea's throat, the jugular opening beneath her mouth, the flood of hot, potent blood infusing her with power and pleasure, driving the lust higher even as the hunger ebbed.

Drea cried out, her release flooding Sabine's hand and coating her thighs.

Sabine moaned, her hips thrusting with each deep swallow. Drea released again, and her pelt riffled down the divide in her abdomen. Her wolf silently howled with pleasure. Sabine gasped and pulled away.

"No," Drea said, "you haven't—"

Sabine rolled off onto her back, her laughter cold as ice. "I cannot, not and leave you breathing."

Drea turned and pushed her hand between Sabine's thighs. "Let me—"

"No," Sabine hissed, grasping Drea's wrist and jerking her hand away. "Your Alpha would not be happy if I drained you tonight."

Drea's sex throbbed, and she was close to release again. She shouldn't care if this Vampire found any pleasure in the act, but her wolf wanted only one thing. To take her, to drive her to the edge, to release again *with* her.

"Is there any way—?"

"No. Rest now. I will want you again before moonfall."

❖

Sylvan caught up to her mate and her young less than a mile from the Compound, yipping with excitement as she barreled down the escarpment to intercept them on the trail. As she came alongside the trio, Drake shouldered her in greeting, and her young nipped at her throat. She twisted from side to side, giving each of them a firm bite on the snout, a greeting and a warning that they mustn't forget who was in charge. Kira and Kendra had grown in size, almost equal in height if not muscle to her and Drake. They were fast leaving adolescence behind, all the more reason they accepted their position in the Pack. They might be her young, but many of the wolves in the Pack outranked them, and unless they wanted to be endlessly and prematurely challenged, they would have to acknowledge the dominance of others. For a while.

They needed to spend their aggressive energy hunting, training, and tangling. Callan needed to keep them too tired to get into trouble.

Sylvan caught the scent of an elk not far away. Just what they needed for a good hard run to tire them out and drain some of their energy.

Kendra, do you scent him?

Yes, Alpha.

Go then, we'll follow.

With a rumble of pleasure, Kendra streaked ahead, Kira close on her heels. Drake and Sylvan kept them in sight as they followed through the lush undergrowth beneath the waning moon.

You'll have to work hard to keep Kendra from challenging everyone who outranks her, Drake's wolf telegraphed.

I know.

Will it be soon?

She'll test her limits for a while yet. Remember, she is beloved by the entire Pack, and she loves the Pack. Some will step aside for her.

I love her, but I'm not foolish enough to think a young dominant wolf has any sense whatsoever.

Sylvan swung her head to catch Drake's eye. *I had plenty of sense.*

Ha, Drake huffed. *Why do I not believe you?*

Sylvan nipped at her muzzle. *Had you been here when I was her age, I would've claimed you then.*

Again, I am not believing. Drake snorted. *And perhaps I would have looked to—*

Sylvan growled. *When does not matter. I knew you were my mate from the moment we met.*

Even when I was human?

Even then.

Up ahead, Kendra turned and splashed across a chest-high, ice-cold mountain stream.

Maybe this wasn't such a good idea, Sylvan thought as she followed into the water. Kendra's hunting sense was strong, but the elk, as Sylvan anticipated, had not grown to his size and stature without having outrun many a predator. A few moments later, Kendra circled and then circled again before trotting over to Sylvan.

I'm sorry, Alpha. He's gone.

He will not be our prey today, but he has given us a good run. Let's go home now. You'll have little time before Callan expects you.

When they neared the Compound, Sylvan led them past the stockade and through the forest to the den she shared with Drake. The *centuri* who had trailed them through the forest on their run took positions at a distance and would keep guard until Sylvan and Drake were once again within the Compound walls.

"Come eat," Sylvan said as she shed pelt on the wide plank porch.

Drake followed, as did Kendra and Kira. Once inside, Sylvan and Drake pulled on pants and T-shirts. They kept clothes for the twins among their stores, but as it turned out, they no longer fit them.

"Here," Drake said, returning from the bedroom with shirts and pants. "You can wear these."

The two young Weres dressed quickly, and Kendra said, "Is there meat?"

Sylvan snorted. "Of course."

As they all gathered to finish off the remnants of a roast, Kira glanced at Kendra before saying, "We want to go with you on the expedition."

Sylvan finished her slice of meat and took in her two young. Not identical, but undoubtedly siblings. Same height, same build, same features but each with distinctive hair and eyes resembling one of their parents. Strong, brave dominants.

"You're not prepared," Sylvan said.

"We will be," they said as one.

Kendra took up the argument. "Callan has promoted us, and we will be training in Jace's squadron. We're ready."

"You're recruits. Not *sentries*."

Kendra's chin came up. "We will challenge for a place, then."

Sylvan growled and let her power flow. "You will fight when and where your Alpha orders."

Both looked away.

"Do you understand?"

"Yes, Alpha," they said.

"Go now," Sylvan said. "You need to rejoin your cadre."

"Kendra," Drake said as the two young headed toward the door.

Kira looked back. "There will be time to find your place. But first you must be strong and skilled. If and when you challenge, you must choose well and fight well."

Kendra dipped her head. "Yes, Prima."

"Good," Drake said gently. After they both disappeared into the night, she sighed. "I don't have firsthand experience with young dominants like this. How soon were you starting to challenge everyone?"

Sylvan laughed. "Just about their age. Maybe a little sooner."

Drake rolled her eyes. "And your Alpha didn't try to stop you?"

"He tried."

"Meaning you are not likely to be successful either?"

"I wouldn't try as hard if we weren't likely to go to war. They're not ready for that, and I won't lose them."

Drake wrapped her arms around Sylvan's waist, rested her head on her shoulder, and kissed her throat. "We won't lose them."

Sylvan dropped her chin on the top of Drake's head. "You, my young, my Pack are my life."

Drake raised her head and nipped Sylvan's chin. "And you are ours. Come with me. This time is mine now."

"All my time is yours," Sylvan said, taking Drake's hand as Drake led the way to their room. "I wish I had more to give you."

Drake raised a brow as she shed her shirt and pushed down her pants. Her body shimmered with the first mist of sex-sheen. The sight and scent of her pheromones brought the blood surging to Sylvan's sex, and she rumbled softly as she pulled off her clothes.

Drake laughed. "We have all the time we'll ever need. Although, if you're going to be this slow—"

Sylvan leapt, catching Drake around the waist and carrying her onto the bed. She straddled her, her face inches above Drake's, her wolf hot in her eyes. "You taunt me. Is that wise?"

Drake swept a hand down the middle of Sylvan's back, the blunt tips of her emerging claws leaving thin trails of fire until she gripped her hips and pulled her tightly between her thighs. "When it brings you to me like this, most definitely."

Sylvan pressed tightly into the cleft between her mate's thighs, locking them as only mated pairs could bond, the breath hissing from her throat as the pleasure roared through her.

"Are you sure we're not breeding?" Her wolf rode her hard, and her voice came out on a growl. "I can't control my wolf. I'm ready to release."

Drake rocked to Sylvan's rhythm, drawing her deeper, and pressed her mouth to the mate bite on Sylvan's chest. She nipped lightly, too lightly to trigger Sylvan's release. "No, I'm sorry."

Sylvan growled again. "Never. Never with me for any reason."

The fire in her loins exploded, and she released to join her essence with Drake's. Drake clenched around her at the height of her release, drawing every ounce of Sylvan's strength from her. With a whine of pure pleasure and surrender, Sylvan finished, her body cradled in Drake's arms, exhausted and sated.

Drake caressed the damp hair at Sylvan's temples and kissed her. "I love that I can do that to you. That I can take your strength for just a moment, and you'll let me."

"I love that you make it easy for me to let go."

Sylvan sighed and faced Drake, one hand cradling Drake's breast. "You already know I want you to stay here when we return to Faerie."

Drake kissed her again. "Of course I know that. And you know that's not going to be possible this time. We'll need all our strength if we need to call on the Pack here at home, and you will need my strength if you are to bond again with Rafe and Torren."

"We should not leave the Pack alone."

"They won't be alone. Max will be here." Drake took a long breath. "And Niki."

"Niki?" Sylvan raised her head, frowning. "She is our *imperator*. The general of our forces."

"We're bringing select warriors, not a full battle force—and you will command them. Answer this—if a Vampire is injured and their host is not available, or injured themselves, would you feed them?"

"Of course," Sylvan said.

"As would I, or any of our Weres. I believe in Niki's loyalty completely, but Niki should not be in that position, even if she was willing. For her safety—and for that of those she commands."

Sylvan sighed. "She'll fight me on this."

"Then talk to her and her mate together."

"As usual, your judgment is what keeps our Pack safe and strong." Sylvan brushed the soft pelt in the centerline of Drake's lower abdomen and lower, until she clasped her sex beneath her palm. "You keep me strong."

Drake gripped Sylvan's shoulders, the wolf in her eyes wild and fierce. "I love you. You are my strength, my passion, and my life."

Sylvan took her again, deep and slow. When Drake's essence flooded her hand, Sylvan pressed her still-full sex to Drake's thigh and emptied.

"Rest awhile," Drake murmured, stroking Sylvan's hair. "There is time yet."

As she could with no other, Sylvan's wolf curled up in the warmth of Drake's arms and slept.

❖

Anya jolted, realizing as the overpowering desire drained away like snowmelt under a burning sun that Rafe had withdrawn her thrall. The sudden absence of the erotic connection was as painful as a fresh wound, leaving a longing that she'd only felt on those nights when she ran beneath the full moon. At the height of moon call, the memories of all the wolves who had come before her, those who had been hunted and nearly exterminated, filled the Pack consciousness, and they howled for their losses and for the love they shared. Even as they sang their songs of joy and freedom, they keened for all those who no longer ran beneath the moon. Now she ached to be filled in a way she'd never ached before, not even then.

She was not used to being so undone by need.

If Rafe felt any discomfort at the loss of their connection, Anya couldn't sense it. The Vampire stared straight ahead, her profile as elegant and sharp as the granite peaks of a mountaintop, and just as remote. Anya's wolf snarled, frustrated at being shut out, simmering with the urge to fight or couple. Anya looked away and met the eyes of Jody Gates, who studied her with unapologetic intensity. Anya wasn't sure how, but she was certain the Vampire Liege knew exactly what was happening between her and Rafe, and the effect it had on her. If Jody was anything like the Alpha, she could sense the power of others. She obviously detected Rafe's thrall. Anya tilted her chin up but was careful to not suggest any challenge with her gaze. She needed the Vampires to respect her, and like all predators, they would respect strength.

"Not much longer," Jody said softly.

A few moments later, Anya sensed the vehicle slowing. They'd been rolling over pavement for the last half an hour. She'd never been to the city. Some Weres not suited to be warriors lived and worked outside of Pack territory, returning to the forest when they needed to reconnect to the spirit and strength of the Pack and for the hunt on every full moon. She had always known she would be a warrior, although she hadn't expected the role she'd been given. She was trained to fight like any other Were warrior, but now it seemed the Alpha wanted her to use her heightened empathic connection to other Weres as part of her duty. That task felt far more challenging than pure combat ever had, but she was a warrior, and she would serve in any way the Alpha wished.

They slowed even further, and the vehicle tilted as if they were headed down a ramp of some kind.

She glanced at Rafe.

"We've reached the seethe," Rafe said. "We will be descending into the underground garages."

"I see," Anya said. "And then?"

"Then I will take you to my quarters."

"Of course." She didn't need to ask anything else. She doubted Rafe would actually answer her, and what was about to happen would happen, whether she anticipated it or not.

"Are you regretting your decision yet?"

Anya cocked her head, surprised. "No."

"Perhaps you should."

"It seems you would like me to. Or be frightened, at least. Does that make things more interesting for you?"

Becca Land coughed, as if covering a laugh.

Rafe's mouth thinned. "Are you always so incautious? It's already apparent you are impulsive."

"It might be that you are too used to routine."

When Rafe snarled, Anya discovered an odd and arousing pleasure in taunting this terribly self-contained and apparently humorless Vampire. Rafe had withdrawn her thrall as if Anya was someone to play with, and her casual dismissal annoyed her wolf enough to make her want to retaliate despite knowing they were in a vehicle with the Vampire Liege and her Consort. Hardly the place for a frenzied tangle, which was exactly what her wolf wanted. Nothing about the present situation was familiar. Ordinarily she had no reluctance at having sex with others around. Weres were not self-conscious about nudity or the natural, instinctive desire to couple. She was at a disadvantage, but she didn't plan to let that show.

She leaned forward until her shoulder touched Rafe's and her mouth was close enough for her breath to warm Rafe's ear. "I think you'll find that being impulsive can be pleasurable. After all, when was the last time you fed from a Were?"

Rafe hissed softly. "The last time I was allowed to take my fill."

Probably Rafe intended to shock her, or frighten her, but Anya felt just the opposite. Rafe was dangerous, as every strong predator was dangerous, but she was not afraid. Maybe she should have been. Maybe she would find herself incapable of defending against whatever need Rafe might demand. But still, she ached to slide her hands under the tight, smooth silk that encased Rafe's slender torso, to feel Rafe's mouth at her throat, and for her sex to empty until the terrible ache inside her ebbed. Her wolf stormed her senses with the urgency to tangle. And more, more that she could not think about now, even as she struggled to ignore the pulsing beat of her wolf's thundering demand. *Bite. Bite. Bite.*

The vehicle came to a halt, and Rafe pushed open the side door. She stepped out, looked left and right at the row of vehicles pulling in beside theirs, and said to Jody, "All is clear, my Liege. With your leave, I will see that the volunteers are escorted to our chambers."

Jody slid out and offered her hand to Becca, who took it and joined her. "I would speak with you at sunfall after you have fed." She glanced at Anya. "You are not obliged to meet all of Rafe's needs, should you find that impossible."

Anya said formally, "I fully intend to meet any and all of the Lord *Senechal*'s requirements, Liege Gates."

Jody nodded and glanced at Rafe. "See to the others, then."

Rafe saluted. "As you wish."

She slipped her hand beneath Anya's elbow again, that odd and unexpected movement one that Anya found she liked.

"Stay close to me," Rafe murmured as they walked forward to join the other Vampires with their Were companions. "The seethe is full of Vampires, and not all of them are as disciplined as my guards. Don't worry. You will not be harmed."

"I can defend myself, Lord *Sene*—"

"You may call me Rafe," Rafe said with a touch of impatience. "And you don't know what you face."

"And you do not know me."

"Then come," Rafe said, leading her down a ramp into a darkened tunnel. "It's time to find out."

Chapter Ten

The tunnels weren't completely without light, although the recesses that branched off at frequent intervals yawned like impenetrable caves. Anya sensed rather than saw the occupants, scented the foreign chemicals in the air, felt the touch upon her skin of whispers of thrall, as if questing hands stroked her. Unlike Rafe's thrall, these searching advances failed to arouse her. Her wolf instinctively bristled, battle hormones stirring the pelt beneath her skin and the first ache of her canines about to erupt.

She hadn't realized she'd moved closer to Rafe until their shoulders touched. When she went to move away, Rafe's arm came around her waist.

"Your blood is richer and stronger than that of our human servants," Rafe murmured, "and there are those among us who are never truly without hunger. You excite them."

"I understand."

"Do you?"

"They do not tempt me."

Rafe's arm tightened around her. "This one is mine," she said, her voice no louder than it had been but somehow reverberating throughout the tunnel, echoing in the air, and rippling along the surface of the walls in much the same way that the Alpha's call reached throughout the Compound and beyond. "The first one to touch her will die."

The seeking sensations abated, and Anya shuddered, aware only after the thrall had been withdrawn how many there had been. The abrupt withdrawal of the pervasive stimulants left her shaking.

"You needn't fear—"

I am not afraid, she signaled mentally, *and if I am to be here, you must let me stand on my own. I will not be prey.*

Rafe's head jerked. "You should not..."

She gripped Anya's hand again and pulled her along. "Hurry. There are others who may feel your thoughts. Your power will only make them hunger more."

They strode rapidly to a bend in the tunnel that opened into a large hexagonal room with doors on each wall standing open to yet more hallways. Anya had the sense of being deep underground, and her wolf bristled with displeasure. How would she find her way out if her wolf could not follow the scent trail? How many Vampires would she have to fight?

"Now you understand," Rafe said.

Anya tensed. Was Rafe reading her thoughts? Could she do that? She knew so little of the Vampires, and now...now she was joined to one, at least by duty.

"This way." Rafe led her down yet another long corridor. The door at the end was closed, and when they reached it, Rafe pushed it open and ordered, "Inside."

Anya stepped through into a bedchamber that was surprisingly opulent. Not in the furnishings, which consisted of only a large canopy bed, as much as in the richness of the colors and textures. Deep maroon silk curtains draped from the canopy, creating a secluded space within covered with dark blue, nearly black sheets. A thick, intricately woven rug warmed the stone floor, and tapestries displaying wild vistas that made Anya's wolf long to run adorned the walls. She was used to the utilitarian surrounds of the barracks, and for a moment, she forgot why she was there.

"How is it you could do that?" Rafe snapped. "Touch my mind?"

Anya jerked, angry at the mental lapse. This was not the den of a lover or a friend she had joined for a tangle. The room held no dressers, no night tables, no armoires. This was a space for feeding—for blood and sex and pleasure-pain. This was the lair of a dangerous hunter, more seasoned and skilled than her. Rafe's eyes had taken on the volcanic color that Anya now recognized as her Vampire unsheathed.

"I didn't intend it," Anya said. "I think because of where we were, I just naturally linked. I didn't want to speak out loud."

"How many?" Rafe hissed, advancing slowly toward Anya. "How many heard you?"

"Only you."

"How do you *know*?"

Rafe's fury rolled over Anya like a blow, and her wolf surged. Pelt dusted her arms and throat. Her canines extended. "I only meant for you to hear."

"And if you are not welcome in my thoughts?"

"You have been speaking to *me* since the moment you and Liege Gates and the others entered the Compound. Haven't you? Isn't that what your thrall is?" Anya snarled. "I don't recall you asking my permission. Or stopping when I didn't respond."

"Didn't you?"

"Not knowingly."

Rafe laughed, an unexpectedly deep and sensuous sound, unlike the laughter that accompanied her faint ridiculing. This almost sounded like pleasure, and the thought filled Anya with unexpected warmth.

"It seems you have been more aware than I suspected."

"You mean that usually those you attempt to seduce are unaware of it?"

Rafe took a step closer, and Anya held her ground, although part of her wanted to retreat, to find a better vantage point from which to fight if she needed to. Allowing this predator so close went against every one of her natural instincts. Rafe traced a finger along the edge of her jaw and over her lower lip.

Anya showed her canines.

Rafe smiled. "What don't you like about that? Don't you like to play?"

"I like to play," Anya said, "as much as any other wolf. Is that what you were doing? Because it felt like you were using your thrall so you wouldn't risk being rejected."

"I don't have to work to seduce my prey," Rafe said, the arrogant tone back in her voice again. "When I want to feed, it's a simple matter to bring them to me."

"As I said," Anya said, "I don't believe you know how to play."

"Is that what you want?" Rafe said.

"What I want," Anya said, tired of the standoff, "is for you to feed. I want you to believe that if you need my blood, I will be able to give it to you."

"You think that's all it is? Blood?"

"What else, then?"

Rafe took another step closer, and Anya was forced to yield or be pressed against her. The bed was behind her, one step, two, another. Rafe was inexorably closing in on her, and she was about to be trapped. With a snarl, she spun and leapt to the opposite side of the bed.

Rafe faced her across the expanse of shimmering silk and laughed again. "I thought you said you weren't afraid."

"Not afraid, but not willing to be forced. I want to understand what you want. Tell me what you want."

"What do I want," Rafe whispered, the lust rising within her, a fire that scorched the air in her lungs, incinerated the nerves in her limbs, set her mind ablaze. The drumbeat of hunger and lust merged, and her incisors throbbed. Anya regarded her defiantly, her anger unknowingly fuel for Rafe's hunger. Anya's power skittered along her skin, skated across her tongue, settled like a torch in her depths. Rafe's mind bled red. "I want you. I want to taste you, to drink you, to fill myself with what I know runs through your veins. Power. Strength. Life."

Anya knelt in the center of the bed, facing Rafe, unbuttoned her shirt, and tossed it aside. Her skin shimmered with sex-sheen, and a feathery soft line of dusky red pelt adorned the centerline low in her belly. Her body was flawless, powerful and lean, her breasts rose-tipped and firm. The wolf blazed in Anya's eyes, gold and fierce, and her skin glowed with sensuous vigor. Rafe took her in, shuddered as the power flowing from her rolled over her in a wave. She rarely considered the physical beauty of her hosts and was stunned to find how much looking at Anya inflamed her.

"Don't play a game you can't win," Rafe warned. Her hold on her hunger grew dangerously thin.

"Tell me what you feel," Anya said. "Tell me."

Rafe unbuttoned her shirt, released the snap on the sheath that held the blades on her back, and pulled it free. She saw when Anya's gaze dropped to scan her exposed torso, and pleasure rippled through her. Shocked, she hissed.

"What?" Anya said. "What is it?"

"Pain," Rafe said, unable to deny her. "Endless, swirling wildfire, destroying everything."

Anya leaned closer and pressed her palm to the center of Rafe's chest. "You have a heartbeat."

"Not for much longer," Rafe murmured.

"And if you feed?"

"Stronger for a while." Rafe fought the bloodlust. She would not ravage this Were. She sent out a mental call. *Zahn, my chambers, now.* "Get away from me."

"No." Anya stroked Rafe's chest and arched her neck, baring her throat as she had never willingly done without a fight. "I choose to feed you."

Rafe was there before Anya could move. In that half a second before Rafe's mouth was at her throat, she realized Rafe could've taken her at any time, no matter how quick she had been, no matter how swift or strong her wolf. She would have been helpless, but Rafe had waited. And then there was pain, fire in her throat streaming into her chest, and she arched, her wolf growling.

Fight! Fight!

Her claws snapped out. Her jaw grew heavy.

A flood of unbearable ecstasy pumped through her limbs, exploded into her belly, and pounded into her sex. A rushing torrent of need consumed her between one heartbeat and the next.

She thrashed, wild to couple, and emptied ferociously, hips thrusting against Rafe's hand. When had Rafe pushed her clothes aside? When had Rafe grasped her sex and massaged her until she exploded? Her wolf howled in triumph and rose hard within her. She dragged Rafe's pants down and shredded her shirt with the blunt tips of her claws. She gripped Rafe's hips and yanked her between her thighs, full and ready to empty again.

Now now. Bite!

Rafe pulled at her throat, each swallow sending another storm of pleasure through Anya's body. She writhed beneath her, soaking them both with her essence, and Rafe took and took and took.

Anya's wolf ascended and reason fled.

Rafe drew back, groaning. "No more."

Anya wrenched the tattered shirt down Rafe's arms and, lost to instincts, let her wolf go. "Yes. *Now.*"

Rafe stilled at the power of the command, felt Anya's sex pulse against hers. She was full now, fed now, potent again. For the first time in memory, she wanted. Rafe rode her thrust for thrust as the pressure built, and when Anya bit her, the agony burst into an ecstasy of pleasure.

The door to her chambers burst open, and Rafe flew across the room, her mind lost to lust, and struck Zahn Logan in the throat.

❖

Niki watched the sky from the ramparts, tracking the tiny flicker of light she knew to be the airborne Vampire security force. As the last trace disappeared in the distance, satisfied that the Vampires had truly returned to their seethe, she strode along the walkway to a dark pool of shadows. The *sentries* would sense when she leapt over the barricades into the forest below, but they would assume she had reason to break the order that all remain within—again. Their orders were to watch for intruders, not monitor the actions of their *imperator*. She needed to run, to still the fury in her blood. The Vampires, so *many* of them, drenching everyone in reach with their thrall, had stirred the need she kept at bay through will alone. Sophia preserved her sanity, by accepting her, by taking her as her mate, by having faith in her to help raise their young. She would not go to her like this, filled with unrelenting dark hunger that had no place between them.

"You think to run from me," Sophia said quietly as she landed softly on the rampart next to Niki. "After all this time, do you think there's anything about you that I cannot, that I do not, love?"

"How can you love this part of me?" Niki couldn't meet the gaze of her mate, the guilt over the addiction she'd so easily succumbed to the night she'd fed Jody Gates tormenting her. She'd saved the Vampire from true death, and in exchange, her body had been flooded with the erotic stimulants that flowed from the scion of the most powerful Vampire line in existence. She'd known the mindless pleasure that lived still in the memory of her very cells, against her will. Sophia had witnessed her helpless surrender that night in the Compound when Lara—her Packmate, her friend—had first awakened as a mindless Vampire newling. Lara had needed only one thing to survive in her transformed state. Lara lusted for blood, and Niki had wanted to give it to her, craved giving it to her, not out of duty, but out of the hunger for pleasure.

Lara pulled Niki beneath her and pressed her mouth to Niki's neck. "I hunger."

Niki arched her back and gave her throat to her Packmate, in submission and invitation. "Feed." Threading her fingers through Lara's hair, forcing Lara's open mouth harder against the bounding pulse in her neck, she begged, "Please, I need you."

Niki strained in Lara's arms, vulnerable and defenseless. Lara wrenched her mouth away, panting, and Niki shuddered in midshift, her eyes wolf-green, her red-gray pelt shimmering beneath her sex-sheened skin. Lara fell away and Niki kissed her, licking the blood from her mouth.

"More," Niki growled, dragging Lara's head down to her neck. "Take more."

"I can't," Lara gasped.

"Yes." Niki slid her hand down Lara's belly, gripped her sex, and squeezed. "Drink me."

"No," a cool voice said from across the room.

Lara stiffened and flung herself to the far side of the bed. Away from Niki. "Get away."

Heed her, little Wolf. The command slid through Niki's mind like a knife.

Niki whipped her head around, snarling as she came up on all fours, inching closer to a full shift. Her jaws ached, her heart thundered. Her pelvis throbbed with the pressure of sex hormones swelling her glands. She was ready to fight or fuck. She focused on the Vampire in the shadows. Gates, lethal as a blade where she leaned against the wall in dark pants and a white shirt open between small breasts, her eyes fiery red, her skin silvery pale in the glow of a morning she would never see again.

Niki growled a challenge. "I can feed her all she needs."

Niki shuddered at the memory, the fire in her blood and the torturous hunger the same now as it had been then. Her blood, her body, had been sensitized to the Vampire's bite, to the thrall that soothed the mind even as it kindled insatiable lust. She couldn't fight it and hated herself for the truth she lived with—deep within, she didn't want to fight it. The aching, rending need never left her.

"I love you," Sophia said, slashing a claw down the center of Niki's shirt, parting the material as she pressed her back to the wall in the shadows. With another flick of her hand, she sliced open the front of Niki's BDUs and slid her hand inside.

Niki's head snapped back against the rough logs of the stockade wall, a growl escaping when Sophia's hand closed around her sex—full, so ready—and squeezed.

"You are mine," Sophia said in her ear. "This is mine. What you need, when you need it, for whatever reason, I will give you."

"I can't," Niki said.

"I say you can," Sophia said, her mouth at Niki's throat, her canines leaving thin red lines.

The pain shot through her, only a whisper of what the Vampires had stirred in her, but carrying the power no Vampire ever could. The power of her mate bond. Her mate claiming her. Her mate taking her. She opened her eyes, and above her the star-filled sky swirled in a dizzying kaleidoscope that flowed through her as the pleasure rose. As Sophia, Sophia her mate, brought her to the edge.

"Who am I?" Sophia demanded, relentlessly working her closer.

"My mate," Niki groaned.

"Yes. *Yes.*" Sophia stroked her just short of pain.

Niki gouged the wood on either side of her as her release tore through her. Not mindless release, but soul-nourishing ecstasy. She grasped Sophia's hips and pulled her tight to her, her mouth on the mate bite at the base of Sophia's throat. "Mine."

"Yes," Sophia cried as Niki claimed her in return.

The fire in Niki's blood faded as she held Sophia close in the circle of her arms. She kissed her temple. "You always save me."

Sophia laughed softly and kissed her throat. "No, my darling. I love you."

"I'm sorry I didn't come to you," Niki said.

Sophia sighed. "You are far too often sorry about things you needn't be sorry about." She tilted her head back and nipped at Niki's chin. "But you are foolish to forget that I know these things about you. I have always known them. I don't love you in spite of them. I love you for who you are, all of you, always."

Niki said, "You and our young are what keep me sane."

Sophia stepped back and took Niki's hand. "You are stronger than you think, but we will always be there for you."

Chapter Eleven

Rafe plunged her incisors into Zahn's jugular, and Zahn's blood, enriched by her decades of serving the strongest Vampires in the seethe and the genetic enhancements of her ancestral line, immediately filled Rafe with familiar power. She'd barely begun to swallow when a rending pain in her shoulder and a blow from behind tore her away from Zahn and catapulted her across the room. She landed on all fours, enraged, and spun around, prepared to attack. A hundred and forty pounds of snarling wolf crouched a few feet away, ready to spring. Rafe hesitated, caught by the beauty of the red wolf's pelt, streaked with gold and rivers of snow white, rivaled only by the silver lightning slashing through the golden eyes.

The wolf's lips drew back in a warning growl, her canines jutting forward in an unmistakable display of aggression. But she did not attack. Behind Rafe, Zahn telepathically summoned the guards. *Rogue wolf! Destroy it.*

Rafe ignored the blood streaming down her chest from the bite wounds in her shoulder and blocked the throng of Vampires storming into her chamber before they could descend on the wolf and tear her apart.

"*No*," she ordered at the same time as another shout joined hers.

"She's not rogue!" Jonathan, one of the Were *centuri*, naked except for his leather pants open nearly all the way down, pushed through the Vampires with fearless disregard.

Jonathan leapt beside Rafe, shoulder to shoulder, forming a barrier between the wolf and the ring of Vampires, all of whom had bared their incisors. The flaming red of their eyes made it clear they were on the verge of bloodlust.

Just behind her, Rafe heard the wolf growl a warning again and gripped the enormous wolf's ruff, twisting her fingers through it. "Do not attack them."

"Anya," Jonathan said, the command in his voice cutting through the growls. "You will stand down."

The wolf snarled and tried to shake free of Rafe's hold.

The circle of Vampires spread out around them and began to converge.

"Put your back to me," Rafe said. "They will all strike as one. You can't stop them on your own."

"I don't care who I kill," Jonathan said, his voice roughening as his wolf rose. "I won't let them harm her."

"Neither will I." Rafe focused on Marrott, the oldest and strongest Vampire present. "You *will* call them off."

"You're injured, *Senechal*." Marrott's blazing eyes fixed on the wolf pressing forward beneath Rafe's grip. "That wolf must be put down. It attacked you."

"That is not your concern," Rafe said. "You will follow my orders. All of you. No one touches her."

One of the young Vampires, new to the seethe, rushed forward, his bloodlust unleashed by the haze of blood and fury clouding the air. Rafe flung out an arm and caught him by the throat with one hand. She lifted him off the floor and flung him back into the crowd who blocked her door.

"The next time I will tear out his throat. Or that of anyone else who challenges me."

Jody Gates's voice rang through the room. "You will disperse as the Lord *Senechal* ordered."

"Marrott," Jody said, suddenly by his side at the front of the mass of Vampires. Her endlessly deep obsidian gaze locked on his. "Do as I command."

"As you will, my Liege." His lips drew back in a grimace of fury, but he nodded sharply and joined Rafe in blocking the wolf from the encroaching Vampires. "Heed your Liege. Leave now, or we will banish you from the seethe."

Banishment meant probable starvation and death for all but the oldest among them, who might survive as lone Vampires without the protection of a seethe. Several of the less disciplined still tried to push forward, but the guards finally came to order, intercepted them, and dragged them away.

Jody pushed the door closed behind them, leaving Zahn, Jonathan, and Rafe alone with the snarling wolf.

"Zahn, are you injured?" Jody said.

Zahn bled from a rapidly closing tear in her neck. She shook her head. "I am unharmed." She narrowed her gaze at Rafe and the wolf now pressed tightly against her thigh. "The wolf attacked the *senechal*. It should be chained."

"No, she didn't," Rafe said coolly, her grip still restraining the quivering wolf. "She sent a warning."

"To whom?" Zahn's eyes blazed. "You were feeding, and she interfered."

"Is that what happened?" Jody asked.

Rafe shook her head. "I summoned Zahn. I…I needed more than I could take from the Were. Anya…reacted."

The wolf growled. Jody studied her a moment and turned to Jonathan. "Can you reach her? Call her to shed pelt?"

"I'm trying, Liege Gates," Jonathan said, a blond dusting of pelt feathering his chest and arms as his wolf struggled for ascendancy. "I don't know why I can't. Anya is usually—" Jonathan abruptly halted and glanced at Rafe.

"We are aware of her abilities," Jody said. "Why can't you reach her?"

"I don't know. She should be open to me—to any dominant, at least."

"She will open to me," Rafe said and knelt before the wolf. She gripped its huge head in both hands and made eye contact. A wave of heat and fury rushed through her. Her blood sizzled with Anya's power, and lust, carnal lust like she hadn't experienced in centuries, pummeled her. Blood and lust—the elemental exchange of a Vampire and its host.

Rafe reached out mentally. *Anya, control your wolf.*

The wolf snarled.

Rafe leaned closer, and the wolf pushed its muzzle against her throat. Rafe laughed. *Oh no, little wolf. I will not submit to you.*

Teeth closed on her neck. Rafe didn't move. She might survive if the wolf tore her throat out, especially with her Liege in the room to give her blood, but even had Liege Gates not been there, she would've accepted the risk. This was a battle of wills and dominance.

Bite me if you will, but I will not submit.

Anya's wolf growled, a dangerous warning.

Nor will I ask you to submit. I ask only that you leash your wolf for now. We will settle this between us another day.

The wolf's teeth closed until Rafe felt the punctures in her throat, felt her blood trickle down her neck. Behind her, Liege Gates said, "Be careful, Rafe. I will not see you damaged."

When the wolf licked at the puncture wounds, Rafe relaxed her grip, and the wolf backed away a step.

"She doesn't want to hurt me," Rafe murmured, understanding without knowing how. "She wants to own me."

"She thinks you're her mate," Jonathan said quietly.

"She's mistaken." Rafe subtly sent her thrall to soothe the wolf. The red wolf shook its head, grumbled discontentedly.

"I'm not sure it works on a wolf," Jonathan said.

"Not as quickly with one as strong as this, perhaps," Rafe said, impressed and intrigued.

"The guards should take her to the isolation chambers," Zahn said, "and bind her with silver until she is subdued."

"No," Rafe said. "She stays with me."

Jody said, "She may be a danger to you, possibly to all of us."

Anya had not moved her gaze from Rafe's the entire time.

"Another moment," Rafe said and pushed her thrall deeper. *Listen to me, little wolf. You will have your battle, but not today.*

The wolf whined softly, and an instant later, Anya knelt before her, naked, her skin streaming with pheromones, her breasts heaving with the effort she'd expended to leash her wolf.

Without taking her eyes from Anya, Rafe said, "You can all leave us now."

Jody said, "Jonathan?"

Jonathan pushed a hand through his hair, clearly unhappy. "I don't know. Anya? Can you leash her?"

"I'm all right," Anya said. "We are all right."

Rafe rose and held her hand out to Anya, who took it and rose beside her. "Moonfall is moments away. We will remain here."

"Liege Gates," Jonathan said, "I need to return to Estella. She will need to feed again."

"And you should return to your Consort, my Liege," Rafe said. "We will be all right."

"Sunfall," Jody said, temper in her voice. "My chambers, Lord *Senechal*."

Rafe tipped her head. "As you wish, my Liege."

When the room cleared, Rafe turned to Anya. "What happened?"

Anya looked away.

Rafe gripped her jaw and turned her face until their eyes met. "What happened?"

"My wolf..." Anya sighed. "My wolf saw you with Zahn. It was so fast, and the blood..." She shook her head. "My wolf didn't want you to feed from her."

"That is not for your wolf to decide. Or for you. I will take whoever I want."

When Anya said nothing, Rafe continued, "What did Jonathan mean that your wolf thinks we're mated?"

"When you bit me, my wolf mistook it as a signal that you were attempting to mate."

"And when you bit *me*?"

"It's what we do to signal we are willing."

"You understand that's not happening," Rafe said coldly.

Anya's chin came up and she met Rafe's gaze, angry and defiant. "Of course I understand. I don't want that any more than you do."

❖

Niki tightened her arm around Sophia's shoulders as they lay together waiting for dawn. "The Alpha comes."

Sophia kissed the angle of her jaw. "Yes, I feel her."

"I'll go."

Sophia sat up and reached for a shirt, pulling it on as Niki slid into her BDUs. She didn't bother with a shirt. Weres often wore as little as possible to make the shift simpler, in addition to having a high body temperature and general tolerance to cold.

Sophia pulled on loose cotton pants. "I'll join you."

Niki cocked her head and studied her mate for a moment. "You feel something from her? Something is wrong?"

Sophia shook her head. "Not danger. More…concern."

Niki pulled her close and kissed her. "I wonder if the Alpha knows that you can sense her moods?"

"I am Omega. She is the Alpha. Believe me, she knows."

Niki strode to the door of their room in the small building that housed the senior staff and their mates. Their young still lived in the nursery with the other young. When she stepped into the hall, the Alpha was waiting.

"Alpha," Niki said in careful greeting. "You have need of me?"

"A moment, *Imperator*," Sylvan said, using her formal title and letting Niki know that this was Pack business. When she turned to close the door, Sylvan shook her head. "If your mate would come also, let's take a walk in the Compound."

Sophia drew up close to Niki and slipped her hand underneath the back of Niki's shirt. The skin contact settled Niki's nerves more than anything else could have.

"Of course," she said and followed Sylvan out into the breaking dawn. She automatically scanned the ramparts and commons. No sign of danger. *Sentrie*s manned the stockade as they did every hour of the day and night. Recruits streamed out of the barracks and formed up on the far end of the Compound, waiting for their cadre and squadron leaders to appear. Sylvan glanced in that direction, and Niki followed her gaze.

"Kira and Kendra are already out there," Niki said.

Sylvan laughed. "Likely been waiting since well before daybreak."

"They're…advancing quickly," Sophia said.

"They are. That's partly why I'm here." Sylvan stopped at the edge of one of the firepits and addressed Niki. "You'll have duties to attend to, so let me take care of this part quickly. I don't intend to wait for Francesca to make the first move. She will only grow stronger day by day, and as soon as Callan feels the squadrons are as ready as they can be, and Snowcrest and the cats are prepared to move, I plan to take a combined force into Faerie."

"How large a force?" Niki asked.

"Not a full battle contingent. We cannot leave the Compound unprotected. We have young and noncombatants here. And we cannot know where Francesca might strike or when. I'm hoping the element of surprise will make up for our smaller numbers when we invade."

"I agree," Niki said. The Alpha did not need her agreement to make a decision, but Niki had learned over the years that Sylvan expected her input. There had been times when they had not agreed. This was not one of them.

"Drake will be coming with us," Sylvan said, "and I will need Max and you to remain here."

Niki stiffened. "You intend for me to stay behind during war. Are you telling me that I am no longer your *imperator*?"

Sylvan reached out and gripped Niki's neck in a firm, just short of painful hold.

"That's exactly why I need you here. These skirmishes in Snowcrest territory, and even Cecilia's petition for aid, may be a ruse to pull some of our most powerful allies and our strongest warriors into Faerie. A full-out attack here while the Prima and I are absent will require a knowledgeable leader to counter it. Max is an excellent soldier, but you are the seasoned tactician. *You* must stand in my stead as the leader of our forces if the Compound comes under attack."

Niki searched Sylvan's eyes and saw truth, but she had known Sylvan since they'd been young together. There was more that she sensed, more that the Alpha had not said, to spare her feelings. A blow to her honor that perhaps she had earned. She had argued against supporting the Vampires with Were blood in battle out of her own discomfort and fear. She had failed in her duty as Sylvan's closest advisor and general. Reading her as only a mate could, Sophia stroked her back, soothing her and giving her strength.

Niki straightened and met Sylvan's gaze long enough for Sylvan to see *her* truth. "I would feed them, Alpha, if I were to accompany you and one was injured. I would not let them die."

"I know that. Your strength was never in question. My duty is to protect every member of my Pack and to see that the strongest survive. Our young are our future. I can only trust them to my strongest wolves. I need you here if both Drake and I are not."

Niki's jaw tightened. "As you command, Alpha. I will meet with Max today to discuss how best to protect the nursery and our noncombatants in the event of an assault. We will begin training the cadres that are to remain behind immediately."

"Good. Kira and Kendra will be among those remaining here." Sylvan pulled Niki close and murmured, "You are my friend, you are my general, and I trust you in all things. Protect my Pack and my family."

"On my honor." Niki stepped back and gripped Sophia's hand as she saluted with the other. "I am and ever will be proud to serve."

❖

"Come," Rafe said, throwing back the deep navy silk sheets on the bed. "We have little time, and I am not yet finished."

"How much longer after moonfall will you be…awake?" Anya said.

Rafe hesitated as if considering if it was wise to answer. She stripped off her pants and, completely naked, slid onto the bed. "Longer than most."

Anya huffed. An answer that was not an answer. Typical of the Vampires.

Rafe raised a brow. "I can call Zahn if you cannot—"

Anya snarled and leapt the distance to the bed, landing lightly beside Rafe. Her wolf rose instantly at the challenge, and she leaned down, her canines pressed against Rafe's jaw. "Do you wish a repeat of the earlier scene?"

Rafe smiled, and Anya caught a hint of amusement in her eyes. She hadn't thought Rafe capable of humor, not without the underlying sarcasm, but that seemed absent now. Her wolf huffed again, this time with pleasure.

"I'd rather not test the discipline of the guards, especially this close to last feeding—I'm not sure I could hold them off a second time."

Anya growled and allowed her wolf the pleasure of nipping at the Vampire's chin. "I can take care of myself. But if you do not wish me to feed you—"

Rafe's eyes shuttered to depthless obsidian and flared instantly to crimson as she gripped Anya's shoulders and twisted Anya beneath her. Anya doubted anyone else, including the strongest Were, could have managed that with such speed. She thrashed for an instant at the sudden show of dominance, and then Rafe was at her throat, and she stilled. Expectant. Excited.

She was here to feed her. Her wolf thought otherwise and howled, hungry for the hunt and something more primal. The agony this time was bright as moonlight, piercingly painful in its beauty, and then the flood of pleasure roared through her, drowning awareness of anything beyond the rush of release. She could no more control her need to spend than she could stop her wolf from trying to claim the impossible. Rafe ranged over her, her body hot and filled with power. Anya wrapped her legs around Rafe's hips, drawing Rafe close to her center where her wolf wanted to join. Rafe's hips thrust rhythmically in time to her deep swallows, and Anya quickened against her. Her glands were full and tight and her clitoris hard. She was ready again, and this time, when her wolf struck, Rafe trembled and groaned and released with her.

Triumphant, her wolf howled with the joy of victory. *Mine!*

Anya's blood burned as Rafe's essence, transferred as Rafe drank, joined hers. She thrust a hand through Rafe's hair, holding her to her throat, urging her to take.

Rafe trembled again and pulled away.

"No," Anya ordered. "More."

Through the haze of lust and pleasure, she watched flames dance in Rafe's eyes.

"I would drain you," Rafe said.

"You won't. Not the way you fear. But I am ready to release again." Anya gripped her shoulders and rose to bite her throat, deep enough to make Rafe hiss. When she lapped at the trickles of blood, Rafe groaned again, and Anya knew she struggled not to take her. She tugged Rafe's mouth down to her neck. *Drink!*

And Rafe did. Anya arched as the power of their blood flowed between them. When Rafe spent again against her thighs, Anya emptied with a shout.

Rafe pulled away a second time and stretched out beside her.

Anya dropped back onto the pillows, stunned and wary. Her body sang with the power they'd shared. Her wolf might have chosen, but she had not.

"It's not what you think," Rafe murmured, and her eyes slowly closed.

Anya expected Rafe to disappear in some way, as if she wasn't there any longer. Dead but not dead. She'd been wrong. She felt Rafe still in her deepest reaches. Her wolf did too and curled up to sleep.

Tentatively, Anya rested her head on Rafe's chest. Rafe was already cooler as the heat of their joining and the blood Anya had given her slowly settled within her, but Anya felt the echo of Rafe's heartbeat deep within her own chest.

Anya slept without meaning to, and when she opened her eyes, she knew instantly sunfall was only moments away. Rafe would need to feed again, and she felt strong and ready for her. Ready in more ways than one. Already her sex pounded, full and heavy. Her body quickened for what was to come. Rafe still lay motionless beside her, but when she pressed her cheek again to Rafe's chest, she felt her heartbeat stirring. Her wolf leapt with joy as it often did when the Alpha would return from the hunt.

The chamber door opened, and she spun around, putting herself between Rafe and whoever might've entered.

Zahn stood in the doorway. "She will need to feed."

"I am here for that."

Zahn studied her for a long time. "I will be just outside. If she needs more, she will decide."

"I understand." Anya kept a firm hold on her wolf, who was already preparing to meet the threat she somehow saw Zahn to be.

"Very well." Zahn pulled the door shut.

When Anya turned back, Rafe was at her throat, fierce and wild. Rafe pinned her beneath her on the bed, both hands on Anya's wrists, holding her down. Anya thrashed reflexively, and Rafe's leg came between hers. Anya stilled as her release exploded and the rushing pleasure built again.

Seconds passed, and Rafe's grip on her wrists relaxed. Anya swept her hands down Rafe's back to her hips and pulled her tighter into the delta between her thighs. She needed the heat of her, and the pressure, to bring her release again. "I need you here. Drink…harder."

Rafe pushed up on her arms, her gaze locked on Anya's. "You should be too weak…"

"I am not," Anya snarled.

"I know," Rafe said, and this time her bite brought no pain but only pleasure.

Rafe's body grew warm, her heart strong against Anya. As the last of the ecstasy ebbed, Anya stretched and her wolf rumbled.

Rafe laughed. "What is that?"

"What?"

"I've heard you snarl and growl and, I think, somewhere," she said, looking perplexed, "howl. But not that sound you just made."

Anya brushed her hand over the spot where she had bitten Rafe, healed now. But still visible to her wolf. "The wolf is content."

"Is she," Rafe said contemplatively. She drew away, and Anya, about to follow, jerked as a barrage of sensation assaulted her.

"Rafe!"

Rafe spun back. "What is it?"

Anya leapt for her clothes. "Danger." She shuddered. The crashing waves of pain and battle hormones shook her to her knees.

Rafe was instantly beside her, lifting her up. "Where? Here?"

Rafe sent out her thrall. All was quiet. The Liege, awake in her chambers. Zahn, outside the door. Her guards, in their chambers, feeding.

"No," Anya choked out. "Snowcrest. And the cats. They're under attack."

Chapter Twelve

"Come," Rafe said urgently and grasped Anya's hand. As they raced down the hallway to the central chamber, she sent out the alert to Jody, Zahn, and the guards. *Secure the seethe. Attack imminent.*

Vampires poured out of the adjacent corridors. Jonathan and the other *centuri* hosts appeared with their Vampires and, before Anya could call to them, seemed to disappear like smoke in the wind. Dematerialized, she realized.

Satisfied that all her forces had mobilized, Rafe wrapped an arm around Anya's waist. She needed to get to Jody. The seethe might fall, but if the Liege survived, the Dominion would be secure. "Hold on to me."

Anya didn't question but wrapped her arm around Rafe's waist. The stone walls of the chamber blurred. Her eyes teared in the wind that blew past her as if she'd suddenly stepped into a tornado. Her wolf pushed into her blood, and battle lust sent her heart racing. Her canines plunged downward, her claws punched through her fingertips, and her jaw lengthened with the first ache of the shift. She couldn't yet hold the massive half-form like many of the older dominant Weres, but she could fight like a wolf without fully shifting to pelt. When the roaring rush of air stopped, she was in another chamber, this one far more elaborate in furnishings than the bare space that led to the guards' sleeping quarters and Rafe's chamber. Jody and Becca, both fully dressed—Jody in black fighting leathers with a handgun in a shoulder holster snugged against her left side and Becca in a sleek black shirt, pants, and boots—stepped through an arched doorway.

"Report?" Jody said briskly.

"Anya received a...warning." Rafe turned to Anya. "What can you tell us?"

"Not so much a warning as the sensation of battle. Lara and Trent—I...felt them both fighting. I couldn't sense the enemy, only darkness." Anya shook her head. So hard to explain the sensations that traveled the Pack bonds—not words, or even images. But the instinctive responses to joy, fear, danger, desire—even death—that joined them all as one. The Alpha, the Prima, and a rare few others could transmit thoughts, and Anya could hear the feelings of others if she opened herself to them. She hadn't intended to link to Rafe, wasn't even aware she could, but that was something else, a connection unlike what she shared with Pack. What she'd experienced in Rafe's chambers had been so strong, she'd been struck physically as if she'd been in the midst of Trent's and Lara's battles. "They've been attacked, at Snowcrest and the Catamount stronghold. Their Pack and Pride are fighting now. They have injured."

"The Timberwolves?" Jody asked.

"I can't feel anything from there, but I haven't tried. I'm not sure what that means." Anya shuddered. Her Pack bonds were there—if they'd been severed she would know instantly. Her mind, her body, would be adrift. Alone for the first time in her knowing. "The Alpha..." She hesitated to expose any Pack information, especially when she knew not where the danger originated. "I cannot feel the Alpha. And the Pack only feels alert, on guard. I don't sense an attack."

"How large are the forces attacking Snowcrest and the cats?" Jody asked. "Can you see them? What they are?"

"I can't," Anya said, glancing at Rafe. "I'm sorry. If Trent and Lara still retain some link to the Timberwolf Pack, even though they are now part of another Pack and Pride, I can sense through them, but I can't *see* them."

Rafe pressed a hand to the small of her back, a comfort Anya hadn't expected and wasn't certain she understood, saying to Jody, "She is a strong empath, and her telepathic range is more than some of ours. The cats are two hundred miles away."

"An attack here, in the heart of the city, is unlikely without substantial forces," Jody said. She turned to Becca. "We'll need to monitor all the communications you can access—news, police bulletins, military mobilization. We need to know if any human installations are targets."

"What about you?" Becca asked quietly.

Jody grimaced. "We must assume reinforcements are needed. We'll send a contingent of guards."

"How?" Rafe said. "Even by air, it will take an hour to reach Snowcrest and longer to reach the Catamount Pride home."

"Then we should alert the pilots." Jody looked to Anya. "Where? Where should we go?"

Anya didn't hesitate. Another time, she would have said Jonathan should be consulted. As the ranking Were in the seethe, he should determine the strategy, but he was not here, and she was. The urgency she'd felt from Trent and Lara—the rage, the determination, and the pain—gave her strength to act. "To the cats. Snowcrest has the larger force, and their soldiers have been training for this. Also, they're closest to the Timberwolves, and if I can reach the Alpha, I can tell her where you're going."

"Try," Jody said. "Rafe, order the helos—"

Zahn appeared at the mouth of the chamber, her face set and grim. "My Liege, there's been a development."

"I don't sense an attack," Jody said.

"No, my Liege. Lord Torren is here."

"I'll be a moment. Where is she?"

"Here." Torren stepped into the archway next to Zahn. She wore a hip-length royal-blue brocade tunic over black pants and high boots, a short sword with a silver pommel and cross guard, and a golden hilt engraved with runes. A ruby ring glinted on her right hand. The emblem of the hawk adorned her chest.

Jody's eyes narrowed. "Exactly how did you arrive?"

Before Torren answered, Zahn said through clenched teeth, "A Gate, in the guards' chamber."

"Interesting," Jody said coolly. "I see there are some things of which I was unaware."

Torren smiled. "I can take a small force over a considerable distance. I thought your aid might be required elsewhere."

"You're correct." Jody turned to Rafe. "Assemble the guards. Zahn, assign a backup security force to this…entrance in the chamber."

"No one else can use that Gate," Torren said mildly.

"We'll discuss that later," Jody said.

Becca grasped Jody's arm. "Be careful."

"You needn't worry." Jody kissed her. "This is not Faerie. We are at strength here, and an attack this side of the veil must be answered with force. I'll be back soon."

Once again, Rafe pulled Anya close, and seconds later they were back in the guards' chamber where the Vampire guards and the *centuri* who had spent the day with them waited. The guards were armed with an array of weapons, sidearms for each of them, swords and shuriken in sheaths, and undoubtedly other weapons that Anya could not see. Like herself, the *centuri* carried only their wolves within with which to fight. Sidearms were of no use when they fought in the open as wolves.

"Follow me through," Torren said to the two dozen warriors, "in pairs, as quickly as possible. Jody, if you please."

Jody stepped up beside Torren, and then they were gone.

"Stay close to me when we arrive," Rafe said and gripped Anya's hand.

They stepped into the shimmering Gate, and within seconds, they emerged in the center of a natural mountainous fortification with a towering black cliff at their backs, a jumble of caves jutting off among stony outcroppings in a semicircle on either side, and a long grassy plain dotted with evergreens that led down to a wide river. The plains below were a swarming mass of cats and something Anya was at a loss to name. Huge thundering beasts that ran on all fours with tusks like elephants, only straight and thicker, cloven feet, flaming eyes, and maws that opened with double rows of saw teeth. The beasts would catch a cat as it leapt, spear it, and toss it aside or trample it where it fell. Blood ran freely, and the sky smoldered. The sights and scent of blood and rage called her wolf, and she and the *centuri* shifted. At Jonathan's command, the wolves formed a wedge and, with howls of fury and power, raced down the slope to join the battle.

❖

Sylvan, in the midst of discussing cadre assignments with Callan for the campaign in Faerie, felt Jonathan and the other *centuri* shift and tasted their battle lust in her blood. Anya's distinct essence overlaid them all, clear and bright and telegraphing a warning. A fleeting image of Lara in a blood rage passed through her consciousness at the same time.

"Prepare for battle," she broadcast to the Pack. "The Catamount stronghold is under attack."

Callan loped away to take charge of the warriors pouring out of the barracks and *sentries* racing along the ramparts. Sylvan leapt to the top of the fortifications, shifting in midair just as a lookout reported, "The Gate has reappeared."

Drake, already in pelt, dropped from the second-floor window at headquarters and raced across the Compound. A moment later she landed beside Sylvan atop the barricades.

I've instructed the sentries *to close the wing to the nursery*, she mind-spoke.

Good. So the Gate never disappeared. We just couldn't tell it was there.

Drake snarled. *There could be others.*

We'll find them. Sylvan, teeth bared, her ruff spiked along her back, watched for what was about to emerge through the Gate, a mere shimmering of air at the edge of the forest. She scanned left and right along the perimeter of the fortifications. Callan had placed *sentries* two deep along the entire length. Whatever was to come through the Gate would have to cross open ground to make an assault, and when they did, she and her wolves would drop on them. She wanted to fight on ground of her choosing and to keep the enemy away from the noncombatants sequestered inside the Compound. Close-quarter fighting gave them the advantage—wolves instinctively fought as a pack, isolating prey and attacking from multiple vantage points at once. When needed, they could just as effectively incapacitate the enemy with a strategic solo assault.

Sabine, Drea at her side, materialized nearby. Sunfall had just barely ended, but the Vampire appeared well-fed and strong. Sylvan sensed that Drea remained at battle strength as well. If anything, she radiated power. The other two Vampires with their *centuri* hosts appeared beside Sabine and Drea.

Sabine murmured, "They don't know we're here, or they would have attacked at dawn."

Or they don't care, Sylvan's wolf mind-spoke.

Sabine laughed. "Fools, then." She studied the Gate, the fortifications, and the ground between. "Close combat?"

Sylvan's wolf growled softly. *That's how we fight.*

Sabine flicked open the sheath holding her shuriken and propelled a throwing star that flew across the space to the Gate and disappeared with a spark of light. "One-way Gate. Whatever is coming through is not expecting to return."

Niki, having just joined them and still in skin, said, "Watch the sky. Something may come that way, and they could drop behind our lines in the center of the Compound. Max is with Callan—they'll post a rear guard for a counterattack should that happen."

That's why you're the imperator. Ash, the former Snowcrest captain, leapt up beside Niki with Jace at her side.

"Alpha Mir," Ash said, "Alpha Constantine reports an attack on Cresthome. A small assault force within the fortifications. The Gate opened inside the perimeter walls."

Can they hold? Sylvan asked.

"If no further invaders appear, she said they will secure the Pack home without aid." Ash's eyes glowed wolf-gold. "They have injured, and she requests medical support."

Callan, Sylvan relayed, *assemble an away team for Cresthome. A support cadre and a medical team, with supplies. Move out immediately.*

"As you command." Callan jumped down from the ramparts and signaled to Vincent, one of his senior captains. A half dozen Rovers roared into the yard from the rear of the Compound, and a cadre of *sentrie*s streamed into the vehicles.

Drake caught sight of Kira and Kendra among those headed into a Rover. Before she could alert Callan, they were inside and the vehicles were moving out through the main gates. She swung to Sylvan. *Did you see? The twins have gone with the troops to Snowcrest.*

Vincent will see to them. Sylvan detected a change in the density of the space within the Gate and projected power to her Pack. *Ready. On my command.*

Down the lines on both sides of her, extending the length of the barricades, Weres shifted into pelt and wolves howled.

A stream of wolves—or what had once been wolves but were now abominations—flowed from the Gate, four across, each twice the size of an ordinary wolf Were, their pelts nothing but char stretched over the sinew and bones of their once-muscular frames. Short, stubby winglike spikes projected from just behind their shoulder blades, and strings of black saliva dripped from their misshapen jaws, which were elongated and widely hinged. Their stunted legs ended in paws tipped with razor-edged claws. Their howls echoed in Sylvan's bones like the cries of dying beasts.

Attack, Sylvan commanded, and wolves in pelt swarmed from the barricades into the mass of approaching monsters. Wolf Weres circled in pairs and attacked in synchrony, striking back and belly, throat and spine, simultaneously. Sylvan and Drake tore through the scattering ranks, slashing with canines and claws. The blood, or what had once carried the essence of life, ran black, smoking the earth. The Timberwolves, faster, more agile, and with the skill the transformed beasts had somehow lost, swept through the stragglers, ripping out throats, severing bone and ligaments, tearing open midsections where organs had once rested. Now only hunks of decomposing flesh spewed forth.

The last to emerge through the Gate, larger and more nearly wolflike in appearance, leapt over the throng of milling warriors, higher than most wolves except an Alpha could manage, and struck Drea in the chest, carrying her down with its jaws clamped on Drea's throat. Sabine materialized next to them an instant later, thrust a hand into the back of the reanimate's neck, and ripped out what had once been its spine. The thing jerked and flailed and, when she tossed it aside, smoldered into an oily black mass. Blood geysered from Drea's throat as the tan and black wolf lay motionless. Sabine knelt, picked up the wolf, and buried her fangs in her neck.

Niki shot from the morass of milling fighters, intent on stopping Sabine from draining Drea. She landed, jaws wide to strike, and discovered nothing but Drea's blood soaking the earth and the scent of lust. Battle crazed, her wolf howled for vengeance.

❖

Trent soared onto the back of one of the winged beasts—half cat, half giant raptor—that had dropped from the sky with no warning beyond an ominous darkening of the sky and a single ear-battering roar of thunder that ripped a jagged hole in the veil between the realms. She clamped her jaws, grown longer and wider since her mating with Zora, onto the back of the thing's neck and shook her shoulders violently from side to side. The spine cracked, and the beast dropped, its four legs splayed, its enormous hooked beak snapping at empty air. Trent's wolf dove over the head of the dead beast as it smoked and withered, spinning to search for the next attacker. The Snowcrest commons smoldered with the flaming carcasses of the enemy. The trio of Snowcrest *medicus* carried the injured wolf Weres, struck down in the first wave of the assault and now too weak to shift, from the battlefield into the sanctuary of the barracks. The hospital infirmary was full. Zora, in half-form—towering over the wolves remaining in the field, preparing to defend against another attack—methodically dispatched those enemies not yet dead with a swipe of her four-inch claws to the throat. She bled from a bite in her flank that had torn muscle from bone, and she limped on her right leg, but Trent's heart eased as she watched Zora move among the Pack—ordering new battle lines, directing the captains to set the watch. Not badly hurt. As soon as the all-clear came, she would make certain Zora's wounds were tended. Until then, Zora would not leave the battlefield.

"Prima!" a soldier shouted. "Behind you!"

Trent swung around as a figure in a scarlet tunic materialized in the midst of the battlefield, tall and slender, with shoulder-length silver hair to match their luminous silver eyes, and pale delicately carved features. Indescribably beautiful in a way only the Fae could be. They unhurriedly unsheathed a longsword in one smooth motion and glided toward Zora.

Zora roared a challenge and stood her ground, protecting the wounded Weres who had yet to be evacuated. Loris, in pelt, raced to intercept the Fae just as Trent leapt from the opposite direction. She would not let this enemy reach Zora.

The Fae's sword was a blur, spinning in an arc that cleaved first through Loris's shoulder, severing muscles, nerves, and tendons, then slashing Trent's flank as Trent's wolf struck the warrior in the chest and dragged them to the earth. Searing pain spread through Trent's side and foreleg as her jaws snapped on empty air. The warrior was gone.

Zora shifted back to skin, shouting, "Medic," as she crouched over Loris and Trent.

Dominic appeared at her side. "Here, Alpha."

"Give me a blade."

Instantly, he handed her a long, razor-sharp knife.

"Hold Loris," she instructed, and Dominic and another of the soldiers pinned Loris's wolf to the ground. She cut out the flesh around the blackening wound in the wolf's shoulder until the oozing black blood turned red.

"Silver," she said grimly. "He can't shift and won't heal until we remove it. Get Loris inside. Quickly."

Dominic called over two recruits, who lifted Loris onto a sling and hurried away. Zora knelt by Trent and stroked her muzzle. "You're hurt, you foolish wolf. Did you think I would lose to the swing of a sword?"

Trent's wolf panted and held out its leg, its eyes trusting and calm. Trent mind-spoke, *I didn't doubt you, but I feared more might come. It's you they wanted.*

"It's me they shall have, but not the way they'd planned," she said grimly and laid the blade to her love's flesh. "I'm sorry."

Chapter Thirteen

As the *centuri* advanced in battle formation at breakneck speed down the bloody slope below the Catamount stronghold to reinforce the cat Weres, Anya lost sight of Rafe and the other Vampires. She'd never fought with them—as friend or foe—and imagined they fought one-on-one as they seemed to do everything else. The Vampires were solo hunters, except when rogue, and as far as she had seen, did not share their prey as did wolf Weres. Small skirmishes dotted the rocky plains, with the smaller cats attacking the massive tusked beasts two or three at a time. This technique Anya recognized, as the cats fought very much the way the wolves did, in numbers. The cats might be more solitary than wolves, but they also lived in a Pride and shared their food as well as the caring for their young.

The closer she and the other wolves drew to the milling mass of bodies, the more she could make out where the assault was focused. The epicenter of the screaming, bellowing morass of combatants was a blood-misted, semicircular rim of the cliff above the rushing river that roared along the border of the plains. The ensorcelled beasts appeared to be closing ranks, crowding closer and closer toward the cats trapped on the cliff above the water.

Anya's wolf growled and nearly broke ranks as the Hound, three times the size of the largest Wolf, massive even compared to the monsters who formed the wall between the cats and the reinforcements, emerged between one heartbeat and the next, shoulder to shoulder with Jonathan. Anya had never seen the Master of the Hunt in true form. Its massive shoulders bunched and rippled with each enormous stride. Its flaming eyes swirled with power, and its cavernous jaws opened to blast an ear-shattering bellow of challenge. Anya's wolf joined the call of the other wolves as they crashed into the tusked monsters, three bodies deep, ringing a handful of cat Weres, their tawny coats matted with blood, their yellow eyes wild with battle rage.

A voice rang in her mind, as clear as the Alpha's, that she instinctively recognized as the Hound's. *They want Raina. Follow me.*

The power in the Hound's command was as compelling as the Alpha's too, and Jonathan along with the other wolves veered behind the Hound. Anya had but an instant to recognize Lara crouched over a cat, who lay motionless on the ground, before a beast turned, lowered its tusked head, and charged.

Anya dove beneath the thundering beast, her claws slashing its underbelly as the *centuri* leapt onto its back. Together they dragged it down and left it, to move on to the next, and the next, dodging tusks and clawed feet, slashing, tearing, severing limbs and opening throats. Her wolf was quickly covered in the black ichor that spurted from the damaged beasts. She ignored the burning in her flank and the bright pain of the gash in her shoulder.

Somewhere a cat screamed, in rage and pain.

Anya dodged a tusk meant to impale her even as it swept beneath her and flipped her into the air. Her wolf tumbled and crashed to the ground, stunned. The earth shuddered as she tried to get to her feet, and the looming beast reared up to drop on her with its massive weight. As the clawed feet, as wide as her whole body, descended on her, a fist buried itself in her ruff and someone dragged her free. Growling, she got to her feet and swirled around, jaws open, ready to die fighting. Rafe, her eyes brilliantly flaming infernos, met hers, and Rafe's voice filled her mind.

With me. We need to reach Raina.

Anya pressed close and, an instant later, was inside the ring of monsters with the other Vampires and the beleaguered cats. Raina, battered and blood-soaked, lay motionless on the ground, and Lara in wolf form, mad with rage, snarled, snapped, and clawed as the beasts closed in.

Protect the Alpha and her Prima.

Anya, Jonathan, and the other *centuri* ringed the cats. Rafe drew a short sword in each hand and, her form a blur, swept the line of beasts, opening throats faster than Anya could follow. More Vampires appeared, while Anya and then Jonathan, on either side of Lara, held back the beasts with fang and claw. And then the Hound roared, an eerie sound that inspired terror in foe and friend. Parts of bodies, withering to ash, flew into the bloody sky, and screams ended in strangled cries. When the last of the beasts lay smoking in the charred field, Lara shed pelt and lifted Raina, still in cat form, onto her lap. The cat Alpha barely breathed, her chest coated with blood, a penetrating wound just below her rib cage bubbling air and fluid.

"I need a healer," Lara shouted wildly.

Another cat shed pelt nearby and called in a guttural voice heavy with sorrow, "Benjamin is gone, Prima. We have no healer."

The Hound, awash in blood and gore, shimmered and Torren appeared, glowing from the power absorbed during the battle. Her tunic, scabbard, and bejewled sword hilt showed not a trace of blood. She knelt next to Lara and put a hand on Raina's chest.

"The lung is punctured, and blood vessels ruptured," Torren said.

"Can you help?" Lara asked. "Please."

"I will try," Torren said.

"As will I," Rafe said and opened her wrist with a quick slash of her blade. She held her arm to Raina's mouth. "Force her to drink."

Lara held Raina's jaws open as Rafe's blood flowed in.

Jody materialized and gripped Torren's shoulder. "As will I. Feed her our power, Lord Torren."

Torren pushed her hand into the wound on Raina's chest, and Anya felt a ripple in the air as if the sun had suddenly broken through a cloud. The air pulsed with the surge of power, and her wolf pressed close to Rafe.

Raina shuddered, a low whine emerging from her throat, as the wound in her chest closed.

"She needs rest and food," Torren said. "When her cat is stronger, she will shed pelt and heal. Until then, guard her well."

"What if there is another attack?" Lara said. "We have many injured, and most of our Pride is scattered throughout the mountains."

"We will not leave this night," Jody said. "If there is a second assault, we will be here."

Rafe stepped back, paler even than the moonlight sweeping over her face. Anya rubbed her muzzle against her thigh, and Rafe reached down to grip her ruff. The tremor in her hand alerted Anya's wolf, who growled unhappily.

You need to feed, Anya's wolf signaled silently. *There is time.*

Do not wait too long, Lord Senechal. *I would not have you weakened if we must fight again.*

Rafe glanced at her, her mocking smile familiar. *I don't intend to wait, little wolf. It is not for you to worry.*

Anya huffed. *And that is not for you to say.*

❖

Sabine, Drea's wolf motionless in her arms, landed silently in the shadows on the wide porch fronting the building where she'd been housed with Drea that morning. They'd called it the infirmary, but whatever it was, this was the building where the wolves, streaming steadily across the Compound, were bringing the wounded. A Were *sentrie* in khaki BDUs who guarded the heavy double doors twitched as she sent her thrall to blunt his senses, enough to lower his aggressive reaction but not enough to incapacitate him.

"I need to know where your best healer is located," she said, gliding in front of him.

He growled, his eyes instantly flashing wolf-gold, but he didn't attack. "That's Drea." He shuddered as thick, dark pelt flowed down his arms and his canines jutted. With a snarl he blocked the entrance. "You may not enter. Give me the wolf."

Sabine hissed. She had neither time nor temperament to negotiate. If she left him in a daze on the ground, Liege Gates would be very unhappy with her. "She is dying. I hoped not to kill you, but I have no time. Decide quickly."

The dominant wolf growled again, but his eyes dropped to Drea, then back to Sabine's before he glanced away. He was dominant, but she was centuries older and exuded power. He reached behind him and opened the door, backstepping so he could watch her as he pushed it open.

"The third door down on your left. Sophia is there, but there are other wounded."

"I do not care about them."

She was gone before he could reply and through the door into the room he'd indicated, as Drea's breath grew steadily weaker. She strode to the center of the large, brightly lit room where injured Weres in pelt and skin lay on the treatment tables. A dozen other Weres hung bags of fluid, sutured wounds, and administered drugs by injection and catheter. On one table a black and brown wolf, smaller than Drea's wolf, twitched and growled, and a dark-haired male appeared in its place. He groaned, and the medic gripped his shoulder.

"Ivan, you've been wounded, but you're all right now."

Sabine announced, "I am looking for Sophia."

A blonde wrapping a bandage around the forearm of a heavyset male sitting on the edge of a treatment table spun around, her eyes the blue of the sky Sabine could barely remember. "I am Sophia." She took in Sabine and the wolf in her arms in one quick glance. "Bring her, with me."

Sabine followed, struck by an odd and long-forgotten sense of tenderness that washed over her. She shook it off impatiently.

"Here," Sophia said and indicated an anteroom with another treatment table. She flicked on a large, round ceiling lamp that flooded the cold stainless steel with harsh bright light. "What happened?" Sophia said as Sabine carefully lowered Drea to the table. She rested her hand on the wolf's chest. "Her heart is barely beating. She can't shift in this state."

"One of the revenants," Sabine said briefly. "I sealed the wound as quickly as I could, but she has lost a great deal of blood. And there is poison."

Sophia looked up sharply. "Are you certain? What kind of poison?"

Sabine hissed impatiently. "I do not know, but I can taste it in her blood."

Sophia's eyes flicked to hers and held them, something another wolf would never do. Again, Sabine sensed calm stealing over the places inside her that roiled with anger and pain.

"What are you?" Sabine demanded.

"A healer. Can you do anything to help her?"

"I can give her the blood that she needs to begin healing, but you must stop the poison."

"Blood first," Sophia said without hesitation.

Sabine put her wrist to her mouth and slashed the large vein in the bend of her elbow with her incisors. She forced Drea's jaws open and held her arm above her mouth as her blood ran freely. "Drink, Drea."

From behind them, Niki snarled, "Stop her. She'll turn her."

"No." Sophia stepped around Sabine, blocking her from Niki's path. "You can't be in here now. Please leave."

"You don't know—"

"I *do* know," Sophia said. "I'll do what I must to save her. Trust me."

"I do trust you." Niki trembled. "I'm sorry."

"I know. What do you know of the poison?"

Niki shook her head. "Nothing. It's black, it burns, and the wounds fester immediately."

"Yes, I've seen it in the others." She turned back as Drea's wolf whined, in pain and terror. "Drea, don't try to shift yet."

Sabine continued to let her blood flow. "It tasted like silver—tarnished silver."

Sophia nodded. "I have a chelating solution that will counteract silver, and that's the only thing that I can think of that would poison a Were."

"Then give it to her," Sabine said without looking at the healer whose gentle voice and calm strength made her uncomfortable.

"If I'm wrong—"

"She'll die anyway." Sabine glanced up. Compelled her. "Give it to her."

Sophia smiled gently, unaffected by Sabine's thrall. "I will. How much blood can you give her before she turns?"

"Unless she dies," Sabine said flatly, "she won't turn."

Sophia injected a clear fluid into the large vein inside Drea's hind leg. When she finished, she placed a hand on Sabine's shoulder. "That's not what I asked you. How much blood can you afford to lose?"

"More than she needs," Sabine said, although as her blood flowed out, her hunger and the pain surged.

"You need to feed, don't you," Sophia said softly.

"Later," Sabine said.

Drea's wolf twitched again.

"Give her more of what you just gave her," Sabine said. "She's getting stronger."

"I don't know what the dosage is. I don't even know if it's the right thing."

Sabine looked up into those pure blue eyes. "You're a different kind of wolf, aren't you?"

The smile, gentle and fleeting, struck her with another wave of tenderness that almost masked the pain that grew greater with each passing second.

"I am a healer." She brushed her hand over Drea's head, and Drea's eyes flickered open for an instant.

"She's better," Sabine said.

"I think that's your blood more than anything else. The antidote is a strain on the system, and she's already struggling."

"Do it," Sabine said. "I can drain her blood, remove some of the tainted blood, and give her more of mine."

"For how long?"

"Long enough," Sabine said and bit the large vein in Drea's throat. The poison-laden blood did not ease her hunger, but it would not hurt her.

The door opened and Niki reappeared. "I've brought one of the others."

Lily, a lithe dark-haired Vampire in black fighting leathers, strode in. "Sabine, enough. Let me feed her."

In an instant she had shouldered Sabine aside, had opened a vein in her own wrist, and pressed the wound to Drea's muzzle. The wolf swallowed steadily.

"You presume," Sabine said.

"We can't afford to lose you," Lily said grimly.

"I'm all right," Sabine said, although her vision dimmed. And worse, her hunger raged.

"Get out of here," Lily said. "The *imperator* said she will take you to feed."

Sophia jerked. "Niki?"

"It's all right," Niki said. "Max is on his way."

Sabine met Sophia's gaze. "I will return."

Sophia gripped Sabine's arm. "Thank you. When she's stronger, she will shift, and she will heal more quickly."

"Don't let her die, then." Sabine followed the wolf general down the hallway to one of the rooms where they'd been sequestered that morning.

"Here," Niki said and pushed the door open.

"I can feel your lust," Sabine murmured. "Are you sure you don't want to feed me?"

The *imperator* growled. "Go."

Sabine laughed. "As you will."

The male who waited was large and strong, and his blood was powerful. He lay quietly, wordlessly, as she took his throat and drank her fill. He moaned once when the erotostimulants rushed through him and forced his release. Sabine had no need or desire for anything other than his blood.

When she stopped, he gasped. "Was it enough?"

"For now."

He turned his head, and gold ringed his eyes. "Take more."

When she left him, drowsy and sated, the *imperator* waited in the hall. Sex-sheen streaked her neck and chest, and her eyes glowed gold.

Sabine traced a rivulet of moisture down the heavy muscle in Niki's throat. "My hunger never ends. You know, don't you?"

Niki lifted her chin, defiantly baring her throat. "I hunger for my mate."

"Is that really enough?" Sabine asked. She'd fed just now, and the pain had dulled to a distant ache she knew would flare again. The Were blood held the pain at bay far more than that of any human host. Her hunger for Drea was just that—hunger for the strongest host.

"Always." Niki gestured to an open door down the hall. "You'll be protected in there if you're here at moonfall."

"We'll be here until the Liege sends for us. Now, I will see what your healer has done for Drea."

❖

Rafe wrapped her arm around Anya's waist as Jody lifted Raina into her arms.

"She's mine," Lara snarled.

Jody turned to Lara, and Anya sensed her extending her thrall. "She needs to be somewhere safe until she is healed. We can take her to your lair. You need to see to your cats and secure the perimeter. Where is your general?"

"I don't know," Lara said.

"Find him. If he's injured, get him inside as well. If he is dead, name another one."

Lara's eyes, the amber glow of wolf and Vampire, flared. "No one touches her until I'm there."

"Only what is needed." Jody signaled Rafe. "See that our Vampires are replenished."

"As you will," Rafe said.

Jody and Raina disappeared. Rafe's orders to the other Vampires flowed through Anya's consciousness.

Follow the Liege inside the caves. Bring the wolves with you.

Rafe tightened her grip on Anya, and the moon blinked out for an instant. Anya shed pelt as Rafe transported them from the battlefield and emerged inside the mountain. The cats' lair was a series of caves and rocky chambers within the cliff face illuminated by moonlight that filtered through the crevices overhead. She instinctively pulled pants from a pile of uniforms against one wall in an automatic move common to all Weres.

A young cat Were, her khaki shirt soaked with blood, some of it her own from a gash in her shoulder, and more from the injured stretched out on the floor of the cave, blinked sharp green eyes and instantly crouched as if to spring.

"I am the Vampire Liege. I have your Alpha," Jody said quickly. "Are you a healer?"

The tawny-haired female nodded. "I am now. My skill is limited, but…"

"We will help you," Jody said.

"How did you know where to bring her?"

Jody's smile was the winter smile of an apex predator. "There are a great many of you here."

Anya now understood that Jody sensed their heartbeats. Even allies could be prey.

"My Vampires will need shelter as well," Jody said.

"There is another chamber, through the passageway," the female said, tipping her head toward a tunnel off to one side.

Lara appeared at the mouth of the cave. "Where is she?"

"Here." Jody laid Raina on a ledge above ground level and pressed a hand to Raina's chest. "Her heartbeat is steady, but she is weak. Too weak to draw strength from the Pride."

"I can help with that," Lara said and stretched out beside her, taking the cat into her arms. She pressed her face to the cat's neck and murmured softly to Raina. "Feel the Pride, Alpha. We are here."

"Come," Rafe said, taking Anya's hand. "They don't need us here. And I need you."

"I know," Anya said. "I can feel your hunger."

Rafe's mouth twisted. "Can you? Can you feel the hunger of the other Vampires as well?"

Anya met her eyes, gloried in the fire that leapt within them. For her, at least for now. "I feel them. They're not my concern."

"You see too much," Rafe said, and then Anya's back was against a smooth stone wall, with Rafe's body pressed against her, Rafe's mouth at her throat. "You still don't know, do you," Rafe whispered in Anya's ear, slicing the front of the uniform pants and sliding her hand between Anya's legs.

Anya's blood flared as her body instantly readied.

"I know what you want," Anya growled and nipped at the angle of Rafe's jaw. "What are you waiting for?"

Rafe's hand closed on Anya's sex. "For you to hunger as I hunger."

"I do." Anya arched as Rafe's incisors pierced her neck, spending her essence with Rafe's first swallow. The pleasure barreled through her, and her wolf exploded to the surface, canines lengthening, pelt rippling down the center of her torso.

Rafe straddled her, one iron thigh between Anya's legs as she pushed deeper and slid inside her. Stroking her, pressing the tense glands that filled again and again. Anya gripped Rafe's hips, her claws scoring the leather of Rafe's pants. She felt Rafe thrust, heard her groan, and knew she was potent and ready.

"Maybe it's you who doesn't yet know," she gasped. She sliced the front of Rafe's leathers with a claw and pushed inside. When she bit Rafe's shoulder at the base of her neck, she squeezed and Rafe flooded her hand with a powerful climax.

For an instant, Anya felt Rafe weaken, drained as she was drained, and wrapped an arm around Rafe's waist, holding her tight against her body. Her wolf rejoiced. *Mate.*

"No," Anya said.

"No what," Rafe murmured, sealing the wound in Anya's neck.

"No," Anya said and licked the bite she'd put in Rafe's neck, "we're not done yet."

Rafe laughed. "We are for now." She pushed away with a hand on either side of Anya's shoulders. "Your wolf is greedy."

Anya met Rafe's gaze and saw something there she hadn't seen before. Satisfaction. "I didn't realize you had your limits." With the hand Anya still had inside Rafe's pants, she stroked her. "I guess I was wrong."

Rafe's eyes bled to obsidian, and she struck again.

Chapter Fourteen

Sylvan, still in half-form, stood in the center of a circle of scorched earth, smoking remains, and charred body parts, searching for more enemy. The air churned with the scent of sulfur and decay. A cloud of purulent smoke clouded the moon, dampening the pull and the power of it. Such a thing had never happened in her memory. Even on the darkest nights, when the moon was at its most distant and clouds masked its glow, the power never dimmed. She could only think the miasma of blood and vaporized revenants, layered like a blanket over the killing fields, somehow responsible. Still, not a single enemy remained. Foolish of whoever had sent those mindless beasts to attack at night when Weres and Vampires were the strongest. She scanned the battlefield, assessing the status of her warriors. *Sentries* and healers lifted injured onto stretchers and into the backs of the Rovers for transport into the Compound. Near the main gate, battered and smoldering in places but never breached, Drake's wolf crouched beside an injured *sentrie*. Sylvan snarled as Drake's pain reached her.

She loped over to her mate, her strides covering the distance from one heartbeat to the next. A large wound running along Drake's right flank bled copiously. "You are injured. Why didn't you tell me?"

Drake's wolf shook her head and spoke inside Sylvan's mind. *It's nothing.*

"That wound is still bleeding. It's festering already. You need to be inside and have that tended to."

The black wolf's eyes met hers, calm and strong. *Theo is badly injured. He blocked a thrust from one of those things as it came up behind me. If not for him my wounds would be much worse. I've stopped the bleeding, but he needs help in healing.*

"That is not for you to do. I will take you inside now." Sylvan's wolf towered over everyone else, her power felt by all the Pack, inside the Compound and without. Her voice, little more than a garbled growl, instilled fear and comfort in equal measure among her wolves. She was Alpha, and her word was law. Her Prima and her young recognized her leadership and regularly ignored her when she tried to shield them from danger, instilling fear and pride in her.

Not yet, Drake signaled. *He is weakening. The medics need to see to him first.*

"Why haven't you shifted?" Sylvan asked. "Your wound will heal then."

Drake shuddered. *I can't.*

"Then you are too weak to help him, and more injured than you seem." With a snarl, Sylvan plucked Drake from the ground. "I will see that he is transported immediately. But you will go first."

Sylvan leapt the fifteen feet up onto the ramparts and then down again to the commons and, in less than a second, stormed across the porch of the infirmary. The *sentrie* on guard duty saw her coming and hastily pushed the doors open. Sylvan didn't slow. Had he not cleared a path, she would have simply kicked the doors down.

"Where is Sophia?" she demanded as she strode down the wide hall. The doors to all the treatment rooms stood open, although the building was eerily quiet—as if even speech required energy best reserved for healing.

One of Jody's Vampire guards pointed to the open doorway. "In there."

Sylvan, twice the size of a Were in pelt, heavily muscled and partially transformed, had to bend to clear the top of the doorframe as she barged inside. "Sophia. The Prima is injured."

Her voice rolled with power, and every Were in the room shivered.

Sophia turned from a young cadet with a series of bloody gouges in his chest. As always, even in the midst of chaos, Sophia radiated confidence and calm. She pointed to an empty treatment table nearby. "Here, Alpha."

Sylvan crossed the distance in two strides and gently laid Drake's wolf down.

Drake's eyes had become glassy, and she panted heavily.

"Drake," Sylvan growled, her voice a heavy rumble in her halfform. She stroked the great wolf's back and caught waves of pain and fatigue as Drake struggled to remain awake. Sylvan looked to Sophia. "She's worse. Her wound shouldn't be serious enough to do this."

"It's the poison," Sophia said as she examined the deep wound that tracked through the musculature of Drake's flank. Ribs showed in the depth of the cavity, and the flesh around the edges had turned black and wept a purulent gray-green substance. "We think it's some kind of altered silver."

"Then you can treat that," Sylvan said. She'd been injured by silver-tainted weapons, and while agonizingly painful, the wounds could be healed when a wolf shifted, especially when given enough strength and power. Drake had given her that when she'd been dangerously injured, and Sylvan had been pouring power to Drake through her Pack bonds from the instant she'd touched her. Any other wolf with a similar injury would have healed already.

"These wounds are not responding the way we expect silver-inflicted wounds to heal," Sophia said, drawing over a large stainless-steel basin and a wheeled rack full of wet packing material. "We've needed to use more of the intravenous chelator than ordinarily, and we're close to running out. I can pack the wound with bandages soaked in the antidote, which should be enough."

"*Should* be?"

"All of our injured are suffering with the poison. Some of them are not recovering, but I can't detect any pattern."

Sylvan held back a growl. All her wolves needed treatment, but Drake would recover no matter what was required. "How long until we can get more intravenous agent?"

"I don't know," Sophia said. "It's the middle of the night. Our sources for the chemicals in the city are closed—"

"They'll open for me," Sylvan snarled.

Sophia regarded her steadily. "Time is critical."

"We have sources available," Sabine said as she walked in from the adjoining room.

Sylvan swung in her direction. "How?"

Sabine smiled. "We do all our business at night."

"How *long*," Sylvan said.

Sabine shrugged. "By transport through your territory? Several hours at least, once secured."

Sylvan's fury flared. "That's too long. Our injured cannot wait. Our Prima *will not wait*."

"If you will allow our helicopters to land in the commons," Sabine said, unfazed by Sylvan's rage, "once our courier has the chemicals, less than an hour."

Sophia said, "That will have to be soon enough. I'll call Becca and tell her what we need. Businesses will break speed records for the Consort of the Night Hunters."

Sabine said, "I will alert the pilots." She hesitated. "If she worsens, I can remove some of the tainted blood, but she will be weaker from the loss. A replacement with my blood would help with that."

Sylvan's golden eyes glowed. "We will wait as long as we can."

Sabine nodded. "I will be with Drea, then."

Leaving Sylvan murmuring to the unconscious wolf, Sophia broke away to call Becca, and Sabine returned to the room where she'd left Drea. In the time she'd been gone, Drea had shed pelt and was sitting up on the side of the treatment table. "You're awake, I see."

"I was always awake." Drea slid off the table and reached for a pair of pants. Shirtless, her torso still held a shimmer of her light brown pelt down the center and along her arms.

Sabine's hunger roared back, a different hunger than she was used to. This was more than bloodlust. Drea met her gaze, her wolf shining in her eyes.

"I feel you in my body now," Drea said. "I remember. You fed me. Your blood is my blood now."

"The connection will fade," Sabine murmured, although the pull was so strong in her she wasn't certain. Of anything.

"Will it?" Drea moved closer and pressed a hand to Sabine's throat. "I'm not sure I want it to. Your blood burns now. I feel that too. I burn to feed that fire."

Sabine sighed. "You do not want that."

"You've fed," Drea said with a growl.

"Yes."

Drea's lip curled, and she snarled softly. "Who?"

"A male. I don't know his name."

"And that was enough?"

"For now." Sabine barely managed not to take her instantly. Her hunger, once only pain, now surged on a wave of need. To touch her, to drink her.

Drea turned her back and pulled on a shirt. "I must report to my captain. There may still be enemy."

Sabine wrapped her hand around the back of Drea's neck and drew her around to face her. "Are you completely well?"

Drea smiled. "I'm starving. But otherwise, I am fine."

"And for what do you hunger?"

"After a shift, everything." Drea leaned into Sabine and ran her canines along the edge of her jaw. "Food, a tangle. And now? Something more."

"I must wait for a helicopter on the commons," Sabine said, lust for blood and more driving her to feed again. "But after…"

"I'll find you," Drea said and walked out.

Sabine watched her go. They'd exchanged blood. A great deal of blood. Her hunger now had a name.

❖

The other Vampire forces joined Rafe and Anya in the cavern where they'd camped while waiting for reports from the perimeter scouts. A few of the Vampires had been injured seriously enough that their inherent healing powers had drained them to the point they needed to feed immediately. The *centuri* who'd volunteered to feed them withdrew into the recesses of the mountain cavern, and the air shimmered with thrall and the scent of Were pheromones. Anya's blood still throbbed with the remnants of battle lust, and now her sex tensed with the storm of stimulants assaulting her. Rafe guided Anya into a shadowed corner with a hand on the small of her back. Anya's wolf stirred at the heat of Rafe's touch, and her clitoris readied.

"Do you hunger, little wolf?" Rafe murmured, pressing Anya's back to the wall with the weight of her body.

Anya's claws erupted, and she pierced the leather vest Rafe had worn into battle until she struck flesh. "Do you?"

Rafe laughed, her mouth on Anya's throat. Waves of relentless lust poured from her, engulfing Anya in a cloud of sex stimulants so dense her essence exploded from her in a torrent that left her body drained and her wolf jubilant.

"Again," Rafe snarled and took her throat.

Rafe's heart pounded against Anya's, and Anya knew Rafe was at full potency. Her blood had given Rafe that. Anya tore Rafe's shirt to bare her shoulder and bit down on the taut muscle. Rafe groaned, trembling, and when Anya released again, Rafe joined her.

Anya stroked Rafe's back, marveling at the power Rafe had given her. "Your Liege is coming," she murmured.

Rafe sighed. "You sense her?"

"You do—and I sense you."

Rafe drew back, her face in the moonlight stark and beautiful. "This wolf of yours is stubborn. And reckless."

"My wolf wants you."

"And you?"

"You know what I want. I want to feed you."

"You are not what I expected," Rafe murmured and kissed her.

When Rafe started to pull back, Anya gripped her nape and took her mouth in a fierce kiss. Her canines drew blood, and when Rafe moaned, her heart surged. She was more than her wolf, but in her heart, in her sense, in her primal needs—she was all wolf. "Neither are you."

Rafe drew away but kept hold of Anya's hand. "Come. We must join the Liege. Moonfall is close, and we'll need to leave soon."

Jody entered the cavern with Lara, Jody, and Torren. She addressed Rafe first. "Raina has shifted and is healing."

Lara added, "She is still weak."

"Not that weak, Prima," Raina said as she strode in.

"You need food and rest," Lara said.

"There will be time for that when the Pride is secured." Raina wrapped her arm around Lara's shoulders and stifled Lara's protests with a soft growl and a kiss. "What is the status of our position?"

Jody said, "The first wave of revenants has been defeated."

Raina turned to Torren. "And the Gate?"

Torren said, "The Gate is closed, but I can sense its presence."

"So it is functional?" Raina asked.

"I don't detect any…energy…within it," Torren said. "The

Sorcerer's power is likely exhausted, and whatever the source, they would need more time to draw from it before they can activate it again."

"But that is possible?" When Torren nodded, Raina said, "How long do we have?"

"Hours, at least, possibly days. We know Snowcrest was also attacked, which would require a great deal of power. For most—even the Fae—replenishing that level of power would take time."

Jody said, "Your forces are significantly diminished. Can you marshal reinforcements?"

Raina hissed. "Most of our Pride hunt solo or in small groups and range widely throughout the mountains. We can call them back, but it will take the better part of two days for us to muster any strength."

"We must be gone before moonfall," Jody said. "Our Vampires will not be secure here from the sun, and we haven't much time left." She glanced at Rafe. "Have we word from the Timberwolves?"

Rafe shook her head. "No, my Liege. I would recommend this site be evacuated."

Raina snarled. "We will not leave our stronghold. We will not let them defeat us."

"It might be more prudent," Jody said mildly, although again Anya sensed the subtle touch of her thrall and the compulsion that rolled beneath her words, "to leave now. If there is nothing here for the enemy to take or destroy, you will secure your Pride to return once you are at full strength."

"And where would you have us go?" Raina said.

"The wolves are your closest allies and have already sworn to an alliance. Snowcrest or the Timberwolves would give you sanctuary."

"Unless they are compromised, as we are," Raina said.

Rafe turned to Anya. "Can you reach Trent or your Alpha?"

Anya opened her senses so her connections to Pack filled her consciousness. She felt the heartbeats of her fellow wolves and sorted through the myriad strands that connected her to all her Packmates, even those like Trent and Lara, whose links to Pack had diminished. She shook her head. "I can't feel Trent at all any longer. The Alpha… the Alpha is there but closed to me."

"And battle? Can you detect if the wolves are under attack?"

"The turmoil I sensed from the Snowcrest wolves remains," Anya said after a moment. "The Timberwolves are…distant. I've only ever felt the Pack like this when the Alpha pulled power and all the energy was focused on her."

"Meaning?"

Anya hesitated. The Vampires and cat Weres might be allies, and she had been ordered by the Alpha to be their link to Pack, but she was a Timberwolf before all else. If she couldn't sense the Alpha because the Timberwolves were in battle—or worse, because the Alpha was injured—she didn't want to expose that vulnerability. "I don't know why they are closed to me, but I might be able to reach someone else. One of the wolves who could give me a picture of what is happening."

Rafe raised a brow. "Someone with a stronger connection than your Alpha?"

"Not stronger," Anya said, "just…different." She'd tangled with Genta only a few days before, and more than once. That link was still fresh if she could find it among the myriad threads that linked her to Pack. "I'll try."

She opened herself to the memory of their lust, their pheromones mingling, their bodies joining, their essences rising, spilling, marking each other however temporarily. She reached out to Genta, and that connection still burned brighter than that with any of the other Weres. An answering warmth flooded through her.

Images flickered, and the sensations of battle frenzy, pain, and victorious elation coursed through her subconscious mind. Excitement, fury, fear, and triumph. And then, the Alpha's call. Strong and comforting.

Anya shuddered. "There was a battle. It's over. The Pack is safe."

Rafe turned to Jody. "The Timberwolf Compound is large enough to house the cats and us. We should not lose any time, my Liege."

"How would we get there?" Raina said. "We haven't the forces to secure a retreat in the open field, and your Vampires cannot travel after moonfall."

Jody glanced at Torren. "Can you activate a Gate?"

Torren sighed. "To the Timberwolves' Compound? Sylvan would be most unhappy with me."

Rafe said, "The Timberwolves will be expecting another assault. If we emerge through a Gate, we might be walking into a trap."

"We'll have to take that chance," Jody said. "Assemble the guards.

Stagger them so that we will go through first. If there's any kind of defensive response at the Gate, do not attack the Timberwolves. I will lead and reach out to Sylvan. She will hear me."

Rafe shook her head. "No, my Liege. We can't risk injury to you. Let me go through first."

Anya grumbled. "Must you all be so stubborn? I am a wolf Were. They will not strike at me. Send me through first."

"Send all of us," Jonathan said, coming to stand by Anya's side. "I will go through with Anya, and she can alert the Pack to our presence."

Jody nodded. "Agreed. I will keep trying to reach Becca or Zahn. Either of them should be able to hear me, but something is blocking us."

Rafe frowned. "I should go through with Anya. If she emerges in the midst of a battle, or the Gate is warded in some way, I can protect her."

"I do not need protection in Pack territory," Anya said. "And you will need shelter as soon as you reach the Compound. Moonfall will be only moments away then."

"She's right," Jody said. "Torren, how stable will the Gate be? There are a great many of us."

Torren said, "I can hold the Gate as long as necessary, but the faster we go through, the better. Those remaining here will be vulnerable until we have all passed into safe territory."

"Then let's not wait." Jody asked Raina, "How quickly can you be ready?"

"I'll assemble my cats immediately," Raina said.

"I don't like it," Rafe said, taking Anya aside.

Anya gripped her arm. "Better I take injury than you or your Liege. Promise me you will not stay to fight, no matter what happens. You must seek safety."

Rafe's eyes glinted with displeasure. "That leaves me no choice."

"I know." At a signal from Jonathan, Anya turned to Torren. "We are ready whenever you are, my Lord."

Chapter Fifteen

"The perimeter is secure, Alpha," Niki said from the archway of the cubicle where Sylvan waited with Drake's wolf for the antidote to arrive.

"Any word from the helicopter?" Sylvan had shed her half-form and wore the pants Sophia had handed her. She knelt with one hand on Drake's flank, feeling her breathe, feeling the distant but steady heartbeat that told her Drake lived. Drake's wolf had curled in on itself, and although Sylvan could still feel her there, she couldn't reach her mind-to-mind. That had never happened before, and just as worrying, despite the love and loyalty and power of every member in her Pack that funneled through her to Drake, she could not give Drake's wolf the strength to shift. During the shift, injuries would heal, broken bones would knit, and internal organs would revitalize. But if Drake remained in wolf form, with her mind and body trapped by the poison in her system while the toxins in the atmosphere interfered with the Pack links, Drake might never emerge.

Sylvan fought the terror while her wolf raged, tearing at her soul.

"I've just had communication from the pilots," Niki said quickly. "They're ten minutes out."

"Meet them. You," Sylvan said, swinging around to meet Niki's eyes. Niki ducked her head, avoiding the wolf riding Sylvan's gaze. "*You* pick up the chemicals and bring them to Sophia."

"Of course." Niki hesitated. "The Pack is with you."

"I know," Sylvan murmured, turning back to her mate.

Niki disappeared, leaving Sylvan alone. This was not the natural order of things. Her destiny, every atom in her body, every cell, every strand of DNA, was programmed by centuries of the strongest surviving, passing their legacy of responsibility and power on to their progeny. Hers was the responsibility to keep the Pack safe, and that included her Prima. Drake would always do battle by her side, for she too bore responsibility for the Pack, but it was not Drake's fate to sacrifice. Sylvan had failed her that day.

The muscles in the great wolf under her palm twitched.

You think too much. Drake's voice came to her, distant but calm and clear.

Trembling, Sylvan rested her forehead on the wolf's shoulder and closed her eyes. She twined her fingers through the ruff, taking comfort in the warmth of fur between her fingers. "I think only of you."

Not true. You carry the weight of many in your soul. Do not worry. I will never leave you.

"Nor I you." Sylvan breathed in her scent, the unique smoky oak aroma of aged wine that was Drake's alone. "Can you shift? Drake?"

Only silence answered, and she knew that the wolf had once again retreated, wounded and weak and struggling. Sylvan bolted upright at the sound of footsteps in the hall and spun around. Sophia appeared, carrying two plastic bags of clear fluid, one in each hand. Elena, the senior medic, carried the rest of the equipment.

"This will only take a moment, Alpha," Sophia said as she gently directed Sylvan to move aside. The suggestion was unspoken, but Sylvan felt the light touch on her arm, and her wolf settled down to wait, watchful but calm. Sophia's power had grown the longer she'd tended to the Pack, and the more the Pack trusted and depended upon her.

Sylvan kept a hand on Drake's flank as Sophia expertly and efficiently inserted a large needle into a vein on the inside of Drake's foreleg. Within seconds, fluid from the bags that hung on the pole ran into her.

"How long will it take?" Sylvan said.

Sophia kept her hand on the wolf's chest, sensing, Sylvan knew, far more than just a heartbeat.

"I don't know," Sophia said. "We haven't had anyone quite like the Prima before. So much of her power was given to the others to keep them alive until we could treat them." Sophia shook her head. "I didn't even know that was possible."

Sylvan growled softly. "Neither did I."

A Pack Alpha could draw on their own well of power to infuse strength to an injured Pack member, as Sylvan had done when necessary. Her ties were so deep and so strong to every single member of the Pack that even when injured, she was not depleted. She'd been silver-poisoned, at the same time she'd sustained egregious wounds, and barely managed to heal. But even then, her wolf had never retreated so deeply. Drake, once human and now Prima, carried altered Were DNA that gave her power other Primas did not have. The extent of those powers remained a mystery, but the cost of those abilities remained a mystery as well.

When the first bag of fluid had emptied, Sophia changed the tubing to the second one.

Sylvan turned to Elena. "How are the rest of the injured?"

"We have been fortunate, Alpha. Our wolves are strong, and though they are recovering slowly, all who we've treated are improving."

All who survived long enough to be treated. Sylvan's wolf howled as sadness filled her. She'd felt each and every loss, even during the midst of battle, as a wound to her heart. And now, Drake still had not moved, and Sylvan knew fear deeper than any other.

Drake twitched, and Sylvan felt a whisper touch her mind. Her heart leapt.

Drake? Sylvan probed silently. *Can you take my power? You must heal.*

There are others who need you more, Drake's wolf answered. *See to our Pack. I will be all right.*

And I will be here until you shift.

I know how to shift without any help, Alpha.

Sylvan laughed, her wolf yipping with joy. "She is stronger. She'll shift soon."

"I think her wolf may sleep awhile," Sophia said, "even as she heals."

"I must see to the Pack," Sylvan said. "Will you stay with her?"

"Of course," Sophia said. "When you can, Becca Land is here. She hasn't heard from Liege Gates."

Sylvan ground her jaws. "You're sure Drake is just resting now?"

Sophia was the only Were, other than Drake, who could hold Sylvan's gaze without fear or anxiety. She looked into Sylvan's eyes now, and Sylvan looked back, finding endless peace in the depths of the blue eyes that shimmered like the purest mountain pool. Sophia was truth. "I've seen it now with many of the others. But I think the crisis has passed."

"I'll go, then. But as soon as she shifts, send someone for me. Where is Becca?"

"Niki took her to the great room."

"You have everything you need here to treat the others?"

"Yes, Becca brought plenty of supplies."

Sylvan took one last look at Drake and felt her wolf settle deep within her. Trusting Sophia and comforted by her ties to Drake that felt stronger every second, she left the infirmary and strode outside to the commons. As she passed warriors still on guard, assembled on training grounds, and gathered around the firepits, her Weres saluted. Pausing, passing her gaze over all of them, she sent a wave of power through their Pack bonds. She was their leader, and they needed to know that she stood strong and certain. As the calls of a thousand wolves echoed in her consciousness, she drew strength from their loyalty and love in turn.

Inside headquarters, Becca, dressed in simple black pants, a white shirt, and black boots, waited beside the fireplace. Pale, Sylvan thought, paler than she remembered her being. Her black hair was tied back at the base of her neck, leaving her throat bare. The faint shadow of Jody's bite adorned the slender column of her neck.

"Sylvan," Becca said in her smooth alto. "How is Drake?"

"Better. You may have saved many of my wolves. And my Prima." Sylvan dipped her head and kissed Becca lightly on the cheek. "I'm in your debt. The Timberwolves owe you a boon."

Becca shook her head. "Nothing is owed. We are friends as well as allies, are we not? I wish there was more I could have done sooner. Had I known what was happening...Have you word from Jody?"

"No," Sylvan said, knowing Vampires, once blood-bonded as Becca and Jody were, could communicate over great distances. "And you haven't?"

"I can't..." Becca looked away.

"Your secrets would not be the first Vampire secrets I know," Sylvan said.

Becca smiled wryly. "I've learned to be careful. I've come to understand how vulnerable we all are."

"Then understand how strong we are too." Sylvan gently grasped

Becca's shoulders. "We—Vampires and Weres—have existed for centuries despite being hunted, despite purges, despite internal and external battles. We prevail. And Jody..." Sylvan shook her head and laughed softly. "I've known many Vampires, but none with her power."

"It's hard for me to think of her that way," Becca said. "To me, she is the one I love. And now I cannot sense her clearly—I know she lives, but I can't tell more." Becca folded her arms over her chest and regarded Sylvan steadily. "Zahn has the strongest link to Rafe, other than Jody, and can't reach her either. What is happening?"

"I don't know." Sylvan paced, frustrated by so much she did not know. "I can't reach my wolves who are with her or Snowcrest either. I don't feel as if I've lost them, but I just find emptiness where they should be. These things that attacked us brought something with them or left something behind that prevents our links from functioning."

Becca said, "I know Jody. She will come here if there is more fighting to be done." She laughed. "She thinks I am safe within the seethe."

"Who did you bring here with you?"

Becca laughed. "You are wise in the way of Vampires. Zahn wouldn't let me out of the seethe without a guard, of course. I barely convinced her to remain behind. I have half a dozen guards."

"It will be daybreak soon. I'll have Niki take you and your Vampires to a secure space," Sylvan said. "If Jody reaches you—"

"She will," Becca said with certainty, "and soon as she does, I'll tell her where I am."

"Good, until then—"

"Alpha," Niki called, hurrying toward them, "a Gate just opened outside the fortifications."

Sylvan spun around, battle hormones driving her wolf to rise. "Alert the captains to prepare for an attack at the Gate."

❖

Snowcrest Clan Home, nearing moonfall

Trent's wolf shimmered, and she shed pelt in a shower of gold. Zora leaned over her, relief and joy in equal measure coursing through her. "You're back."

At the sound of Zora's voice, Trent opened her eyes and pulled Zora into her arms. She kissed her and ran both hands over her neck, her shoulders, her back. "Are you all right? He didn't touch you?"

"It wasn't me who took the sword. Don't ever do that again." Zora stroked Trent's cheek. "I am the Alpha. It is for me to risk a wounding in defense of my Pack."

"I am your mate," Trent said, drawing Zora down beside her on the cot. The room held the murky gray light of predawn, and Trent placed the time as shortly before moonfall. The memory of her wounds was still a bright flare of pain in her memory, but her body was healed. "You are Alpha, and all recognize it. But I will always protect my mate."

"Always so stubborn." Zora kissed her, threading her fingers through Trent's hair. "I was worried."

Naked still, Trent opened Zora's shirt and drew her down beside her, body to body. She was healed, but her wolf needed the contact. She stroked her breasts and kissed her back. "I am well now. The Pack?"

"We have injured but lost only two." Zora mourned those deaths and would forever. The loss of one of her wolves was an injury to her heart, and a wound she would carry forever. "We did not know how to fight them at first, but we are learning."

"And the Gate?"

Zora growled. "It remains. Weaker, nearly invisible, but still there."

"As long as it remains, we are at risk of further attack," Trent said.

"I know. Sylvan sent a squadron of warriors, and they are guarding it now."

"Has Sylvan sent word of when we attack?"

"How? We are still tending to our wounded." Zora shook her head. "Besides, I have had no word. Sylvan's young are with the squadron, and they report they cannot communicate with their Alpha."

"All the more reason for us not to wait," Trent said, pushing upright on the cot. "If we are cut off, we can not expect more aid."

"We cannot move until the scouts return. I have called them back. For now, the Timberwolves guard the Gate."

"I should see to them," Trent said. "This is our Cresthome to protect."

"And we will." With an impatient growl, Zora pushed Trent back on the cot and straddled her hips. "I had to watch you struggle to heal from the poison in your blood and from the wound *I* created when I cut the poison from the festering wound. We will fight again, but right now I need you."

"I feel your need," Trent murmured, sliding a hand down Zora's torso to cup her center. "As I need."

Zora arched, her sex full and pounding to release. "You are my strength and my heart."

Trent reared up and dragged her canines down Zora's throat. "I am yours in all ways."

Zora's wolf slid into her mind, eclipsing reason and obliterating fear, as she spent her essence at the instant her mate filled her.

❖

Moments to sunrise, at the edge of the veil

Francesca turned to Philip, where he waited beside her, naked and already in the throes of lust. She needed to feed, needed to be at full power, or as close as she ever could be with such weaklings to sustain her, to deal with Maester Finngar. She could remain awake past dawn in Faerie, as the sun, or what passed as such, was no threat to her, but her strength diminished more quickly than ever each day she remained trapped in this in-between place. Automatically she took Philip's throat and drank her fill, his moans a distant imperceptible sound. When she'd taken what she needed, or as much as she could and still leave him strong enough to survive for another feeding, she turned away, the process a boring necessity. Passionless, as passion for her stemmed from dominance and power, and there was little of that to be found in the steadily fading surrounds of the barren knowe, her refuge and, now, her prison. Time was running out, something she'd had for millennia and that now felt for the first time precious. Her sanctuary was disappearing, the passages and caverns closing day by day as the knowe died, lacking the presence of the Fae to feed it with their spirit and their magic.

Magic, as if that was what mattered. She swept to her feet and grasped a dressing gown. She would see to Finngar and demand that he finish whatever pathetic rituals he required to give her the last of the forces she needed to leave this place behind forever. She found him, as predicted, in his foul workshop that smelled of sulfur and decay. At her entrance, he turned to her, noticeably paling.

"Mistress," he blurted, falling to one knee. "I am honored. I did not expect—"

"You have good news for me, I hope," Francesca said, holding out one hand for him to kiss.

"The attacks all were executed as planned," he said, his voice quavering.

Francesca recognized what he was not saying. So, not as successful as he'd led her to believe they would be, perhaps.

"And have we succeeded in preventing the Weres and Vampires from coming to Cecilia's aid?"

He hesitated. "They will be severely hindered for some time."

Do not lie to me. Francesca projected her voice and an image of his own creations feasting on his naked body into his mind.

Finngar whimpered and sweat ran down his hollow cheeks. "The blocking spell carried by our creatures might not have had quite as potent an effect on Weres as it does on humans," he said, hastening to add, "but their ability to communicate over distances will be diminished."

"So we don't know *if* or *when* they might regain strength." Francesca hissed. She should drain his worthless carcass now. She gripped him by the throat and lifted him to his feet. Before she struck, she detected a faint ripple in the air at the chamber entrance and swiveled her head. "Yes?"

Beatrice, one of the last of her blood servants strong enough to feed her, appeared.

"Forgive me, my Queen," Beatrice said timidly, "but there is..."

"What is it?" Francesca asked impatiently.

"Outside at the entrance. The Fae, my Queen."

Francesca's heart hardened. It could only be Cethinrod. Unannounced. "Who is with him?"

"A number of others. Warriors, my Queen."

"Yes, well, we'll see about that."

Tossing Finngar aside, she thought quickly. She had only a handful of Vampire guards, but she reached out to them mentally. *Gather your weapons and assemble at the entrance.*

She hurried to her bedchamber, pathetic as it was with the

tapestries crumbling to dust and the furniture rotting day by day, and pulled on her finest gown. The blood-red satin dipped low between her breasts and hugged her waist and hips. She had fed, and she was as strong as she would be at any other time. She felt her beauty and power fill her. After adorning her neck and hands with jewels, she made her way to the entrance.

Her guards awaited, forming a corridor for her, and she swept between them and out into the glade. Cethinrod awaited in the glow of the red dawn, a phalanx of gold-clad warriors behind him.

He bowed low, reached for her hand, and brushed a kiss across her fingers. "Francesca, Queen of the Vampires. How lovely you look this morn."

"Cethinrod, Lord of the Southern Realms. To what do I owe this unexpected honor?"

"I've come to tell you it's time to make war on Cecilia."

"And how have you decided that?" Francesca calculated if she had the strength at arms to hold off a coup should Cethinrod decide to exclude her from what was to come.

"Cecilia's allies are in disarray, and before they have time to regroup and invade at strength in her support, we should strike the throne. Once a new King sits upon the throne, it won't matter what her allies decide upon. They will not wage war against the Fae King."

"The Fae King," Francesca murmured. "And what of the Vampire Queen?"

"Of course, as my strongest ally, you will have an army of Fae at your command when you return to the human world to claim Dominion over all the Vampires."

"How have you come to this decision?" Francesca said.

"The judgment to attack all three Were strongholds at once was sound. Their forces are fragmented, and they will not be able to launch an attack immediately. My general has seen this on his passage through the Gate."

"Of course," Francesca said, "I've never doubted your martial expertise."

Cethinrod's silver eyes gleamed in the moonlight, but his gaze was cold. "Nor have I ever underestimated yours, my Queen."

"And what of the losses?"

He lifted a shoulder and said in an almost bored tone,

"Inconsequential. The beasts were not living, after all, and incapable of independent thought. They're designed for one act, to be loosed and to kill until killed. Enough remain for our purposes."

Francesca cursed inwardly. Without those forces, she was at a disadvantage should Cethinrod decide that he no longer needed allies.

"When we have taken the throne," Cethinrod said, "and you rule over all the Vampires, you will have no need of that mindless army. You will have an army of your own. An army of Vampires that in time will rule the human world."

She smiled. "And you will have a reach beyond the veil that Cecilia has never been able to establish."

He smiled, and the air shimmered with a rainbow of power. "Our time is now."

"When?"

"Instruct your Sorcerer," Cethinrod said, "to cast whatever spell is necessary to animate the last of your beasts. Then we will strike."

"It shall be done."

"By the morrow, then." He bowed again, and when he rose, his smile was winter. "I have waited a thousand lifetimes. I do not wish to wait any longer."

Chapter Sixteen

"It's time," Torren said. "Once the Gate opens, you'll need to pass through immediately and warn the defenders there is no risk. Otherwise we may find ourselves in a battle we do not want."

"Stay close," Jonathan said as he and Anya stepped forward to lead the wolf Weres through the Gate. "We're arriving unannounced through an unauthorized Gate. We are at war, and we might be Timberwolves, but the warriors defending the Compound will not know what to expect from us."

Rafe's voice filled Anya's mind.

This is foolish. I can be inside and by your Alpha's side before a single Were even senses me. I can announce—

No, Anya ordered. *You would be dead before you had time to explain. You don't understand what any Alpha will do to an intruder in their territory.*

You think too little of me, Rafe said.

And you think too much of your invincibility. Anya pushed a pulse of power, and Rafe jerked back in surprise. *In the seethe your word is law, but out here? The Weres rule.*

Jody appeared beside Rafe. "The Weres have the right of it. With our communications blocked, the enemy has isolated us and put everyone in a defensive position. Sylvan will not trust anyone coming through that Gate in those first few moments, even another Were. A Vampire? Even an ally?" She shook her head. "The Weres must relay what has happened and secure our passage."

Rafe bowed her head. "As you will, my Liege."

At Torren's command, Anya stepped through the Gate with Jonathan at her side and the other *centuri* flanking them, automatically assuming defensive positions although they remained in skin. Had they appeared in pelt they could easily be mistaken for an aggressive force.

For a moment, Anya imagined Torren had miscalculated and sent them into some other dimension. This could not be Timberwolf territory. She barely recognized the land that had once been as much a part of her as her own heartbeat. Rancid air blanketed the charred earth beneath a dank, swirling gray sky and obscured the forest that should have ringed the Compound. Her senses failed her—and for a terrifying few seconds she knew the soul-killing isolation of an outcast Were.

Jonathan growled a warning, and Anya sensed him start to shift.

No! she signaled. *Wait. I can reach them.*

She pushed against the curtain of fog separating her from the collective consciousness of the Pack—searching, calling, struggling—and met a wall of silence. She pushed harder, her power surging, as she felt the distorted edges of those links just out of reach. Her vision blurred, as if she peered through a film coating her eyes. She tensed for a blow or the rending bite of canines at her throat.

"Take my hand," Rafe said, materializing beside her.

"Go back! You cannot be here."

"Where else would I be," Rafe said coolly and gripped Anya's hand. "Take my power and use it. Hurry."

Anya trembled as a jolt of energy speared through her depths, and her mind sharpened. The Alpha's call pulsed like a heart beating—it *was* a heart beating. The Pack's heart, and Anya opened herself to it. Sylvan's call rolled through her, reading her mind, her blood, her very bones.

Rafe shuddered, but Anya did not let go of her hand.

She could not let Rafe stand alone now—the Alpha might not recognize her as a friend. Anya shaped the images of the *centuri* in her mind, ever loyal, for the Alpha to see. The fog thinned as her link to Sylvan, to all the Pack, grew stronger.

The power of the Alpha filled her, and Sylvan's voice resounded in her mind.

Where have you traveled from? Sylvan demanded. *What lies on the other side of the Gate?*

The Catamount stronghold, Alpha, Anya answered through their mind link.

Who else gathers at the Gate?

Only friends and allies. The cat Weres are with us, and Jody and her Vampires.

Sylvan dropped from the top of the fortifications, in half-form again, towering over Anya, Rafe, and the *centuri*, her limbs ending in claws longer than Anya's forearms, her wolf eyes a glittering gold that dispelled the thin fog as if the sun burned it away. A ring of warriors circled the battleground, all in pelt, all dominant senior Weres prepared for battle.

Sylvan's gaze passed over the Weres and fixed on Rafe. A low growl of warning rumbled from her chest. "Vampire. You arrive through a foreign Gate and release your power in my territory. Vampires have long hunted Weres. You live only because Anya is at your side."

"Alpha," Anya said, turning her head to expose her vulnerable throat, "Rafe doesn't—"

"I beg your indulgence, Alpha Mir," Rafe interrupted evenly, her hand now resting on the middle of Anya's back. "I violated your boundaries only because our circumstances were dire. I seek refuge for my Liege and our Vampires. And for your cat Were allies."

"And the Gate? Of whose making?"

"Lord Torren," Anya replied. "When we—*I*—could not reach you, Torren created a passageway for Liege Gates and her forces to reinforce the cat Weres."

"The Vampires took my *centuri* into battle with the cats." Sylvan's canines gleamed. "On whose word? Lord Torren?"

"No, Alpha," Anya said quickly, "mine. Any responsibility for the consequences of the decision is mine alone. There were injured."

Rafe hissed. "The Vampires take responsibility for our own decisions and ask leave of none as to when and where we fight. Anya is not at fault for the place or outcome of the skirmish."

Jonathan spoke up. "All the *centuri* have recovered from their injuries, Alpha. Anya advised Lord Torren to open the Gate to the cats as I was…detained…with Estella. If there is any responsibility to bear, it should be mine."

Sylvan regarded the other *centuri*, as if assuring herself that none were affected by any spell or compulsion that might be a danger to the Pack.

"Alpha," Anya said, "it is nearly moonfall, and the Vampires must be sheltered before then."

Sylvan considered Anya for a long moment. "Signal them to enter. Niki will see Rafe to safety."

"I must return through the Gate, Alpha," Rafe said. "I cannot reach Liege Gates in the usual fashion."

"So be it," Sylvan said.

Anya gripped Rafe's arm. "Don't linger. There is little time."

Rafe touched her cheek with her fingertips. "Time enough, little wolf."

She was gone as quickly as she had emerged, without so much as a ripple in the air.

"The rest of you, remain here," Sylvan said to Anya and the *centuri*, "until all have emerged."

Moments passed, and then the cat Weres came through the Gate with Raina and Lara in the lead.

Raina said instantly, "Alpha Mir. I seek refuge for my Pride. We have injured."

Sylvan looked first into her eyes, then to Lara's, and nodded curtly. "You are welcome."

At a silent command from her, the phalanx of warriors behind her parted, and the way to the main gate was clear. Callan waited with a cadre of *sentries* at the archway.

Niki appeared at Sylvan's side. "At your command, Alpha."

"Take the injured Catamount Weres to the infirmary. Have quarters prepared for Alpha Carras and the others."

Anya glanced anxiously at the sky. "The Vampires will need—"

Rafe stepped through the Gate with Jody, followed by the rest of the Vampire guard. As if she'd heard Anya, she said, "We have done this before. There is no emergency."

Anya growled. "You taunt the fates. Many of you are Risen—you don't have *time* to be stubborn. Or proud."

Rafe laughed.

Jody said to Sylvan, "Apologies for the lack of warning. We have a few moments, but it is best if we don't linger. If you are unsure of our intentions, I will stay behind, but my Vampires—"

Sylvan shook her head. "Then there is no need for you to risk the sun. We will speak inside. Anya—escort our friends to the council room."

As Anya turned to Rafe and Jody, Torren arrived. Sylvan stepped into her path.

"This is becoming a habit."

Torren nodded. Power shimmered about her in a shower of light. "Only when absolutely necessary, and my apologies for not seeking invitation first."

"As long as we understand each other," Sylvan said, unconcerned by Torren's ancient strength. "Can you close it completely?"

Torren's eyebrow arched. "Of course. But if more of Raina's cats arrive at the stronghold, they may need passage."

"If they do, I'll decide when and how they arrive," Sylvan replied.

"As you will."

Torren made a small gesture with one hand, and where the Gate had stood, a vison of a world beyond with a crimson sky and orange mountaintops shimmered for an instant and winked out.

"Come," Sylvan said to those still gathered. "We have much to decide and little time."

❖

Anya walked beside Rafe as everyone followed Sylvan and Torren across the commons. "Why do you take such risks?"

"Don't we all?" Rafe murmured. "Had your Alpha been less trusting, you might have been on the way to the healer's now, or worse."

"I'm used to your evasions now," Anya said. "The danger to me was far less than to someone like you appearing without invitation in the midst of a war. The Alpha had no way of knowing what had happened to any of us."

"Someone like me?" Rafe sounded annoyingly amused.

"A powerful predator, and a potential enemy in some circumstances."

"Is that how you see me?"

"Powerful? Yes. Dangerous? Yes. An enemy? No." Anya huffed. "You haven't answered me. Are you testing death, or seeking it?"

Rafe's eyes flashed fire for an instant. "Have you forgotten I have already seen death?"

"How could I? I carry the shadow of your bite on my throat."

"And I carry yours," Rafe said, a tinge of anger replacing the amusement.

"That bothers you," Anya said as they entered the meeting hall. The protective shutters were closed along the rows of windows that flanked the wide walkway.

"Not as much as it should," Rafe said, her tone perplexed.

Anya's wolf chuffed, pleased. Rafe didn't accept their connection—yet—but she didn't fight it either. Anya had no doubt Rafe could block their mental link and mask the potency of their blood bond if she wanted to. She hadn't, and each time they shared blood, the strength of their bonds grew. "How much time will you have before you'll need to sleep?"

"Long enough," Rafe said. "Our guards, though, will not be as tolerant once the sun has risen. The Liege has already ordered them to shelter. We will be outnumbered in this meeting."

"You still don't trust the Alpha?"

Rafe glanced at her. "Trust does not come easily when you've spent centuries being hunted…and betrayed."

"The Alpha will not betray her word. She has sworn allegiance." Anya gripped Rafe's forearm. Her connection to Rafe had begun with duty and been strengthened by desire. The blood they had shared had forged a physical bond and intensified their mutual need. But what linked her now, body, blood, *and* soul, had grown from the moments when Rafe let her see what no one else could—her tenderness, her caring, and her vulnerability. Rafe had stood for her when her wolf was in danger and had given herself in the midst of passion. Anya recognized what her wolf had known the moment Rafe had appeared. *Mate.* "And I will not betray you in any way."

Rafe said nothing.

"You will need to feed before you sleep," Anya said.

"That's not all I will need," Rafe said.

"I know."

❖

Becca met Jody halfway along the passageway to the great hall, linked her arm with Jody's, and kissed her. "You weren't hurt? The others?"

"I'm fine. We lost none. I did not expect you here," Jody said, sliding her arm around Becca's waist as they walked on. "You are not safe outside the seethe."

"And I suppose you were somewhere that was?"

Jody sighed. "I have ways of protecting myself that you don't."

"Remember you promised you would not lead these forces, but somehow you ended up in a battle. My guess is on the front line."

"What kind of leader would I be if I didn't take the first step onto the field?" Jody said.

"A live one, making the decisions your Vampires depend on you to make. Leading them with your mind and heart. Your Dominion is more than just a seethe, and without you, chaos would reign. The younglings would go untrained, and newlings would go mad from bloodlust. The Risen would fight for dominance, and Vampires would feed when and where they wanted. If the less disciplined went rogue and fed to the death, there would be a purge."

"You're right, and I know it. But I don't like it."

"I know," Becca said, "but you are here, and you will lead by the decisions you make to protect your allies and your Dominion."

"This Compound may be attacked again," Jody said. "Our Vampires may not number enough to protect you. You must return to the seethe."

"If you are staying, then so am I."

"I must stay," Jody said, exasperated. "I cannot order my guard into Faerie from the safety of the seethe."

"I know," Becca said. "I've already sent for Zahn and the rest of my guard. They'll be here any moment along with human servants to feed them."

"If we take more of our soldiers into Faerie, they will not be able to remain for long without hosts," Jody said.

"If needed, I think the Timberwolves or the cats will volunteer." Becca frowned. "Sylvan isn't planning a siege—once Francesca is eliminated, Cecilia must look to secure her throne with her own forces."

"I agree—our task is not to keep the Faerie Queen on her throne." Jody stroked Becca's arm. "Who remains to protect the seethe?"

"I've ordered the senior guards to stay behind—I don't believe even Francesca would be foolish enough to attack in the heart of the city without an unbeatable army. She cannot have that yet."

"So you have mobilized our army," Jody murmured.

"I suppose you could say that."

"You have truly assumed the mantle of Liege Consort now." Jody whisked a hand up Becca's back and ran her thumb along the column of her neck. "Your decisions are sound."

Becca laughed softly. "You mean there's more to it other than being in your bed?"

"There and all places."

"Then you will need me soon. It's nearly moonfall, and you must have expended a great deal of power in the fight at the stronghold," Becca said. "You will need me unless you've fed already."

"I always need you." Jody smiled as Becca's eyes flashed with desire and possessiveness.

"So you *have* fed."

"My love, why would I ever take another?"

"If need be, you know I would want you to."

"*You* are my strength," Jody murmured as she and her Vampires drew to one side of the council room in the positions they'd taken when they'd first talked of war. Sabine and Drea, along with the other guards and their Were hosts, joined them.

Jody signaled them to form behind her, Becca, Rafe, and Anya in a formal show of strength. Now they were no longer discussing possibilities. Now they were in the midst of war, and when the outcome of war was uncertain, she had to prepare to protect her Dominion at the cost of even her alliances.

The cat Weres, missing their general and many of their senior fighters, held the space on the opposite side of the broad hearth. They'd taken losses before Jody and the others had been able to reach them and would be weakened in the field as a result. The Snowcrest Weres were missing.

Sylvan stood at the apex of the circle, in front of the roaring blaze, with Torren, Niki, and Callan at her side. She'd shed pelt and had found leathers somewhere along the way inside. Drake was absent, but Jody sensed no inner turmoil from Sylvan. Drake was in no danger, or Sylvan would not be able to hide it from her.

"Time is short," Sylvan said. "The Vampires need seclusion, and Raina must see to her injured."

"What of Snowcrest?" Jody asked. "How have they fared?"

Sylvan's eyes flashed gold, and her jaw grew heavy with a hint of canines. Her wolf rode close to the skin, and fury bled from her on a wave of battle lust. "Their status is uncertain. Anya, can you reach Trent?"

"I have tried, Alpha." Anya shook her head. "I'm sorry, but I cannot sense Trent." She paused, unsure of how much to reveal.

"Speak," Sylvan said, her gaze passing slowly over the gathering, a rush of power filling the room. "Now is not the time for secrets."

Several of the Weres present whined softly, and even the cat Weres bristled with a flush of pelt. Jody was immune to Sylvan's power, as only the strongest Risen could be, but she registered the combination of calm certainty and absolute command that flowed from her.

Unflinching at the barrage of Sylvan's power, Anya straightened and answered steadily, "Soon after I felt the initial attacks at both Snowcrest clan home and the Catamount stronghold, my ability to sense others was…blocked. Even now, it is hard for me to link."

Sylvan surveyed the room. "Is that what you've all experienced?"

Rafe shot a warning glance to Jody.

"Yes," Jody answered, appreciating Rafe's caution but seeing no advantage in hiding what must have been obvious to Sylvan considering the way they'd been forced to flee the Catamount stronghold with no advance communication.

"We must assume that is why we cannot reach Snowcrest," Sylvan said.

"How do we counter this?" Raina paced, her cat unhappy at being caged while her territory and her Pride were at risk.

"It's an obfuscation spell," Torren said into the silence. "A clouding of the senses. Such things were not uncommon in past times when humans fought wars and used Sorcerers to subdue or confuse their enemies. They require a great deal of power to create and maintain. The effects will fade given time."

"How much time?" Raina snapped.

"That depends on the Sorcerer."

Raina hissed and flashed a canine at Torren. "Or a Fae?"

"The spells are ancient, but the skill to cast them has mostly been lost," Jody said smoothly. "Many of the battle Mages died as they drained all their power to hold the spells during battle, or the spellcasting ability disappeared as fewer Mages remained to pass on the skill. This spell is far less potent than what a powerful battle Mage would have been able to cast."

Torren added, "Francesca's Mage likely needs time and sacrifices to restore their power after creating the Gates and launching the beasts that carried the spell across the veil."

"How much time before this Mage is at full strength again?" Sylvan asked.

"That depends on how much blood is available to them. A powerful Vampire like Francesca could probably restore them with a single feeding—if she's at full strength." Torren leaned back against a pillar, lithe and somehow resplendent in a simple tunic and soft leathers, the bejeweled hilt of her sword jutting over her shoulder from a sheath on her back. "If they have other sources of blood—Weres, particularly—then again, not long."

Raina snarled. "What does any of this talk matter? We cannot know what the enemy will do or when they will do it. We cannot wait for another attack. I say we use the Gates, before they disappear, and kill whatever we find on the other side."

"And if all of Faerie awaits to strike you down?" Jody asked.

"I thought the Fae were our allies," Raina said, her gold eyes fixed on Torren.

"We have not heard from the Queen," Torren said, "but these creatures are not Fae. Cecilia has had a millennium to attempt to destroy the Praeterns on this side of the veil and has been too wise to attempt it."

"Then I say again," Raina said, glaring at Sylvan and Jody in turn, "enough talk. We must strike before this Mage regains strength and our territory is destroyed."

Sylvan turned to Jody. "Liege Gates?"

"I concur. If Francesca is to be defeated, we cannot let her rebuild whatever strength she may have lost in these recent battles."

"How do you expect to find her?" Raina said.

Sylvan glanced at Torren.

"Once we cross the veil, there are ways to use our combined power to seek her out," Torren said in typical Fae fashion, her answer a non-answer.

Niki turned to Sylvan. "And what of Snowcrest? We will need them."

Sylvan nodded. "If Anya cannot reach them soon, we will send a courier. By nightfall, when the Vampires are at strength, we will ride the Gates into Faerie."

Chapter Seventeen

With only a few minutes left before moonfall, the Timberwolf Weres, led by the *centuri*, escorted the cat Weres from the great room to their quarters. Jonathan, Dasha, and Mila remained behind with Jody's Vampire guards, who would need to feed.

"My apologies," Sylvan said to Jody. "Zahn has arrived with the rest of your Vampires, and they're already securely quartered. We don't have enough space there to accommodate all of you. This hall and the adjacent alcoves, however, are well protected from daylight."

"We will be fine here," Jody said. "I hope you don't take offense if we post a guard at the main door."

"I would expect nothing less," Sylvan said. "I must see to Drake if there's nothing else you need."

"She was injured?"

Sylvan's canines flashed. "Healing now. But yes."

"You should know that I will not lead our soldiers tonight. Rafe and Zahn will have command."

Sylvan nodded. "I understand. It's a wise decision. You are not replaceable."

"And you are?"

Sylvan smiled faintly. "I was born for this."

"So was I," Jody said with a sigh. "To wage war, yes, but born for a very different kind of war. We have ever protected our own. Until now."

"Before the humans came to power, and the Fae withdrew from this realm to Faerie, we hunted each other. Now we hunt common enemies." Sylvan grinned, a feral smile that spoke of hunts to come.

"A better arrangement. But still, your Vampires require something different from you than what I provide my Pack. My Weres take comfort, strength, and a trust in the order of our Pack from me. Your Vampires are at heart lone hunters, but they accept the constraints you dictate. They survive because of you."

Jody grimaced. "You always have known too much."

Sylvan laughed and gripped Jody's shoulder. "You are my friend, and I trust you at my side in a fight. But I would not want to see anyone else hold your position in the Dominion, for many reasons, so your consort is right in insisting you remain behind."

"And now you read our minds?"

"I didn't have to. That was a given." Sylvan laughed.

"Will you take your Prima?" Jody asked.

"She wouldn't have it any other way," Sylvan said, a rumble rising in her chest, "and her power will be needed if we are to locate Francesca quickly."

"Watch out for my Vampires."

"You've placed your best in charge. But you have my word on it."

Jody grasped Sylvan's forearm in an ancient gesture of unity. "You are my friend, and I trust you will return safely."

Sylvan returned the gesture. "I will see you here again."

❖

When Sylvan left to find Drake, Jody wrapped her arms around Becca and drew her down onto the long leather sofa facing the fireplace. Her Vampire guards and their hosts had already dispersed to more secluded parts of the great hall to feed and nest until sunfall. Lethargy had begun to steal through her as the sun rose outside the shuttered windows, and she would soon surrender to the torpor that held her captive during daylight hours. But first, the need rising within her to feed…and more…raged.

"I hunger for you," Jody whispered to Becca and kissed her.

"I know." Becca stroked her face. "I feel it, your need. You fill me with it. Fill my heart with joy and drive me mad for release all at once. I hunger for you."

Jody brushed the hair away from Becca's throat and kissed her again. "When this is done, when our Dominion is secure, you shall have whatever you need to keep your heart full."

"I love you," Becca whispered, "and that is all I need."

Becca brought Jody's face to her throat, and Jody slid her incisors deep within her, releasing the hormones to transform pain to pleasure as she fed. Becca whimpered as ecstasy stole through her, infinitely deep, exquisitely sharp, the power of Jody's essence joining hers, forcing her to orgasm again and again. She gripped Jody's hair and held Jody's mouth to her vein until Jody, full and potent from *her* essence, climaxed.

"I love you," Becca murmured as Jody released her and closed her eyes.

When Jody slept, flushed and sated, Becca lay awake thinking of what was to come at day's end. Vampires—hers now as well as Jody's—would risk true death to secure the safety of others like them. To protect their species.

She had been born to a different world, a human world where the supremacy of those like her was a given. She'd never feared being hunted or having her love torn from her by the beauty of a sunrise. Now she lived in the night, and each time she and Jody shared their love, she became a little less human.

Watching the logs burning in the great hearth, she pulled the wool throw from the back of the sofa and covered them both. Jody would not feel the heat as her body slowly cooled, but Becca would keep her warm until she rose again, nonetheless.

❖

Sylvan had sensed when Drake had left the infirmary, and her wolf had settled, knowing her mate was healed. Still, Sylvan would not rest easy until she had seen her. Touched her. Connected again on a primal, intimate level. Just as her wolves needed her touch to feel secure and safe, she needed Drake's to right her world. She slowed when Niki hailed her as she crossed the commons.

"Callan has three squadrons prepared for battle," Niki said. "They will assemble a half hour before sunfall."

"Good," Sylvan said. "Have we identified more donors for the rest of the Vampires?"

Niki nodded. "Every *sentrie* volunteered."

"Let's hope we don't need them. What of the medics—none of them have yet crossed the veil."

"Elena says if their equipment and supplies do not cross with them, their ability to treat the injured will be hampered, but they'll be able to shield them until they can shift." Niki hesitated. "Sophia is going."

Sylvan gripped her shoulder. "Our warriors will protect them, but we need them with us. Just as I need you here."

"I know."

"Our mates are Weres—we cannot ask them not to fight for their Pack." Sylvan held Niki's gaze. "My young are with Snowcrest. Until they return or the Prima and I do, you are my second. You will lead if we do not return. There is no one I trust more to assume the mantle."

"I am honored," Niki said, "but I will never be Alpha. Your Weres await your return."

"As quickly as we can. Now, I must see to my mate."

Niki saluted and stepped away as Sylvan turned and leapt onto the porch of the adjacent building. Drake, she knew, waited in their rooms, and she hurried upstairs and down the hallway to their private quarters.

Drake, in battle fatigues, stood at the window overlooking the commons. She turned as Sylvan entered, and Sylvan felt the warm embrace of her wolf as their eyes met.

"They look ready," Drake said.

"They are," Sylvan answered. "And you? Are you well?"

"Fully recovered. I'm sorry to have worried you."

"I would spare you pain if I could."

"I know." Drake crossed to her and kissed her. "But you can stop now."

Sylvan wanted to take her instantly. Her wolf was ready and so was she. They had little time and much to do, but as urgent as her need, she wanted something more. She wanted to fill herself with Drake in every possible way. She pulled Drake close and kissed her again. Deep inside, her wolf reached for Drake's. As their wolves joined, their power merged, grew, and pulsed through her. The Pack bonds flared brightly.

Kira's voice rang sharply in her mind. *Alpha?*

I am here. You and your sister? You are well?

We are.

And the others?

None injured. Snowcrest lost some soldiers. The Alpha and Prima live.

Bring them this message. Sylvan quickly relayed the battle plans, unsure of how long she could hold the link.

As you command.

The link faded and Sylvan said, "You heard?"

"Yes," Drake said. "When Snowcrest joins the battle, our Weres will be with them. Including our young."

Sylvan nodded. "They are strong and well-trained. And they were born for this."

"I wasn't, but our bond has given me the memory and the instincts to understand what they must do. It doesn't make it any easier." Drake pulled her toward the bed in the alcove. "We have only this day before we all do what we must do. I need you now."

"I hunger for you," Sylvan murmured as she pulled Drake's shirt from her trousers and unbuttoned it. Her wolf wanted *now*, but still, she went slowly. She traced the curve of Drake's breast with a gentle claw and followed the line of her torso down her abdomen to the top of her pants.

Shivering lightly, soft pelt feathering low on her abdomen, Drake carefully stripped the tight T-shirt off Sylvan's torso. "I hunger for you."

Wordlessly, they undressed each other, until Sylvan, trembling with the effort to hold back the driving need to fill and be filled with her mate, lifted Drake and carried her the last few feet to the bed and lowered them both. Drake wrapped her legs around Sylvan's hips, drawing her between her thighs, gripping Sylvan's shoulders as she traced her canines along the column of Sylvan's neck.

"I've been waiting for you. Every moment, all my life."

Sylvan raised herself on both arms and pressed her center to Drake's, their bodies naturally cleaving, their essences readying to fuse. Her breath came quickly, her heart pounded, and pressure filled her loins.

"You make me weak and stronger than I've ever been." Sylvan rocked her hips, and Drake answered the rhythm as they rose and fell together, steadily approaching the moment they would empty into each other. Sylvan slipped her hand between them and stroked her, waiting for the instant she was ready to erupt to fill her.

"I love you," Drake whispered and set her canines to the mate bite on Sylvan's shoulder. Sylvan groaned as the flare of pain and passion erupted through her. At the peak, she filled Drake, claiming Drake with her bite, and their wolves howled in triumph.

❖

"Come this way." Anya grasped Rafe's hand and drew her away from the recesses of the great room where Sabine and Drea, Jonathan and Estella, and other Vampires with their hosts had settled to await moonrise at the end of the day.

"The Liege may need me," Rafe protested.

"The Liege is safe with her Consort, and Zahn guards the door," Anya said. "And I need you." She slid her hands up Rafe's back and pulled Rafe against her as she leaned against a wide pillar. Rafe's incisors glinted, and her eyes of infernal red gave way to obsidian when Anya bared her neck. "I hunger for you."

Rafe cursed inwardly, Anya's scent igniting lust for far more than blood. For more than she could fight—or cared to. "I hunger for you."

Rafe took Anya's throat, and the fire of ten thousand suns that she had failed to witness burned through her as Anya's blood filled her. The words formed in her mind, echoed in Anya's. *Only you.*

Anya shuddered, the first surge of Rafe's thrall rushing through her, forcing her to release. She found Rafe's hand, pushed it between her thighs. "Take me. Drink me."

Rafe clasped her sex, squeezing her distended clitoris, milking her glands as she pulled Anya's essence into her with every swallow.

Anya released again and again, the pleasure a brilliant starburst blinding her. Her wolf keened, wild and victorious. Her claws erupted, and she shredded Rafe's shirt, baring her chest. "I want you."

Rafe's head snapped up, power lashing out, setting Anya ablaze. "Do it."

Anya's wolf struck, sealing the mate bond with her bite.

Rafe jerked, and for an instant, her spirit soared beneath the clear blue sky, the scent of the forest filling her, the taste of sunshine enveloping her.

❖

Trent lay with Zora's head on her shoulder, feeling the rush of Zora's blood, the beat of Zora's heart in time with her own, the soft whisper of Zora's breath against her throat. She traced the muscles in Zora's back, down the delicate curve of her waist to the strong rise of her hips. A fierce, beautiful warrior's body. Trent had been born and raised a warrior, a dominant Were whose primal call was to protect and serve. Zora and the Snowcrest Pack were traders and merchants and protectors of the land, but now they too were soldiers.

"We will not turn our backs on what has happened," Zora murmured, her lips brushing the angle of Trent's jaw. "We will answer with all the power of our Pack."

"When?" Trent said.

"As soon as—"

Zora paused, sensing the approach of her *imperator*. "Loris is coming."

"Yes." Trent tensed as the male, one of the most dominant in the pack, drew closer to their quarters. Her wolf's first instinct was always to guard her mate. "He is not alone."

"No." Zora sat up and pulled on a pair of pants.

"Forgive me, Alpha," Loris said from beyond the door. "Kira and Kendra wish to speak with you."

"Come," Zora said, rising as Trent also dressed.

The door opened and the two Timberwolf twins, young dominants—strong, proud, and respectful—entered.

Kira, gaze carefully fixed below Zora's, said, "Alpha Constantine, our Alpha has reached us. There has been an attack on the Compound."

"As there was here," Zora said. "And how do they fare?"

"The attack has been repulsed, but the Alpha plans to counterattack at sunfall. She requests the Snowcrest Weres join the battle."

"Where?" Trent said.

"She wishes you to take your force through the Gate. The Timberwolves who are here now will join with you in support."

"I see," Zora said. "Thank you. Loris, I will be with you soon."

"As you command, Alpha."

The twins saluted crisply in unison. "At your command, Alpha," they both said and turned and followed Loris out.

Zora glanced at Trent. "And so it begins." She brushed her fingers over Trent's cheek. "I need you to be careful. I need you to protect our wolves and trust that I will do the same."

"I am yours to command." Trent pulled her close and kissed her. "I love you. Where you lead, I and the Snowcrest Weres will follow."

"Tonight, then."

Chapter Eighteen

Sunfall, the dying knowe

Francesca tightened her grip on Philip's slender torso as he arched convulsively in the throes of orgasm, his heartbeat growing steadily more distant as she drank her fill. The power filled her, hot and vital, and she took all she could, needing all the strength possible for what was to come. His cries of ecstasy turned to whimpers as his blood trickled to a stop, and she rose to dress, leaving the lifeless shell of his body amidst the twisted satin sheets. He had been the strongest of her blood servants, and the one she had carefully preserved until the final moment to ensure she was at her most potent when the battle began. When this night was over and Cethinrod sat on the throne of Faerie, she would have all the blood slaves she would need. She would cross the veil once more into the human world with an army at her command, and her Vampires would feast as they were meant to, as was their right.

She dressed as the Dark Queen to meet the Night Lord in a black leather bodysuit laced down the center of her torso and thigh-high black boots. A triple strand of ruby-encrusted gold necklaces nestled between the pale mounds of her breasts and reflected the red glow in the depths of her eyes and the blood-red fullness of her lips. She summoned her Vampire guards, three dozen—all who remained from her hurried flight from Nocturne—and the fiercest of her fighters. She'd allowed them to feed from the Were captives they'd taken for Finngar's experiments in anticipation of the coming battle, and they were at full power. They waited at attention in two lines, their expressions hungry, their eyes already alight with battle lust.

"Soon," she crooned, lightly brushing each one with the tips of her fingers as she passed between them on her way to the exit from the knowe, "we will be free to hunt once more. Follow me, destroy my enemies, and you shall take what is yours by might and right for eternity."

"Hail, Francesca, Vampire Queen," they answered as one.

Francesca swept from the knowe into the glade followed by her Vampires. Finngar waited at the head of an array of the countless creatures he had created—reanimated Were beasts with clawed feet and jaws filled with sharklike teeth, giant vulturelike birds with curved razor-edged beaks large enough to sever limbs, tusked warthogs with triple sets of eyes, spiked hooves, and gaping maws capable of biting an enemy in half.

Francesca surveyed the monstrosities and smiled. Finngar, his hands tightly clasped, looking gaunt and tremulous, bowed.

"My Queen," he began in a reedy voice, "I have assembled your army as you ordered. You have only to command them—"

"Oh no, Maester," Francesca said softly. "It is not I who will lead them, but you. The honor, after all, should go to the creator."

"I, my Queen? But I am no battle Mage. I—"

"Tonight you will be," Francesca said, draping him in the cloud of her thrall. What color had been present in his hollowed cheeks leached away. He looked scarcely able to stand. Perhaps she should have let him feed a little more recently, but then after all, she hated to waste good blood on expendable subjects.

"Don't worry," she murmured, "you need only do as I order, and all will be well."

"Of course, my Queen."

"Come," Francesca said, motioning her guards forward. "It is time to join with Lord Cethinrod and reclaim our rightful place at the head of the Vampire legions."

She did not look back as she left behind the sanctuary that had become a prison.

❖

Sylvan surveyed the array of allied warriors in front of the main fortification ready to file out through the Gate that Torren would open into Faerie—wolf Weres and cat Weres in pelt, the Vampires in fighting leathers with sheathed weapons at their backs, swords and knives of cold iron, the only weapon capable of disabling and potentially destroying a Fae. Mechanized weapons would not function in Faerie, so their usual sidearms were useless.

Torren, bejeweled longsword sheathed at her back and short swords at each hip, wearing the colors of her house and the sigil of the hawk on her chest, silver hair wafting in the breeze, waited a few paces away. She wore the weapons and her regal attire, Sylvan suspected, along with the symbols of her rank more for the formality of treating with the Fae Queen than for battle. In the fight, the Hound would command the field. Torren's mate, Misha, already in pelt, leaned against Torren's thigh as Torren slowly stroked her ruff.

Drake's wolf stood by Sylvan's side as well, both their wolves straining to begin. The Timberwolves and the cats carried no weapons into battle but would fight as they lived—by fang and claw, as Weres. In ranks behind Sylvan and Drake came first her *centuri*, those who had partnered with the elite Vampire guards with them at their sides, then Callan at the head of Sylvan's warriors, followed by the cat Alpha and Prima, Raina and Lara, and finally the rear guard, Zahn and the remaining Vampires.

If we emerge in the midst of battle, Drake signaled, *the cats might not hold the ranks.*

Probably not. They're solo fighters for the most part, Sylvan answered, *and most effective that way. Raina will command them, as they would likely only follow her orders regardless. Since our numbers may be smaller than the enemy's, unpredictably is a good thing.*

Drake, who loved order even more than Sylvan, huffed. *Cats.*

Sylvan shot her a wolfie grin. *Hopefully, Cecilia is not already engaged in battle, but for now at least, Torren must command. The Fae will trust no other—if they even trust her.*

Torren was right, Drake said, *not advising Cecilia we are coming. Every court has its spies.*

Sylvan snarled. *We are fortunate our wolves are loyal to the last one.*

Your wolves will always follow you, Drake said.

They follow us, Sylvan replied.

Drake grumbled. *Try not to get injured tonight.*

Sylvan bumped her flank. *You as well. If we are separated—*

I will find you, they finished together.

Sylvan turned to Torren. *We are ready.*

❖

Anya waited beside Rafe in the front line with the *centuri* and their Vampires. If battle was imminent, she would fight by Rafe's side and, if Rafe was seriously injured, feed her until her power was restored. She'd been in battle now and knew how easy it was to become separated from the others.

"You need only call me," Anya said quietly. "I will hear you, no matter where I am."

"I won't need to feed again this night. As I am sure you remember," Rafe said with her usual hint of arrogance tinged with amusement, "I've already fed. As, I believe, you enjoyed."

"As do I always," Anya said. Her blood still thrummed with the power that coursed through her. When Rafe emerged from her torpor at sunfall, her hunger had been greater than usual and Anya's need greater. Each time they exchanged blood, her connection to Rafe strengthened. As did her pleasure. "I'm always happy to feed you, but I would rather not again this night. So be careful."

Rafe gave Anya a long look. "And you as well, my wolf."

Anya's wolf preened. *My wolf.* No longer *little wolf.*

The Alpha's voice rolled through the Pack bonds, pulling all the Timberwolves into pelt.

I don't need to tell you why we go to battle or how to fight. We will emerge near the Faerie Queen's royal knowe. If her army is engaged, Lord Torren will command us in battle. Cadres, fight well and protect each other.

Then Rafe spoke in her mind. *When we attack, Torren will send the wolves to break the enemy's line—once their formation scatters, my Vampires will slip among them and feed them cold iron. Stay with the wolves—that is where you fight best.*

I will not leave you, Anya replied.

Rafe's power pushed into her, not a compulsion, but a demand she could not ignore. *If I need you, I will call.*

Your word, Anya shot back.

My word.

Then guard your head. No matter how much blood Anya could give her, if Rafe was beheaded, she could not save her.

Rafe laughed, the sound tinged with irony. *You seem to be the only one capable of making me lose it.* Her grip tightened in Anya's ruff. *Do not come to harm this day. If you are mortally injured, I will not let you go. Do you understand?*

Anya understood completely. Rafe would turn her if she had no other choice. Anya'd seen how Lara had suffered when she'd been turned, had witnessed the agony of a newling's bloodlust, and she'd viewed what Lara shared now with Raina. She would not let Rafe perish while she lived. She would not deny Rafe the same. She would not relinquish what they shared. She was a wolf, and her wolf would survive. *I would not leave you. Do what you must.*

❖

Lord Torren along with her mate, Misha, strode outside the fortifications and into the glade where the last battle had scorched the earth. Anya couldn't see a Gate, but she'd seen Torren fashion a portal where only rock had been to provide passage for them from the Catamount stronghold to the Timberwolf Compound.

Where will she take us? she asked Rafe silently.

Rafe shrugged. *Wherever she likes. Your Alpha puts a great deal of faith in one of the enemy.*

Torren is Fae—that doesn't make her the enemy. And you've seen her fight with us, risk her life to save us.

Rafe glanced down, met her steady golden gaze. *You're right. Much has changed.*

Anya's wolf chuffed. *For me as well.*

As Torren raised a hand and swept a circle in the air at the edge of the great forest and a Gate appeared through which the magenta sky of Faerie glimmered, Rafe murmured, "Take care of my wolf."

Torren turned to Sylvan. "Quickly now, but remember we come unannounced. Keep your wolves on a leash."

The Alpha's wolf called to the Pack, a howl that reached the primal core of every Were, and the army sped through the Gate.

Anya and the *centuri* leapt through the portal after the Alpha and Prima in a powerful surge, and when they landed on the other side, their

Vampires materialized beside them. Anya touched down upon a vast plain of blue-green vegetation that came halfway up her forelegs and smelled faintly like crushed lavender. A brilliant crimson sun washed the land in fingers of fire.

Her heart clutched. *Rafe!* The sun. Somehow Torren had miscalculated and they'd entered Faerie not at moonrise, but sunrise. She spun to Rafe and clamped on to her arm, intent on dragging her toward a ring of towering trees with gleaming ebony trunks and leaves the color of ripe plums. *Take shelter.*

Rafe stilled her with a thought. *This sun will not harm us, my wolf.*

Quivering, Anya swung her head from side to side to see that all the Vampires who had emerged were unharmed. She huffed. *Someone could have warned us about this.*

Sensing the others crossing the veil and spreading out behind her, she surveyed the terrain. A stone path resembling polished river rock, twice as wide as a highway, wound through the gently wafting grass and toward an archway at the base of a hill ringed by more trees. Glittering stones encrusted the arches, and just within stood two massive dark wood doors carved with sigils and, in bas-relief, dragons with forms so lifelike Anya expected them to swing their massive heads toward the rapidly assembling troops and spew fire.

A phalanx of Fae guards in sky-blue tunics, black leggings, and gold boots that came to midthigh flanked the stone road on either side. Golden helmets emblazoned with dragons' heads and elaborately etched cheek guards covered much of their faces. Trumpets blared, and the guards, lowering their long pikes and bringing their swords to the ready, swung as one to face Torren, her mate, and the Alpha wolf pair, who stood alone at the forefront of the forces.

Expecting an attack, Anya's wolf growled and prepared to spring, her ruff flaring and a rush of battle frenzy speeding through her. On either side of her she felt the *centuri* readying as well.

"Stand easy, wolves," Rafe murmured.

Quivering, Anya held.

Torren unsheathed her sword and tilted the point to the ground. On either side of her, Misha and the Alpha and Prima crouched on their haunches, their wolves poised to spring but restrained. Anya detected a shimmer in the air, and archers appeared in three rows behind the phalanx of guards as more flooded through the archway, spreading out to either side in wings, effectively encircling Sylvan's forces.

She felt as much as heard Torren's voice. "We have come as allies to Cecilia, Queen of Thorns and All of Faerie."

A tall Fae in full armor strode through the gate. "Cecilia, Queen of Faerie and All the Realms beyond the Veil, has not summoned you. You are in violation—"

"I am the Master of the Hunt," Torren said, "and I present my allies—and those of your Queen—to begin the Hunt. We do not answer to you."

The Fae stiffened and his hand went to the sword sheathed at his side. He stilled as the most beautiful female Anya had ever seen appeared beside him. The air around her glowed, as if the sun burned within her and flowed from her pale, near translucent skin. Her golden hair kissed her bare shoulders and teased the wisps of the diaphanous royal-blue and ivory gown that hugged her voluptuous breasts. Her smile held a hint of predatory interest, and her emerald eyes radiated power that at once seduced and terrified.

"We have visitors, I see," the Queen—for she could be no one else—murmured in a voice that stirred Anya's loins in an unexpected and unwelcome way.

Torren took a knee but did not lower her head.

"Cecilia, Queen of Thorns and All of Faerie," Torren said, "I come to you as Master of the Hunt to declare the time is now. Enemies have encroached beyond the veil and attacked your allies, declared in faith with you at your request. May we have your leave to hunt down the enemy and destroy them?"

Cecilia surveyed the forces arrayed before the royal knowe, her cool gaze lingering on Sylvan and finally Torren. "You may rise, my Lord Torren, Master of the Hunt. You and your commanders may treat with me this—"

A wild scream pierced the air, and every Were readied to attack, an avalanche of growls and feline screeches thundering over the plain. The magenta sun winked out and shadows fell over the gathering.

"Hold," Torren said, and Sylvan signaled the same to her wolves.

A blood-red dragon, clawed feet jutting from huge hind limbs, black-veined blue and crimson wings sweeping the air like great flames, landed on the square between Cecilia and Torren with an earthshaking thud. Turning one enormous glittering golden eye toward the gathered forces, it surveyed them with a gaze that brought Anya's hackles rising. Here was the ultimate predator. The dragon bent its scaled head on a long sinuous neck to Cecilia, who reached out to stroke its cheek.

After a moment, the dragon lowered its belly to the ground, and Cecilia, in a movement too quick for Anya to follow, mounted the beast and grasped the thick fringe—a darker shade of red, like old blood—that ran in a line down its neck to its back. She turned to Torren.

"It appears the battle is at hand. The Night Lord of the South and an army approach." She raised a hand as the dragon lifted into the sky with a great beating of wings. "I declare the Hunt has begun."

Chapter Nineteen

Zora stood with Trent before the shimmering Gate that the enemy had used to launch their attack on Clan home. She couldn't make out anything through the haze that filled the portal, and her wolf bristled unhappily at the thought of leaping through it. She would be leading her Weres into an unknown world with no idea of what—or who—awaited them, or even where they would emerge. She turned to face the forces arrayed behind her. Ash, the former leader of her *centuri*, and Ash's mate, Jace, stood with the Timberwolves who had arrived as reinforcements. Kira and Kendra, the Timberwolf Alpha's young, led a cadre. They looked eager but also calm. Zora wasn't surprised. Sylvan's young bore the heritage of generations of Alpha Weres, and the memory of battles long past was carried in their genes. Her Snowcrest soldiers had not been born for battle, but they had trained for it unstintingly, and she was as confident in their abilities as she would've been had she led a battalion of seasoned warriors.

Now she would lead them against an enemy she could neither see nor name, and they would follow to the last wolf. They trusted her to lead, and she would not fail them. She unleashed her call and felt the Weres, one and all, come to attention.

"We may emerge in the midst of a battle. If that is the case, you know how to fight. Protect each other, and we will all return home together. Those we fight this night showed no mercy when they encroached on our territory and abducted our Packmates. Show none in return."

She shifted, pulling them all into pelt, and glanced at Trent. *See that you take care of my mate.*

Trent's eyes shone as they met Zora's, and her muzzle opened in a wolfie grin. *Have no fear, Alpha. When the battle is done, I will be at your side.*

Zora looked to Loris, her *imperator*. *Establish defensive positions until we can assess where we are and make contact with Alpha Mir. Should we fall, bring my wolves home.*

On my honor, Alpha, Loris answered.

Zora swung away and dove through the portal, Trent at her side.

She landed in a clearing covered in brittle brown vegetation that looked and smelled dead, under a sky with what she imagined to be daylight, as the magenta orb that emanated heat and light must be this world's sun. The air, murky and gray, held a taint of decay, as if the very land was rotting around them. Her wolves came through behind her, spreading out in a defensive crescent on either side of her and Trent as Loris ordered.

Trent growled, her wolf uneasy. *What is this place—everything looks...dead.*

I don't know, Zora said. She sensed nothing living around them, no sound or scent of other creatures. Even the foliage appeared dead or dying. On the far side of the clearing, a dense forest climbed to a far-off mountaintop, although the trees bore no resemblance to those of her home world. Gnarled trunks fashioned from twisted braids of what might once have been wood now appeared stonelike. Leafless branches carried needlelike projections as long as her foreleg, and what might've been sap oozed from the notches between the twisting limbs, running like tears down the slick surface to coat the ground in fetid pools.

Something has leeched the life from this place, Zora said, and the images of the reanimated monsters that had attacked her clan home flashed through her mind. They had come through the portal from this place—had the life force that fueled them been stolen from all that once lived here? Her hackles rose.

We can't stay here. We must reach Sylvan. Whatever—whoever—was once here is gone.

Kira and Kendra are the only ones likely to reach her, Trent said. *My link to the Timberwolves is weak, clouded.*

Ask them to try, Zora said.

Trent signaled Kendra and Kira to join her, and they trotted over, the black one slightly in the lead. She lowered her head and brushed her muzzle against the undersurface of Trent's jaw in greeting.

Can you find your Alpha? Trent asked.

We will. Kendra's golden eyes, so much like Sylvan's, deepened, and her silver twin, Kira, leaned against Kendra as she lifted her head to scent the fetid air. Zora suspected that Kira was adding her power to Kendra's. After a moment, Kendra shook herself as if coming out of a cold lake and laid her muzzle on Trent's.

Over that far ridge, at the far edge of the forest, Trent relayed to Zora after a moment. *Kira...they...sense the Alpha and Prima and many Timberwolves. They sense something else—a hunt.*

Zora huffed. *A battle, then.*

As we expected. Trent's wolf chuffed. *That's where we should go.*

Zora judged they could cover the distance in less than an hour at a full run and signaled her orders. *Loris, the left wing, Ash and Jace, the right. If we meet the enemy, we will not let them pass. Hold the line.*

With a howl, Zora pushed her call to all the gathered wolves and raced for the forest. Her wolves followed, filling the silence with the sound of the hunt.

❖

Trumpets blared and cordons of Fae soldiers appeared on either side of the royal knowe, four across and in rows extending back farther than Anya could count. Dressed in Cecilia's colors, royal blue and snow, they carried pikes and wore swords at their sides and back. Attillus, the Fae whom Cecilia had called Consort, approached Torren.

"The Queen has designated you the Master of the Hunt, and we are at your command." Expressionlessly, he saluted, fist to shoulder.

Anya's wolf growled softly. Something about this Fae felt... wrong. She scented the air, tasted a plummy sweetness that might have come from the fruit hanging heavily on the surrounding trees, and beneath that, the familiar tang of copper. She knew Rafe's taste as well as her own, and the blood she sensed was not hers. The Fae who regarded Torren with the cold eyes was something else beneath the glamour.

Rafe tugged her ruff. *Trust no one in Cecilia's court, my wolf, and do not stray from the Pack in battle.*

"We will follow the Queen," Torren announced in a quiet voice that filled the glade as Cecilia and her mount circled high above them. "She will lead us to the field of battle. Our Weres will take the center with the Vampires as rear guard, and the Fae will attack on the flanks. Once their line breaks, the Fae will sweep in and close the pincer."

"And you will collect the souls," Attillus said.

"My Hound will clear the field of the spirits that remain."

Once more Attillus saluted. "As you command, Hunt Master."

As the Alpha trotted to Torren's side, her command sounded in the mind of every Were. *When we engage the enemy, target the revenants. Attack in pairs, strike in concert, incapacitate them.*

Anya, attuned to Rafe, heard her orders to the Vampires as well. *Target the Fae commanders.*

Torren shifted, and the Hound, three times the size of the Alpha with leathery brown hide, blood-red eyes, and huge gleaming canines, bounded out in front of the battle line and roared. The Hunt had begun.

❖

Sylvan trotted beside Drake with Jonathan and his Vampire counterpart on her other side. Overhead, Cecilia's dragon trumpeted a battle cry and spiraled toward a series of forested mountain ridges. The dragon skimmed the surface of the earth and blasted a stream of fire into the forest at the far edge of the plains. As the trees lit up like a thousand enormous candles, figures burst from cover and swarmed onto the broad field.

As Sylvan had expected, the revenants led the charge. They were expendable but also capable of doing vast damage. And the Fae had not faced them before. If the Fae line broke, their forces could be surrounded. Torren must have read her mind as the Hound leapt forward. The ground trembled as Cecilia's dragon settled to the earth, and the Were legions closed around her, Torren's Hound at her side and the Alpha and Prima on the other.

A line of helmeted Fae warriors in crimson tunics and shining silver breastplates, several rows deep, erupted onto the field behind the charging abominations. First came the archers with longbows and crossbows, then the foot soldiers carrying shields and pikes.

In the center of the army rode a Fae with a golden helmet and matching armor on a beast with the head of a great predator bird, its razor-like beak snapping at the air, and the body of a winged cat with talons for feet. His gleaming hair floated to his shoulders from beneath the helmet and he wielded a longsword shimmering with power.

Cethinrod, the Hound signaled. *And the sword is enchanted. One strike, no matter how minor, will bring death.*

The dragon trumpeted again, and its command formed in every mind.

Attack!

Sylvan and the Weres raced to meet the oncoming horde of beasts with clawed feet, bladed wings, curved tusks, and maws filled with spiked canines. Sylvan and Drake fought together, attuned in this as in all things. When one charged at the head of a beast, drawing its attention, the other leapt on its back from the opposite side to crush a spine or shred a wing. When one raked a flank with teeth and claws, the other struck at the throat, tearing the head from what remained of a body. All around them the revenants crumbled to ash, black blood fell like acid rain, and tarry smoke blotted out the sky. An arrow sank into Sylvan's shoulder as she sprang at a thing that had once been a cat Were, and she stumbled and fell. Kira, with Kendra at her side, appeared out of the murk, streaked past her, and snapped at the beast's head as Drake rushed to shield Sylvan. Kira dragged the monster down by the neck as Kendra crushed its spine. Leaving the creature twitching and melting into a tarry mass, the twins raced back to where Sylvan struggled to get back to her feet.

How bad? Drake demanded.

Sylvan twisted and snapped at the bolt buried in her shoulder. *Not lethal. Pull it out.*

Drake clamped the shaft in her jaws and jerked her head. The bolt came free, and bright red blood arced after it.

Retreat to safety, Drake said.

When this is done. Sylvan fixed on Kendra. *Where are the Snowcrest wolves?*

Working their way along the far ridge—behind the enemy. Alpha Constantine sent us to report.

Find her. Tell her to hold there and block their retreat.

Yes, Alpha. Kira and Kendra hurried away.

Sylvan's wolf shook herself and raced toward the nearest enemy. Drake howled and sprinted to join her.

❖

When Cecilia's dragon spewed fire and the revenants charged, Anya raced forward with the *centuri* into the midst of the transformed Were animals, the violated remains of wolves and cats and other things she couldn't identify. The air vibrated with the whistling sound of spears and the bolts of crossbows, launched from both sides, and the enemy and the allies began to fall. She saw the Alpha take an arrow in the side, stumble, then right herself as the Prima rushed to guard her. Then the Alpha rose and surged into the melee with a howl that energized the Pack. Anya searched for Rafe, saw a blur that for an instant became her lover, short sword slicing across the throat of a Fae warrior. Then the warrior was falling, the armor awash with blood the color of his tunic. Anya lost sight of Rafe again as she fought with fang and claw, darting among the soulless beasts who were not as quick as Weres but not as easy to incapacitate as a living enemy. She tore at limbs and throats, leapt onto backs to bite through skeletal bones, clawing at what remained of their bodies. Talons raked her flanks, fangs bit at her neck, but she twisted and dodged and hunted with her Pack as she had since her first hunt. Everywhere trumpets sounded, wolves howled, cats screeched, and the dragon screamed.

As she whipped around to strike a Fae archer, the Fae on the griffin charged the Queen's dragon. An instant later, a gray mist floated over the field, and she lost sight of the Queen. Black-garbed warriors materialized out of the choking fog, striking down the royal Fae and Weres alike and disappearing before the bodies fell.

Rafe appeared beside her. *Francesca's Vampires.*

The Hound bounded to them. *Magic. There must be a Sorcerer. Where? Can you find them?*

Give me what power you can, the Hound said.

Rafe gripped Anya's ruff, drew on Anya's links to her and the Pack, and pushed their combined power into the Hound.

The ridge above the tree line. The Hound snarled and bounded into the oncoming line of crimson-clad Fae, its great head swinging from side to side, crushing limbs and hurling bodies to the side.

Stay with the Pack, Rafe ordered and disappeared.

Anya opened her senses and followed Rafe, sensing another power as she raced through the corridor the Hound created in the swarming mass of warriors. A power devoid of light, soulless and dark, poisoning the air.

She leapt over the smoldering body parts of the revenants littering the field and dove into the thickest part of the heavy, choking fog. She twisted away from the blade of a Vampire, ignoring the searing pain along her flank. There, on a small knoll above the battlefield, a figure in a dark cape, both arms extended to the sky. And beside him, a woman in black—shimmering with unearthly power.

❖

Francesca looked down on the field of battle and turned to Crista, the strongest of her remaining soldiers, the one she had allowed to feed, to preserve her strength and bind her will, for just this moment. She had hoped that some of her most loyal Vampires would survive this battle, but if that was not to be, she could always find more loyal minions once she was restored to her rightful glory. And for that, Cethinrod had to defeat Cecilia. "Lead the others to attack Cecilia's front line. Target the leaders—the Alpha Weres and the royal Fae guards. Take half your number and stop the Hound. See to that yourself. Without them, that ragtag army will scatter, and we will feast on their bones."

Crista's expression remained stonelike as she saluted briskly. If she knew the mission was suicide, she didn't show it. "Yes, Mistress."

"Move quickly. Your silver weapons will incapacitate the Weres, and the Fae can be slowed long enough for Cethinrod to finish them."

"As you command, my Queen." Crista disappeared into the swirling mist that shrouded much of the slope between Francesca and the field of battle.

Francesca's rage rose as she watched Cecilia on her dragon cutting a swath through the archers with great sweeps of the dragon's tail and felling Fae soldiers with burning tongues of lethal power that Cecilia flung from her outstretched hands. She had power, the Fae Queen, but

Cethinrod had power as well. When the lightning bolts of blistering power that Cecilia launched arrowed at him, he countered them with power of his own. Her power struck his shields, and the sky blazed. The earth shuddered as their powers clashed. Cecilia opened chasms in the earth, and Cethinrod's foot soldiers were swallowed up, their screams rising above the clash of steel, an eerie accompaniment to the roars and screams of the beasts. Cethinrod whipped coils of lethal power, shimmering like golden lassos across the line of advancing royal Fae soldiers, severing heads from bodies.

Cecilia's allies advanced as the archers retreated, giving way to the foot soldiers. Finngar's monsters fell before the speed and skill of the Weres, and when they did, royal Fae warriors filled the breach and pushed deeper into the midst of Cethinrod's pike bearers. Cecilia's dragon reared with a scream and incinerated Cethinrod's unprotected flank with a blast of fire. Dozens of Fae drifted to ash. Cethinrod's line broke. A path appeared through the center of Cethinrod's Fae, and the Hound tore its way to the base of the ridge.

Francesca reached out to her Vampires. *The Hound. Destroy the Hound.*

Even as her Vampires converged on the Hound, Cethinrod's griffin charged the dragon. They met in a great clash of sound and fury, of screams and bellows and gnashing teeth. As the beasts battled, Cecilia and Cethinrod exchanged lightning bolts of power. Cecilia's dragon unfurled its wings and rose to fight from the air, its great talons raking the griffin's neck and tearing open a wound that geysered blood. The griffin stumbled, dropped to its forelegs, and the dragon whipped its head around and plucked Cethinrod from the back of the dying beast.

Cethinrod's screams of rage ended abruptly as the dragon closed its jaws and flung what remained of Cethinrod's torn body to the earth to lie beside the griffin.

Cecilia's command thundered across the plain and echoed from the mountainside.

Teine!

The dragon spewed fire, and the griffin, its dismembered rider, and Cethinrod's soldiers in the way were consumed by flame. The rest of Cethinrod's army broke and retreated in chaos.

The Hound roared and Francesca, watching the disaster unfolding below, snapped, "Finngar. I need more power. Feed me what you have."

"I have no more, Mistress," Finngar gasped, already on his knees, his body sunken, his skin withering.

Francesca snarled and grasped him by the neck, draining what remained of his life force. She forced her thrall outward to trap and confuse the Hound long enough for her Vampires to return—whatever of them were left—and aid in her escape.

Not enough.

Crista appeared. "Mistress, my Queen, we were unable—"

"All of you—gather here and stop that Hound."

Crista hesitated.

"Do as I command," Francesca ordered, and Crista bowed her head.

A half dozen Vampires materialized to join Crista. They would fail. Cecilia's forces, led by the Weres and the royal Fae swords, were already climbing to the ridge. But her Vampires were fierce assassins and would slow them long enough for her to escape. With one last look at the carnage below, she glided off into the cover of the forest. Cethinrod's secret knowe would have to shelter her awhile longer.

Chapter Twenty

The mist Finngar had created to shroud the ridgeline and hide Francesca and her Vampires slowly dissipated as Francesca fled the ridge and penetrated deeper into forest. She traveled through the shadows, avoiding the shafts of magenta light that speared through the gnarled limbs overhead. When she had left the knowe with her Vampires and climbed the mountains to the ridge overlooking Cecilia's royal knowe, she'd mentally mapped a line of escape if Cethinrod proved no match for the Queen of Thorns. She'd witnessed too many battles with every combination of humans and Praetern to rely on the outcome, no matter how strong one side appeared at the outset. Cethinrod had assured her he would marshal forces to far outnumber Cecilia's royal Fae, and that together with her Vampires and Finngar's monsters, their army would be unbeatable. He had underestimated Cecilia's strength and misjudged the power of the Hound, the Weres, and the Vampires who had joined her. Even as she'd abandoned the ridge, on the field of battle below, Cecilia and her royal Fae surrounded the remnants of Cethinrod's army. Many of the Fae rebels knelt, pledging allegiance to Cecilia. Apparently those who did not were given a swift end by the sword.

Now Cethinrod was nothing but ashes, and Francesca was forced to flee from her archenemies once more. Her rage boiled, the frustration like acid in her blood, her hunger growing more ravenous. She'd expended almost all her power holding back the Hound and feeding Finngar's pitiful attempts to cloak them on the ridge as she directed her Vampires against her enemies. She might have aided Cethinrod in his final confrontation with Cecilia, but that would have drained her, dangerously, to the point she might not have been able to save herself. By that time, he and his forces had proved themselves too weak to vanquish Cecilia and her allies. Unfortunate, but she could not risk all for a weaker ally.

She halted abruptly at the sounds of battle where none should be—mad screeches, growls, howls of triumph, and roars of challenge. Pressed against the slick trunk of one of the massive black trees, she breathed in and sorted through the miasma of aromas in the cloying air, dismissing the unidentifiable creatures, the tendrils of death and decay, the blood and ash, until *there*—unexpected and unexpectedly exciting. Wolf Weres. Dozens. Just ahead, in the path of her descent to the glade and safety. Where had they come from?

Hunger tore at her, a beast clawing her mind and body. She had to feed if she was to escape, and the prey she needed was close. She ghosted from tree to tree, following the ever-stronger scent of wolf Weres. She avoided the area where the scent was strongest, searching for individual scent-markers, singling out the lone wolves. The sounds of battle grew louder, nearer now. Soon. Soon she would strike. The wolves' attention would be on their enemy, and she would have opportunity. She had hunted all her many centuries of existence but hadn't hunted prey like this in a millennium. Strong, healthy prey worthy of her bite, not weak-blooded humans or, weaker still, blood addicts of all species. The hunt thrilled her, filled her with excitement for the life that would soon be hers to take, and her bloodlust filled her with agonizing expectation. No restrictions now. She could take her prey, feed at will, and replenish her power to a pinnacle she hadn't experienced in recent memory.

She drifted closer as the single scent line grew stronger, her movement so stealthy even the air did not ripple, until she was only yards from the golden-brown wolf crouched behind a downed blackened tree trunk. A *sentrie*, on guard and watchful, but its muzzle lifted in the direction of the battle. Searching for an enemy. Slowly, Francesca released her thrall and sent the pheromones in the direction of the wolf. Most Weres had never encountered a Vampire, had never felt the subtle lassitude filling their consciousness, had never experienced the loss of will. Slowly, she enticed the Were from its cover, and the wolf padded toward her.

Francesca smiled. Oh, what a pretty one, so young and full of life. The golden eyes regarded her curiously but without fear as she beckoned it closer. Compliant now, the wolf joined her, brushed against her leather-clad thigh. Nearly as tall as her waist, the she-wolf radiated power. Power that would soon be hers. Fleetingly Francesca recalled the taste of Sylvan's blood, the power greater than any other she'd absorbed flooding through her, driving her to a sexual peak and leaving her stronger than she'd ever been. This wolf would do for now. Her incisors lengthened and her blood filled with the chemicals to subdue the prey. She drew it into the cover of the underbrush, took a moment to stroke its muzzle before she knelt, wrapped an arm around its powerful withers, as she might a lover, tipped its muzzle up to bare the soft fur on its throat, and struck the vital vessels pumping below the skin. The wolf quivered once but made no sound. She drank, pouring hormones into its blood to subdue it. The wolf went to its knees and then its side, and she lay over it, rejoicing in the warmth of the body beneath hers. Heat flooded through her, the erotic power of the wolf's lifeblood returning life to hers. When the wolf lay still, she rose, its blood streaking her neck and pooling between her breasts.

She exalted, the power glorious, triumphant. She blurred away from the Were forces, her speed now a dozen times faster than what it had been all these long weeks imprisoned in the knowe. She'd have to return there now, but only until she could find a way out through the Gate Finngar had created to unleash his monsters across the veil. She just needed a little time. And much more blood.

❖

Rafe, along with Sylvan, Drake, and the *centuri* with their Vampires, crested the ridge seconds after the Hound. A crumpled body partially obscured by a black cloak lay among the tall blades of grass. Francesca's Mage—drained and true dead. Rafe recognized the Vampires in black fighting leathers who swirled around the Hound, blades slashing at its legs and body. Francesca's elite guard—the best and most loyal of her inner circle who had escaped the failed attack at Nocturne with her. The Hound snapped and twisted, driving them off with swipes of its clawed paws and gnashing teeth, but as the assailants flickered away from her, their blades drew blood.

Defend the Hound, Sylvan commanded.

The Weres leapt to intercept Francesca's Vampires as they circled their prey, forming a protective ring around the laboring Hound. Pools of bright red blood stained the ground beneath its huge body. As the Vampires swept forward as one, Rafe blurred among them, her own blades flashing as she opened throats faster than they could detect her. She'd take their heads, but that could wait until the Hound was safe.

Within moments, more Weres flooded the ridge, and the last of the enemy fell. Exhausted, bleeding from multiple wounds, the Hound slouched to the ground.

Rafe methodically beheaded the downed Vampires, those still aware snarling feebly but unable to recover quickly enough to heal. One who had taken a spear to the chest hissed and said, "You will never defeat her. The Queen of the Vampires will rise—"

"Your Queen will die, true dead, like the rest of you," Rafe said as she swept her blade and removed the head. When she'd finished with the last of Francesca's Vampires, she signaled to Sylvan, who padded over to her. "Francesca is not among them. She left them to cover her retreat."

We'll pursue her, Sylvan signaled. *The Snowcrest Weres should be downrange from here, and they may intercept her first. But first we must see to the Hound. We may need you.*

"I must find Anya," Rafe said. "She is injured."

Sylvan tipped her head, gold eyes flashing. *Hurry.*

Rafe spun away and blurred among the mass of Weres and Vampires steadily filling the ridgeline. *Anya!*

Anya's wolf emerged from the far side of the knoll and limped toward her. Blood flowed from a long gouge in her side, matting her red-brown fur. Muscle, still oozing, showed through the gash.

"I thought I told you not to get injured today." Rafe swept her up, carried her to the seclusion of a large rocky outcropping, and knelt with the wolf draped across her lap. She sliced open the large vein in her forearm with her blade and held it to the wolf's muzzle. "Drink."

Anya's wolf-gold eyes, hazy with pain and blood loss, fixed on hers as she lapped at the blood. After a moment, Anya whined softly, and her wound began to close.

When Anya's wolf attempted to pull away, Rafe ordered, "More."

Anya's words came to her then. *You're not without injuries. I don't need more.*

Rafe grasped Anya's ruff and pressed her muzzle firmly to her vein. *I'll say when you stop. Drink.*

This time, Anya growled, and Rafe laughed. *Better.*

When the wound closed and Anya got to her feet with an impatient shrug, resettling her fur, Rafe rose and surveyed the ridge. More Weres had flooded up, congregating around the Alpha pair and the Hound.

I tried to protect the Hound, Anya said. *But there were too many.*

Rafe registered a sensation she'd long thought impossible. Fear. Fear she might have lost something she could no longer do without. "You were brave—and lucky. I'd rather you were less brave at times. I…I do not want to lose you."

Anya's wolf leaned in to her. *You will never lose me. I swear it.*

Rafe stroked her neck, turning to listen to the sounds floating up from the forest on the far side of the ridge. "Francesca has escaped. She can't be far away—all her Vampires were starving. Her power must be diminished too. Those are Weres, fighting close by. They'll need us. This time, stay with the Pack."

Anya gripped Rafe's arm in her jaws. *Wait. You can't go alone.*

Rafe glanced down at her. "You command me now?"

When you're foolish.

"I must join Sylvan first. The Hound is injured too."

Anya snarled. *I'm coming with you. You can't heal everyone without draining yourself.*

"I'm far stronger than you think."

Anya shouldered her thigh. *I know just how strong you are. And just how stubborn. Let's go.*

❖

The revenants surged over the ridge like a black cloud and crashed through the forest. Trees toppled, crushing many of the rampaging beasts. The raging monsters raced toward the wolf Weres, seemingly with no organized plan of attack. If they'd ever had a leader, there was none now. The Snowcrest line held as the beasts struck.

Kira and Kendra fought side by side, as did Zora and Trent and many of the other wolves—hunting and striking as they were born to do. Vastly outnumbered, despite being faster and more intelligent, some fell. The pain of every loss reverberated through Snowcrest and Timberwolves alike, and the pain became fury that drove their battle frenzy.

Kira raced to intercept a charging beast, its deformed head lowered, its massive tusks set to impale her sister. Howling, Kira launched herself onto its back and bit deep into its back to crush what was left of its spine. As it stumbled forward, she warned her sister. *Behind you.*

Kendra spun, felt the graze of tusk tearing across her shoulder, and with a snarl, clamped her jaws on the beast's throat. She whipped her head from side to side and tore out the remnants of its flesh. Black liquid spurted, and the thing tumbled to the ground.

Kira leapt free of the smoldering ash. *Is it bad?*

No, Kendra said. *Listen.*

Kira raised her head and answered the familiar call with a howl of her own. Her eyes blazed as she shot Kendra a look of triumph. *The Alpha comes.*

We're not done yet, Kendra replied.

Kira chuffed, and together, they launched themselves at the nearest beast.

❖

Can you heal these wounds? Sylvan asked Torren.

With time, the Hound replied. *A day perhaps.*

The sounds of continued battle filtered through the forest. The unearthly cries of the revenants warred with the battle howls of wolves. Kira and Kendra and a squadron of her Timberwolves were in battle. Sylvan crouched next to the Hound and draped her head and torso over the Hound's thigh. *Snowcrest Weres are fighting the monsters that escaped us. There may be Fae among them. We need you now. Take my power.*

Drake shouldered close to Sylvan and pressed against Torren's flank. *And mine.*

And mine, Rafe added, pressing a hand to the Hound's chest over its heart.

The Hound shivered, absorbing the strength shared by its allies, its friends. Its power rose, and with it, its magic. The bleeding slowed, severed muscles healed, and torn flesh closed. With a deep-chested rumble, the Hound shook them off and lumbered to its feet. *I am strong enough. And we have an enemy to defeat, and one last Vampire to destroy.*

Sylvan rose and called to her wolves. *Into the forest.*

One more time, Anya leapt into battle at Rafe's side.

Chapter Twenty-one

The sounds of the battle faded as Francesca blurred down the mountainside. When she reached the dead glade that she'd left behind with such visions of triumph at moonfall, something she hadn't experienced since she'd been a youngling during the dark centuries in Europe whispered in her depths. Tendrils of fear rose along with the return of burning hunger, and with it, a gripping sense of terror and unease that had plagued her during the centuries when prey was scarce and she was hunted. The silence that pervaded the surrounding skeletal forest, the absence of life in the earth and the sky, and the scent of decay that lay over the barren land reminded her that she was alone, without minions to protect and serve her. Without human servants and blood slaves to feed and satisfy her.

Fury rose to quench the fear. All that would change. She had only to access Finngar's Gate to escape this place and return to the human realm where she would soon regain her power and her position. Those wolves up on the ridge had come through the Gate, and she could just as easily pass into their world. The hunger burned inside her, and she couldn't wait long, but she couldn't risk being caught out in the open while the enemy was so close. No, she'd take shelter within the knowe, the hidden sanctuary that only Cethinrod had remembered. She smiled to herself as she slipped through the entrance. Cethinrod had been useful after all.

The silence echoed tenfold within the empty hallways. The moans and cries of Finngar's subjects that had unceasingly drifted through the passageways were absent, as were the cries of ecstasy from the minions feeding. The pathway to her chamber had somehow changed location, and she was forced to backtrack and search until she found her way. When she finally reached it, a new surge of shock twisted within her. The walls had closed, leaving barely enough room for the bed where she had last fed. The body she'd left on the floor was gone, only a mound of ash in its place. Spiked branches of dead wood protruded from the walls where previously her tapestries had hung. The ceiling had been replaced by a mass of snarled roots and fetid earth. The scent of decaying leaves tainted the air.

Abruptly, she spun about and rushed from the barren chamber. No matter. She didn't plan to use the space again. She laughed. She would soon have a bed large enough for as many servants as she wanted, with silk sheets and endless pleasures. She blurred along the passageways, chased by the growing hunger and the ghosts of the past. She wouldn't wait any longer. She would search Finngar's laboratory to discover the location of the Gate. She'd never bothered to witness his pathetic efforts to attack the Weres with his creatures, but the Gate must be nearby. If she was lucky, one of his specimens might still be imprisoned and she could feed. Once again, the pathway she usually took ended in a dead end, and for the first time, the fear inside her overwhelmed the hunger. The knowe was changing, collapsing in on itself. But then, she didn't need much time.

Finngar's lab was as empty as her chamber had been, with no evidence of the Weres he had kept imprisoned before draining their life force and reanimating them to follow his commands. Fetid water seeped through the ceiling of the cavern, cold and dank, and collected on the crumbling rocks. There was nothing here to help her.

She spun about and rushed back into the passageway, one that seemed wholly unfamiliar.

❖

The Hound, her mate Misha, and Sylvan and Drake charged down the mountainside at the head of their army and trapped the revenants between their forces and the Snowcrest line. The revenants, churning in an incoherent mass, were quickly surrounded and destroyed. Zora and Trent, both bloodied but not appearing to be seriously injured, trotted over to Sylvan and Drake as the Hound finished moving among the dead, absorbing the power of the few remaining fleeing souls. Sylvan flicked a glance past Zora and Trent, saw Kira and Kendra approaching with the Timberwolf cadre, and her worry lifted. Her young were safe. Beside her, Drake chuffed softly, her relief matching Sylvan's.

As the leaders converged, Torren, once again in the colors of her house, swords sheathed at her back and side, appeared at Sylvan's side. Sylvan called her wolves to shift and heal as Zora and Raina did the same.

When everyone emerged in battle attire, Sylvan looked at Torren and indicated the black battle BDUs. "Is it real or an illusion?"

Torren laughed. "Does it matter?"

Sylvan grinned as Drake muttered, "Typical."

"What of Cecilia?" Zora asked, her wolf still riding her eyes. "I must see to my wounded if we are secure."

"She has triumphed," Sylvan said. "The rebel Fae army has broken, and these are the last of the revenants."

"What—"

"Alpha!" A young Snowcrest *sentrie* raced up to Zora. "One of our scouts…I found her, dead. Drained." He hesitated. "I think…there is a bite on her neck, but she did not struggle."

Zora growled, pelt dusting her throat and chest, and glared at Rafe. "A Vampire? A Vampire has attacked one of ours?"

"Quite possibly," Rafe said calmly, "but not one of mine. If the kill was recent, I should be able to pick up the scent trace."

"The *kill*," Zora said softly, dangerously. "My Weres are not prey."

Sylvan rumbled softly, her power spreading to encompass the wolves. "Our allies would not turn on us."

Zora stiffened before slowly letting out a breath. "Of course. My apologies, *Senechal*."

Rafe nodded. "Of course. Where is this body?"

"Show us," Zora said to her *sentrie*.

Rafe and the others followed the Snowcrest *sentrie* and crouched by the body of a Were that lay in a shallow depression beneath a tree. Gently, she lifted the wolf's muzzle and leaned closer. After a moment, she glanced up at Sylvan and Zora. "Francesca. Not long ago."

Sylvan growled. "Can you track her?"

"Yes, but it will be easier with help." She stood and asked Torren, "Can you scent her as well?"

Torren nodded. "Together we should be able to find her."

"Then let's get started," Sylvan said. "We must find her before she gathers reinforcements."

"Or accesses a Gate," Torren said.

"Can she do that?" Sylvan asked.

"If she recognized it and the Gate still maintains enough power, perhaps."

"Then we must stop her first."

Zora edged forward. "That is my wolf. I claim the hunt."

Sylvan said, "The right is yours, but it may take all of us to end her."

❖

Sylvan signaled to Kira and Kendra and Ash. "Form your cadres and take the left flank. The Snowcrest Weres, take the right. We'll sweep through the forest behind the trackers."

All three saluted. "Yes, Alpha."

The Hound, Rafe, and Anya, the Timberwolves' best tracker, led off with Sylvan, Drake, Zora, and Trent and close behind. The sky lightened as a magenta sun and its twin, a paler crimson crescent, rose into the sky.

A mile down the mountainside, Torren slowed beneath the gnarled black trees and looked to Rafe. "There is a large clearing just ahead. The trail is faint now. Can you sense her?"

"She is here," Rafe said, "close by, but shrouded somehow."

"Shielded," Torren murmured, "but the magic feels wrong. Fae magic, but something else, something tainted."

"The Mage's doing?" Anya said. "The air tastes poisoned."

"Everything about this place is corrupted," Rafe said. "I sense no life. Even the earth is empty, barren, stripped of its very essence."

Sylvan drew up beside them. "Is this where the Mage siphoned the life force to animate the revenants?"

Torren nodded. "The inherent life force of the captives wouldn't have been enough. He needed to infuse them with magic drawn from other living beings."

"Why would she come here, then?" Sylvan said. "She needs the living to feed from."

"We have destroyed her minions. She needs to cross the veil," Rafe said. "To hide, regain her power, and gather minions to her again."

Sylvan growled. "She's looking for the Gate. Torren, can you sense the Gate?"

"No. It will be close and so will she. I'll need to search for her."

Misha spoke up from just beside her. "You're not going out there alone."

"No one tracks her alone," Rafe said. "She is not without great power, even alone."

Torren shook her head. "I am best able…"

A piercing cry from overhead brought everyone's attention to the sky.

"Two of them," Sylvan murmured as the dragons soared beneath the blazing suns, the red wyvern they'd seen in battle, and beside it, another brilliant gold wyvern with wings of silver, glinting majestically. Instinctual terror washed over Sylvan, the primal fear of the ultimate predator, and her hackles rose. "Are they…?"

Her wolf rose, pelt feathering her torso as the golden dragon arrowed toward them.

"Something we haven't seen in millennia," Torren murmured.

A shower of brilliant color burst across the glade and Cecilia appeared before them in a silver breastplate laced with gold and studded with gleaming sapphires. A diadem centered with a glittering diamond encircled her forehead. Overhead, the red dragon circled once more, trumpeted a roar of triumph, and soared for the sun.

Torren stepped into the glade and went to one knee. "My Queen."

Cecilia laughed, a sound like rainbows bursting in the air. "You have done great service this day, Lord Torren. You may rise." Cecilia took in the gathering. "So, she's here, is she? The one who took sanctuary in my kingdom and planned to wage war with the traitor, Cethinrod."

Beneath her brilliance, something dark and dangerous roiled.

"She is," Torren said.

"Ah." Cecilia tilted her chin, her eyes blazing like the diamond she wore. "She hides," she said, turning slowly, "in the dying knowe."

"I will seek her out," Torren said. "In the light you cast, the entrance is visible to me now."

"No one goes in there alone," Sylvan said. "There may be others with her."

Torren looked over her shoulder. "This is for the Fae now."

Sylvan growled.

"I sense only her," Anya murmured.

"Then we should not delay," Sylvan said, rising into her half-form. Many of the Weres shifted into pelt at her call.

Torren shimmered, and for an instant, the Hound reared. "You challenge now?"

Cecilia laughed again, a sound so sensuous it was like a caress, a touch filled with seduction and danger. "I would so like to see the two of you in challenge, but I'm afraid I must agree with Lord Torren." Her eyes flamed, and a flood of power swept across the glade and into the forest. "She waged war in my kingdom."

Drake rumbled. "She waged war on us as well."

Cecilia nodded. "And all shall have their vengeance." She glanced at Torren. "The knowe is dying, and without magic to feed it, it will disappear from this realm. We will seal it now."

Rafe hissed. "If she is inside, she will not die."

"No," Cecilia said airily, "but she will never emerge. The knowe will collapse as Faerie reclaims the last of its magic."

"She will be entombed," Rafe said softly. "Eternal hunger. The cruelest of punishments."

Cecilia tilted her head from side to side, her smile chilling. "All that she deserves."

Zora snarled. "A just ending. I consider that vengeance is done."

"As do we," Sylvan and Drake echoed.

"As do the Vampires of *Chasseur de Nuit*," Rafe said.

Cecilia held out a hand to Torren. "Join your power with mine, and let this be done."

"As you wish, my Queen."

When Torren's hand touched Cecilia's, the sun burst in the glade, forcing those watching to close their eyes against the brilliance. A scream of fury pierced the air and died with a howl of despair.

The glade erupted into life, and blue-green blades burst from the ground, capped with magenta flowers that captured the radiance of the sun. The gnarled tree branches uncoiled and exploded with fuchsia leaves and bright green fruit. The air filled with the scent and sound of creatures moving once more through the lush vegetation.

"There," Cecilia said with a beguiling smile. "It is done. And I owe you all a boon."

Sylvan, wise to the ways of the Fae, knew better than to hold the debt of any, especially the Queen. "Cecilia, Queen of Thorns, all I ask is a path for my wolves and allies to return home."

"Granted." She turned to Torren. "You, however, are Fae, and this is your home."

Torren straightened. "I have no home here. My lands—"

"I am restoring your house to its rightful place in the court," Cecilia said, "and proclaiming you Lord of the Southern Realms."

Torren glanced at Misha, who nodded.

Torren unsheathed her sword and laid it on the earth between them. "My Lady and I accept, my Queen, and pledge our lands and our allegiance to the throne."

Cecilia waved a hand in the air. Brilliant flashes of light coalesced into a gilt-edged Gate that glowed as if lit from within. She turned to Sylvan and the gathered forces. "Wherever you wish to go, the Gate will take you."

Sylvan called her wolves to her. "Might I ask, Cecilia, that the Gate close when we have all returned home."

Cecilia raised a brow. "Still don't trust me, Alpha?"

Sylvan smiled. "It is not a matter of trust, Queen of Thorns, but merely one of duty to protect my Pack."

"Once you and your allies have reached your chosen destination, the Gate will be gone. And the boon is paid."

Sylvan nodded, and at her command, the Timberwolves leapt through and returned home.

Epilogue

Anya crossed through the Gate with Rafe and stepped into the center of the commons, surrounded by the Pack and Rafe's Vampires. The Alpha surveyed the gathering, then led the *imperator* who had hurried to meet her and the Prima, inside the headquarters. A full moon bathed the training grounds as Jody and Becca emerged from the building. Anya's wolf, caught in the wash of moonlight, immediately roused and urged her to run.

Anya grasped Rafe's arm as the others moved away to join their Liege.

"I should've considered that it might be daylight," she said, a fist tightening in her chest. "You could have been injured."

"You worry too much," Rafe murmured, stroking Anya's hair as she often stroked her pelt when her wolf was ascendant. "When will you learn I—"

"When will *you* learn the answer is never?" She gripped Rafe's shirt with both hands, jerking her closer. "I worry because I love you. I know you know that, but you're too stubborn to admit it."

Rafe smiled, her smile etched in sadness. "Stubborn? No. Realistic. Our worlds are too different. It's foolish for us to speak of love."

"Why? Are our worlds—are *we*—so much more different than that of your Liege and her Consort?" Anya refused to loosen her grip. Refused to deny what she felt, and what her wolf had always known. Rafe was *hers*. "The Consort is human—and I am a Were. I respect her strength, as I know you do. Why can't you respect mine?"

Rafe cupped her cheek. "I know who you are. You are a wolf, strong and fierce. You are also a creature who needs the attachments to others, to your Pack. Vampires are the opposite. We are solitary hunters."

"Maybe all those centuries ago when you were turned, that was true. But that's not the way of things now." Anya blew out a frustrated breath. All around them, Weres drifted to their mates or rejoined their cadres, but the activity might have been in a different world. All Anya cared about was making Rafe understand she would not give her up. "You are the *senechal*, and you live within the seethe. You're pledged to protect your Liege and the others. And besides, what does my Pack link have to do with being your mate?"

"If we are mates," Rafe said slowly, "then you would not tangle, as it were, with anyone else."

"That's already the case. My wolf wants you and no one else. I want you—and only you."

"And how would your wolf feel if I were to feed with another?"

Anya growled, her wolf bristling, as did she. "Why would you?"

"I know you understand, but now you're just being stubborn," Rafe said, echoing her words back to her.

"Why?"

"When I emerge at sunfall, the hunger, even for one like me, is not something that's easily controlled. I am dangerous when the hunger surges."

"I know that. I will be there, and at moonfall before you nest for the day."

"You cannot live in the seethe. Your wolf would never tolerate it." Rafe hissed softly. "And I would be forced to kill any who attempted to feed from you. You would be in danger."

Anya shook her head. "I have duties here, as do you at the seethe. But what prevents you from nesting here? We would have as much time together as many mates share, before you nest and when you awaken—perhaps more."

Rafe laughed. "Here? You would have me spend the daylight hours in the Timberwolf Compound? This is truly what you want?"

"I would have you as my mate."

Rafe gently traced the pulse bounding in Anya's throat. "And I would have you, my wolf. I love you, but you know that, don't you?"

Anya wrapped her arms around Rafe's waist. "I know. Just as I know you hunger now, as I hunger."

"I must speak to my Liege," Rafe murmured, "and then I will find you. I will always find you—I swear it."

Anya nipped at her lip. "Hurry."

❖

Sylvan wanted nothing more than to be alone with her mate, to lie with her, to join with her, to take comfort from her. Drake's wolf called to hers, and her body thrummed with the need to take her. When she'd finished briefing Niki and her captains and ensured the Compound was well guarded, she turned to Drake. "I'm sorry. Just a while longer. I must speak with them."

Drake stroked the center of Sylvan's chest, her blunt claws a tantalizing torture. "I know. I need you, but I will wait."

"I'll be quick," Sylvan growled, and silently called for her young.

Kendra and Kira appeared in the briefing room an instant later.

"You left the Compound without permission," Sylvan said. "You could have endangered the others."

Kendra bristled. "We fought—"

"You're right," Kira said. "We...we were insubordinate."

Kendra stared at her.

Kira shrugged. "You know it."

Sylvan met Kendra's gaze and held it. Kendra shuddered and looked away.

"It was my doing," Kendra said. "I—"

"It looked to me like Kira was willing," Sylvan said flatly. "You're both all right?"

"Nothing serious that didn't heal when we shifted, Alpha," Kira said.

"You've been tried in battle, and you fought well." Sylvan gripped their shoulders. "You're *sentries*. You've earned it. Remember this—Callan has my leave to relieve you of that duty if you fail again to follow orders."

Kendra took a deep breath. "As you will, Alpha."

Kira grinned. "Thank you, Alpha."

"Go, join your squadron."

As they left, Drake said, "You were easy on them."

Sylvan clasped her nape and kissed her. Her skin tingled with the first flush of sex-sheen. "They deserved the promotion and the reprima—"

"My apologies," Jody Gates said as she appeared at the entrance. "A word, Sylvan?"

She looked up as Drake stepped away. "Of course, come in."

Jody shot Drake an apologetic glance. "I won't take but a moment."

Drake said, "I'm going to check at the infirmary to be sure that all of our injured have fully recovered."

"I'll find you," Sylvan murmured.

A few minutes later, Sylvan met Drake just leaving the infirmary. She slung an arm around her waist and pulled her close. "It's time for us to return to the den. Alone."

"None too soon. I'm ready." Drake's pheromones rose to envelop them both as they hurried from the Compound. "Is everything all right with Jody?"

Sylvan smiled. "It seems like we'll have to do some remodeling. Rafe will be spending a good deal of time with us in the future."

"Good for Anya. Now, if you want me, come run with me, my love." Drake shifted and her wolf raced into the forest.

Sylvan howled joyfully and gave chase.

About the Author

In addition to editing over twenty LGBTQIA+ anthologies, Radclyffe has written over sixty-five romance and romantic intrigue novels, including a paranormal romance series, The Midnight Hunters, as L.L. Raand.

She is a three-time Lambda Literary Award winner in romance and erotica and received the Dr. James Duggins Outstanding Mid-Career Novelist Award from the Lambda Literary Foundation. A member of the Saints and Sinners Literary Hall of Fame, she is also an RWA/FF&P Prism Award winner for *Secrets in the Stone*, an RWA FTHRW Lories and RWA HODRW winner for *Firestorm*, an RWA Bean Pot winner for *Crossroads*, an RWA Laurel Wreath winner for *Blood Hunt*, and a Book Buyers Best award winner for *Price of Honor* and *Secret Hearts*. She is also a featured author in the 2015 documentary film *Love Between the Covers*, from Blueberry Hill Productions. In 2019 she was recognized as a "Trailblazer of Romance" by the Romance Writers of America.

In 2004 she founded Bold Strokes Books, one of the world's largest independent LGBTQ publishing companies, and is the current president and publisher.

Find her at facebook.com/Radclyffe.BSB, follow her on Twitter @RadclyffeBSB, and visit her website at Radfic.com.

Books Available From Bold Strokes Books

A Heart Divided by Angie Williams. Emmaline is the most beautiful woman Jack has ever seen, but being a veteran of the Confederate army that killed her husband isn't the only thing keeping them apart. (978-1-63679-537-9)

Adrift by Sam Ledel. Two women whose lives are anchored by guilt and obligation find romance amidst the tumultuous Prohibition movement in 1920s California. (978-1-63679-577-5)

Cabin Fever by Tagan Shepard. The longer Morgan and Shelby are stranded together, the more their feelings grow, but is it real, or just cabin fever? (978-1-63679-632-1)

Clean Kill by Anne Laughlin. When someone starts killing people she knows in the recovery world, former detective Nicky Sullivan must race to stop the killer and keep herself from being arrested for the crimes. (978-1-63679-634-5)

Only a Bridesmaid by Haley Donnell. A fake bridesmaid, a socially anxious bride, and an unexpected love—what could go wrong? (978-1-63679-642-0)

Primal Hunt by L.L. Raand. Anya, a young wolf warrior, finds herself paired with Rafe, one of the most powerful Vampires in the Americas, in an erotic union of blood and sex.(978-1-63679-561-4)

Snake Charming by Genevieve McCluer. Playgirl vampire Freddie is on the run and a chance encounter with lamia Phoebe makes them both realize that they may have found the love they'd given up on. (978-1-63679-628-4)

Spirits and Sirens by Kelly and Tana Fireside. When rumored ghost whisperer Elena Murphy and very skeptical assistant fire chief Allison Jones have to work together to solve a 70-year old mystery, sparks fly—will it be enough to melt the ice between them and let love ignite? (978-1-63679-607-9)

Aubrey McFadden Is Never Getting Married by Georgia Beers. Aubrey McFadden is never getting married, but she does have five weddings to attend, and she'll be avoiding Monica Wallace, the woman who ruined her happily ever after, at every single one. (978-1-63679-613-0)

A Case for Discretion by Ashley Moore. Will Gwen, a prominent Atlanta attorney, choose Etta, the law student she's clandestinely dating, or is her political future too important to sacrifice? (978-1-63679-617-8)

The Broken Lines of Us by Shia Woods. Charlie Dawson returns to the city she left behind and meets an unexpected stranger on her first night back, discovering that coming home might not be as hard as she thought. (978-1-63679-585-0)

Flowers for Dead Girls by Abigail Collins. Isla might be just the right kind of girl to bring Astra out of her shell—and maybe more. The only problem? She's dead. (978-1-63679-584-3)

Good Bones by Aurora Rey. Designer and contractor Logan Barrow can give Kathleen Kenney the house of her dreams, but can she convince the cynical romance writer to take a chance on love? (978-1-63679-589-8)

Leather, Lace, and Locs by Anne Shade. Three friends, each on their own path in life, with one obstacle…finding room in their busy lives for a love that will give them their happily ever afters. (978-1-63679-529-4)

Rainbow Overalls by Maggie Fortuna. Arriving in Vermont for her first year of college, an introverted bookworm forms a friendship with an outgoing artist and finds what comes after the classic coming out story: a being out story. (978-1-63679-606-2)

Revisiting Summer Nights by Ashley Bartlett. PJ Addison and Wylie Parsons have been called back to film the most recent *Dangerous Summer Nights* installment. Only this time they're not in love, and it's going to stay that way. (978-1-63679-551-5)

BOLDSTROKESBOOKS.COM

Looking for your next great read?

Visit BOLDSTROKESBOOKS.COM
to browse our entire catalog of paperbacks, ebooks,
and audiobooks.

**Want the first word on what's new?
Visit our website for event info,
author interviews, and blogs.**

Subscribe to our free newsletter for sneak peeks,
new releases, plus first notice of promos
and daily bargains.

SIGN UP AT
BOLDSTROKESBOOKS.COM/signup

Bold Strokes Books
Quality and Diversity in LGBTQ Literature

*Bold Strokes Books is an award-winning publisher
committed to quality and diversity in LGBTQ fiction.*